W9-AAD-877

DIRTY WATER

A RED SOX MYSTERY

ALSO BY MARY-ANN TIRONE SMITH

FICTION

The Book of Phoebe

Lament for a Silver-Eyed Woman

The Port of Missing Men

Masters of Illusion: A Novel of the Great Hartford Circus Fire

An American Killing

THE POPPY RICE MYSTERIES

She Smiled Sweetly

She's Not There

Love Her Madly

NONFICTION

Girls of Tender Age: A Memoir

For Bette —

DIRTY WATER

(Go Sox 2009)

A RED SOX MYSTERY

by Mary-Ann Tirone Smith
and Jere Smith

Hall of Fame Press

Kingston, Rhode Island

Published by Hall of Fame Press
copyright © 2008 by Mary-Ann Tirone Smith and Jere Smith

Hall of Fame Press
The Feinstein Building, University of
Rhode Island, 3045 Kingstown Road,
Kingston, Rhode Island 02881-1710

First Edition, 2008

LIBRARY OF CONGRESS
CATALOGING IN PUBLICATION DATA

Tirone Smith, Mary-Ann and Jere Smith
Dirty water: a Red Sox mystery/Mary-Ann Tirone Smith and Jere Smith.—
Smith, Mary-Ann Tirone and Jere Smith
1st ed.
256 p.   cm.
1. The Number One Place (Fictitious blog)—Fiction. 2. Patel, Rocky
(Fictitious character)—Fiction. 3. Boston Red Sox (Used fictitiously)—
Fiction. 4. Boston Police Department (Used fictitiously)—Fiction. 5.
Government investigators—Fiction. 6. Politicians (Used fictitiously)—
Fiction. 7. Sports agents—Fiction. 8. Boston (Mass.)—Fiction. 9. Los
Angeles (Cal.)—Fiction.

813'.54—dc22   2009024141   2008
ISBN: 978-09776240-2-7 [cl]   CIP

Hall of Fame books are available for special promotions
and premiums. For details contact publisher.

Distributed in North America by Midpoint Trade Books,
27 West 20th Street #1102, New York, NY 10011,
212-727-0190, www.midpointtrade.com
and
in the United Kingdom, Eire, and Europe
Gazelle Book Services Ltd., White Cross Mills, High Town,
Lancaster LA1 1RN England,
1-44-1524-68765, www.gazellebooks.co.uk

Printed in the United States of America
13579108642

ACKNOWLEDGMENTS

We would like to thank all our friends, family and legal advisors (regardless of favorite team). Also, everyone at the Institute for International Sport: Dan Doyle, mover of mountains; Jerry Creamer, our man under fire; Deborah Burch, who steered this book through shoals, submerged rocks and a couple of hurricanes; and Laurie DeRuosi, consummate professional. We appreciate the efforts of the kindly Jeremy Kapstein, who did his best by us. Another thank you to Joe Castiglione for his support and twenty-five great years of making us feel like we're there; the ever-gracious Jan Castiglione; and of course, the Boston Red Sox.

Jere Smith adds: I'd like to thank the smart, funny, talented, tireless (and usually unpaid) members of the Red Sox blogging community, many of whom I've had the pleasure of meeting in the "real" world; the readers of my blog for their feedback and unending support; and my mom, who has taught me so much, the least of which being how to write a book.

For Kim

And for our fifth-generation Red Sox fans:
Amanda, Joe, Emily and Chris

DIRTY WATER

A Red Sox Mystery

CHAPTER

1

A Sunday morning in Boston—just like a Sunday morning in any big American city—is quiet and traffic-starved, except for the ribbons of church-goers making their way to both large and small bastions of Christianity. Then, too, there are the groggy couples slogging along in the direction of museums or brunch spots, the tempo of their walk bogged down by the lingering saturation of Saturday night sex.

But smack in the middle of this city—Boston—a greater edifice is about to open its portals hours earlier than usual to welcome a milling throng of tens of thousands: The Red Sox are scheduled to play a make-up game at noon, the first of a day-night doubleheader. With that, the routine at Fenway Park is awry in order to accommodate the shift.

The previous night's game went into extra innings and lasted four and a half hours. That, plus the shift, will make for bleary-eyed personnel and strained ballplayers. The grounds crew arrives at 5 AM instead of seven; the food vendors and souvenir concessionaires are already prepping the microwaves or tidying the t-shirt piles by eight; and at nine, the ushers gingerly remove their blazers from the closets. Also at nine o'clock, the venerable clubhouse manager Joe Cochran enters the special players' door on Van Ness Street. Not until ten does the press begin trickling in, generally hung over and grouchy, slugging down coffee out of giant cardboard cups.

Finally, right on their heels, manager Terry Francona and his team drive their cars, SUVs and pick-ups into the players' lot tucked under the ramp at Gate D. Most come alone, but some are dropped off by wives, who get a goodbye smooch. To the family dog astride the back seat—a pat on the head. God forbid the kids left the back door open and allowed the dog to escape; ballplayers need their rituals.

The guys will enter their clubhouse, not only tired out, but still feeling the vestiges of jet lag. They'd arrived from KC a few days earlier, a flight that landed at Logan at 3 AM, though each one—to a man—would insist, if pressed, that he's never affected by a missed night's sleep. Denial and superstition go hand in hand.

It is now 8:55. A good-looking guy, maybe Hispanic, wearing a press tag around his neck and shouldering a bulky, black, mesh backpack, strolls along Van Ness Street, past the player's parking lot. He turns the corner onto Yawkey Way and arrives at Gate D during the morning's most hectic moments. Sacks of change—a quarter of a million dollars worth—are being unloaded off the Dunbar armored truck to be wheeled into the park under heavy guard, where they will be dispersed among the concession and souvenir stands.

The lumpiness of the guy's backpack should have raised the eyebrow of the low-level security guard at D, his boss off to see to the money truck. Sportswriters' backpacks are flat, though thick with their laptops layered between notebooks. But this particular guard's usual duties are to make sure no one is sneaking under turnstiles. So he doesn't even take in the backpack; he actually gives the guy quite a friendly wave in hopes of one day maybe making it into his column.

Also, the sportswriter is dressed sharply, and has a presence about him what with the high-end sunglasses and hundred-and-fifty dollar haircut. He's briskly entered the park with the superior air of a sportswriter on a deadline. He will go directly to the clubhouse when only the clubhouse manager is inside—the coaches and trainers won't arrive until just before the players do.

Joe Cochran is in a poor frame of mind because DeMarlo Hale, the third base coach, impulsively decided to get in some work in left and center with Coco Crisp and Jacoby Ellsbury, the player brought up from Pawtucket to share left field duties while Manny Ramirez recuperates from a painful strained oblique. DeMarlo, Coco and Jacoby are about to arrive, so that the kid could practice positioning himself to play the tricky caroms off the Green Monster.

Cochran is frustrated that his clubhouse isn't in the top state of preparedness he prides himself on. The threesome came barreling in. Despite this extra disruption, he quickly has them organized and out to the field.

When the slick sports writer peeks in, Cochran is in the shower room unloading a box of toiletries, lining up the players' brands of choice on the shelves under the mirrors. He is cursing actually, digging frantically for *Soothe Sensation Post-Shaving Therapy Solution*, the aftershave Manny insists on splashing over his face or else he won't come out. This attitude, described in a term now embedded in baseball lexicography—*Manny being Manny*—is also reflected in Manny's work ethic; though sidelined for a few days. He's arrived early too, so he can give more detailed tips to Jacoby. Manny is already out in left field stretching and jogging.

Perfect.

The sportswriter walks swiftly across the lounge area, past the soda and juice machines, and to the nearest inner door which happens to be the new interview room. He opens the door, slides his backpack from his shoulders, and places it on the floor just inside. He eases the door shut again and walks out.

The only thing Cochran ever heard was his own grumbling.

The guy takes the same route back out, waves to several vendors, and to the bathroom attendants and ushers arriving in force. Any of them who might have registered his counterfeit press pass tag didn't make much of the fact later that they couldn't recall his face. These press guys come and go.

The sportswriter strode right out through Gate D, now mobbed with personnel rushing past a just-forming line of tourists waiting to start their guided tour of Fenway, twelve bucks apiece. They will end up quite thrilled at their good luck—getting to see the unexpected mini-training session going on at the foot of the Green Monster. Manny will be sure to toss a ball or two to their group.

The sportswriter heads around the corner and up Van Ness. At the gas station, he jumps into a Cadillac Escalade, its engine idling. The SUV immediately speeds off past the ticket-holders heading toward Yawkey Way, and past the non-ticket-holders hot-footing it to *The Cask'n Flagon* as well as several other bars of lesser renown along Lansdowne Street, all opened early on this beautiful Sunday morning.

THE NUMBER ONE PLACE
Sunday, 8:05 AM

I know it's mid-season, but I want to give new readers of this blog a sense as to what goes on here. My name's Jay, I live near Boston, and I've been doing this website for five years. At least once a day, I'll give you updates on our beloved Boston Red Sox, or whatever else I've got an opinion on.

I'll give you my take on last night's game, but don't expect a traditional rundown. I'm assuming you've watched the game, are familiar with the players, know the bases are run counterclockwise, etc. After all, you *are* probably a Red Sox fan. When I see people in Sox hats, I can assume they are die-hards. When I see people in Yankees hats, well, I don't ask them who played shortstop before Derek Jeter, because they probably don't know anyone *ever* played shortstop other than ol' Mr. Calm Eyes. (All apologies to *true* Yankee fans.)

While the newspapers might talk about how much "respect" we all have for Derek Jeter after a game against the Yankees, I'll tell you how much I can't stand looking at his face. Because that's what *fans* really say, and that's how I really feel. I'm not auditioning for a spot at the *Boston Globe*. I also go to a lot of games at Fenway Park, and will post here any pictures or videos I shoot at Sox games.

I'm always getting questions about the name, *The Number One Place*. People think I'm implying that they should turn here first for everything Red Sox. I hope so, but I'm not that arrogant. It's actually an ad-lib from the song that's been played after every Red Sox win at Fenway Park for about ten years now, "Dirty Water" by the Standells. After the line *Boston you're my home*, the singer snarls, *Aw, you're the number one place.*

But you should've known that, Red Sox Nation! Yes, I know "Red Sox Nation" is now a copyrighted term for a team-sanctioned fan club you have to pay to get into. But I've been using it since "Red Sox Nation" was just a term describing the team's global following of fans. The "official" RSN gives you some good benefits, and I understand the ownership's desire to snatch up the popular title and market it, but to me, that term will always stand for all the Sox fans who have lurked in every town in the country— even before the media noticed we were every-where. That's got nothing to do with the team's suc-cess. If it had, we would've given up a long time ago. . .

Day-night doubleheader today against Toronto. I smell a sweep.

COMMENTS:

MattySox said: Thanks for the update, I never knew *what* the hell was going on here. ☺

26Rings said: same old shit with you boston fans. one title in a hundred yrs, it'll be another hundred till you win anuther. the usual boston choke is on, looks like the yanks will win the al east again this year! go yanks!!!1

ConnecticutSoxFan said: This is what I deal with, day in, day out around here. The Red Sox could win the next 30 World Series, and Yankee fans would still make us out to be losers, and themselves winners: "Sure, the Sox have more championships now, but ours are *classier*."

Jay said: Mr. 26rings, I see you're still a little bitter over 2004. You Yankee fans called us "chokers" my whole life. Now that you guys have committed the ultimate choke to us, maybe it's time to lay off that word. Three years later, it's just as sweet: We were down three games to none to you guys, came back to win the American League Championship Series, and then went on to win our first World Series in 86 years. I'd say "I know how you feel," but I don't—my team never choked *that* bad. . . .

RebGirl said: Ouch! Good call, Jay. And just because our huge lead has been cut to eight games, I'd hardly say we're "choking" anyway. By the way, Jay, what's with this "us" and "we" stuff? Do you think you're on the team?

Jay said: Reb, when a team has been part of your family your entire life, you can refer to them as "we," heh. Just the way I was raised, I guess. I'm a lifelong Sox fan, you know. My great-grandfather learned to speak English listening to the Sox on the radio.

CHAPTER

2

So that's how it all started, innocently enough, but rife with treachery as the law understands all too well. And it started in the heart of Fenway Park, in the Red Sox clubhouse, on the first series following a long successful road trip.

According to the police interview with Michael Sullivan, one of Cochran's several clubhouse assistants, known as *clubbies*, he'd arrived at the park not too long after Cochran. Sullivan was called Sully, just like every other Boston Irishman named Sullivan.

Cochran had called out to Sully from the shower room to expect Coco, Jacoby and DeMarlo early. So before he got the coffee going, Sully took out his cell, and told another clubbie in charge of laundry to hurry up with the practice jerseys because the three guys were expected any minute. He started putting out some fruit and snacks, when in a few short minutes the laundry clubbies came rushing down the corridor with racks of freshly laundered Red Sox practice jerseys and pants, followed minutes later by the early birds who were soon on their way out to left field. Manny preferred to practice in his T-shirts, sleeves ripped off.

Then the uniforms were rolled in, and Cochran helped hang everything in anointed, open, wood lockers lining the walls.

"Nah," is what Cochran said to the cop, the first of the Boston Police on duty at Fenway to arrive on the scene. "There was nuthin' unusual. Nuthin'."

At that hour, the clubhouse having been thoroughly cleaned the night before in preparation for the early game, Cochran had found no necessity to enter Terry Francona's office just off the locker room, or go into the trainer's room, or the interview room either.

When the police officer asked Cochran the next question, one he would ask over and over again—"Did you see anything unusual?"—Cochran responded, "Well, not right then."

The question after that: "Did you *hear* anything unusual?"

Cochran didn't answer immediately so Sully chimed in, "Not right then, either."

The first player to walk into the clubhouse after Manny dashed through, and DeMarlo, Coco and Jacoby got out to the field was Tim Wakefield, scheduled to pitch the day's first game. He smiled to himself for he'd noted the lack of humidity despite the early-morning heat, and had taken a glance at the flag. It was blowing toward left-center field out over the Green Monster. Just what hitters hope for against any other pitcher. But Wakefield's knuckleball darted and danced better when a breeze was blowing right in his face. Hitters have enough trouble making contact against it; when they're swinging for the fences they have even less of a chance. And with low humidity, any ball a batter was able to get up into the jet stream would be a little less likely to reach the Monster Seats. Sometimes the difference between a solid performance and an early shower.

The grateful Wakefield knew that weather was one of so many things he couldn't control. Tough enough trying to control his infamous knuckleball, something near to impossible.

Before starting his day's routine with a shower, Wake must

let Sully know whether or not he's decided to go with the red jerseys instead of the usual snow-white home uniforms. The occasional red jersey plan was some front office idea that made no sense to the players and certainly not to the fans. As if they needed yet another over-priced "authentic" jersey. But it was more bucks for the brand. However, bottom line? The decision is left to the pitcher as the game pretty much rests on his frame of mind.

Wake said to Sully, "Stuff the red shirts."

Soon Sully was aware of more footsteps approaching in the corridor. He would say to the cop, "I knew it was Lowell and Lugo and Cora. Tavarez, catching up, dropping his stuff. Good friends. Always laughin'. Could hear that laughin' a mile away."

The rest of the team arrived in staggered groups of two or three, along with their manager who called out a greeting to everyone. Then Francona ducked into his office and closed the door behind him so he could review the trainer's report from the previous night before filling out the lineup card. His lineup hinged on the health of the players.

Paul Lessard, the trainer, arrived too, with his assistants, and they prepared for an hour of wrapping ankles, checking blisters and bruises, after which he'd consult with Francona one last time.

In the hallway, Kevin Youkilis met up with Dustin Pedroia. The first and second basemen were in competition for the slowest baserunner award. Their joint appearance elicited calls of encouragement for one to beat the other to their lockers.

The final group was led by David Ortiz, known throughout baseball and beyond as Big Papi. He walked with Daisuke Matsuzaka, who he had in a headlock. His other arm was draped around the shoulders of Hideki Okajima. The two new Japanese pitchers also had nicknames: *Dice-K*, the pho-netic pronunciation of his name for the benefit of Americans who needed a clue as to how in God's name to say, *Daisuke*. And *Oki*—a no-brainer choice.

Their translator hung back, still a little afraid of Big Papi's physical demonstrations of affection. All recollected later to the police officer that it was Doug Mirabelli, Wakefield's per-sonal knuckleball catcher who'd first said, "What the hell was that?"

Wakefield, at his locker, still damp from the shower, asked him, "What was what?"

His catcher said, "I don't know. I thought I heard a squeak or something."

Lugo called out, "Thas' Cora farting away. I smelling it from here."

The clubbies laughed but clammed up when Cora told them to shut up: "*Cállense, cabrónes.*"

All of a sudden, the squeak that Mirabelli had been the only one to hear sounded again. Everyone heard it this time and they stopped what they were doing, posed in the act of either, buttoning or tying, all conversations stopping in mid-stream.

"Is there a fucking cat in here?" Youkilis was allergic to cats.

The players shushed him, and they listened, cocking their heads, their expressions intent.

"Would somebody turn off the goddamn television?"

Someone did.

But there was nothing.

And then Curt Schilling, father of four, said, "Ya know. . . Don't think I'm crazy, but it sounded like a baby."

Good-natured derision ensued—"What the hell time did you get to bed last night, Schill?"—and after another minute, just as the guys went back to their routine and the clubbies had begun bustling again, the squeak sounded one more time, only now it was more of a cry. Once again, the players froze in mid-motion. Then Daisuke made a cradling motion with his arms, and Dustin, who had no children, said, "That was a baby, I swear to God."

The players were all on their feet, not moving, concentrating, listening. Cochran was at the wall phone, dialing security.

Squeak. . .

Papi shouted, "Tito!"

Sully started banging on the manager's door, "Tito! Tito!"

Everyone called Terry Francona by his ballplayer father's nickname, Tito, which Francona loved.

Francona's door opened just as the players, like statues come to life, moved at the same time. They spread out through the clubhouse, dashed though the shower room and bathrooms, rifled through the lockers, looked in the wastebaskets, under the trainers' tables, rummaged through the equipment cases. Tito tried to make sense out of what Cochran was trying to tell him.

It was the Captain, Jason Varitek, who opened the interview room door. The room was brand new, and doubled as a chapel for the many evangelical players who held prayer groups there. They, in fact, referred to the room as the chapel when it was time for a service. It was windowless and pitch dark. Varitek switched on the light, and his gaze fell to the movement at his feet. Instinctively, he went into his catcher's squat, opened the black backpack lying there, and lifted out a baby.

The infant was wrapped in a piece of dirty rag stained with grease, the kind all these men had stuffed into the wheel wells in the back of their array of vehicles.

Varitek shouted, "Somebody get a towel," and began to pull open the filthy piece of cloth.

The baby was wearing a yellow onesie with a bunny hand-embroidered on the chest. Knitted cotton booties to match.

Lugo yanked off his shirt. "Wrap him in this. Is warm, at leas'."

Tito broke into the huddle of players around Varitek. He squatted down too, knees cracking. Later, he would say to the police officer, "Someone shouted to turn off the air conditioner. The baby was wet."

Schilling unsnapped the onesie at the crotch and took off the soaking diaper.

The baby was a boy.

Then he wrapped Lugo's shirt around him, and Varitek took up the baby again holding him to his chest. He shouted for the trainer, "Where the hell is Paul?"

Paul Lessard was just now dashing out of his office, along with Jonathan Papelbon, wearing nothing but a newly wound elastic bandage hanging from his wrist.

The players proceeded to describe to the officer what the commotion sounded like:

"Man, we were all shouting at once."

"Yeah, like, *Somebody get the doc*. But the doc wasn't there yet. So then somebody else yells, *Get the fucking ambulance guys!*"

"We couldn't figure out how the hell to turn off the god-damn air conditioner."

"Dustin yanked some cord out of the wall and half the fucking lights went out."

"The air conditioner stayed on."

"So Cora says, 'Shouldn't we give him some milk or something?' So I says, 'Shut up, you asshole.'"

"And Tito kept saying, 'Jesus Christ, Jesus Christ.'"

The men told of the trainer staring down at the infant who was quiet, but whose eyes were open, gazing up into the face of Varitek.

"He's a few weeks old, I think," was what Varitek whispered to Schilling, the veteran pitcher with the four kids.

And Schilling agreed. "Bout a month."

The trainer remained speechless.

Varitek said, "He seems weak."

"Like he's all cried out." Schilling's eyes welled up.

Finally, the trainer came out of his trance. He put the palm of his hand on the baby's head. "He doesn't feel hot. But. . . I hate to say it. . . I think he's drugged."

Varitek held him closer as the players expressed dismay.

Just then, Amalie Benjamin, *wunderkind* of the *Boston Globe* walked in, yawning, there to gather info for her televised, pre-game, clubhouse report. She asked, "What's the ambulance revving up for?" She hooked her thumb over her shoulder. "Did Lugo pull an ass muscle hustling to get to the doughnuts?"

Tito went right at her, put an arm around her shoulder and pulled her to the door. "We've got a situation. You're out."

"What *situation*? Tito, you can't. . ."

He shoved her out the door and closed it.

The baby, at that moment, let out his pathetic little squeak again. Sully elbowed his way into the scrim of players huddled about him. He held a cup of warm water in his hand. While Varitek continued to cradle the infant, Sully sprinkled a few drops on the little head and said, "I baptize you in the name of the Father, the Son, and the Holy Ghost."

Several players blessed themselves. Dice-K and Oki bowed their heads and closed their eyes.

Big Papi whispered to Kevin Youkilis, "Don't take it personal. That baby's Hispanic."

Youkilis said, "There's a lot of Jewish Hispanics, Papi."

Amalie, outside the door and wits collected, got out her cell and pressed 8, which was a direct line to the sports editor to be used only when there was a breaking story. She said to him, "There's some kind of shit goin' down here."

He told her to stay where she was, something she'd certainly planned on doing.

Then the EMTs came flying past Amalie and into the clubhouse. Cochran had told them what to expect and they were prepared.

Upon laying eyes on the baby, one said quietly to the other, "He's not a newborn."

"Nope."

"Put away the suction stuff." The senior EMT took the baby from Varitek and said to his co-worker, "Something's wrong with him. He's too flaccid."

The trainer gave them his opinion.

They agreed. The baby had likely been drugged.

They went into action, preparing him for his swift journey to Beth Israel Deaconess Medical Center, the nearest hospital to Fenway. The doctor on call at the Deaconess station within the park still hadn't arrived yet. The players watched, and then Varitek made an announcement which he directed at his manager. "I'm going with him, Tito."

Later, Tito said to the officer, "I knew I wouldn't talk him out of it. I didn't want to talk him out of it, either, tell ya the truth."

Varitek's decision was easier to accept since Wakefield was pitching that first game, which meant Mirabelli, trained to handle the knuckleball, would catch. Varitek told Tito not to worry—he'd be back for the second game which wasn't until eight o'clock. Then he and the EMTs ran out with their little bundle. As it would turn out, Varitek returned to the field in the sixth inning of the first game with news of the baby's treatment and diagnosis. The news was good—the baby had been transferred to the hospital next door to Deaconess—

Boston Children's—and by the time Varitek left for the park, he was much stronger, really carrying on, crying like a champ.

"The drug was pretty much worn off," he told the team, who'd mobbed him in the dugout.

THE NUMBER ONE PLACE
Sunday, 12:30 PM

Craziness at Fenway right now. As I type, Jason Varitek is not in the dugout (he wasn't gonna catch the first game anyway with Wake on the mound). He's at Deaconess. A baby was found in the Red Sox clubhouse before the game started, and Tek went with it in the ambulance.

As you can see if you're watching on TV right now, the game's going on as normal, and NESN hasn't mentioned anything. Who knows if they will or if they'll wait until after the game. More on this as it develops.

COMMENTS:

ConnecticutSoxFan said: If the Yanks were in town, I'd have said A-Rod planted the baby, only to "rescue" it later. But the Red Sox found it first, foiling his attempt to find the spotlight. Man, that guy never comes through in the clutch. By the way, you ARE joking about this baby thing, right?

MattySox said: Do you think A-Rod used a Cabbage Patch Kid, or one of the babies he had with his mistress?

Jay said: Haha. I knew you all would somehow weave A-Rod's failures into this story. But no, this is all true. The baby story is real.

KGNumber5 said: Yeah, this news is up now on the Joy of Sox blog, quoting AP.

RebGirl said: And now Remy's mentioning it on the air. Holy shit!

AJM said: Jay, come on, you're really Curt Schilling, right? You were right on top of this one.

Jay said: Nah, Curt's got his own blog. . . .

CHAPTER

3

The nurses at Beth Israel Deaconess Hospital named the baby Ted Williams, what else? The ambulance had required three minutes to reach its destination. It left Fenway Park from under the grandstand, and as the EMT hit the siren and lights, it turned right onto Van Ness and sped toward Brookline Ave, crossed the invisible Muddy River diverted underground, pased Emmanuel College, and then zipped into the emergency entrance to Deaconess.

As the charge nurse in the emergency entrance carefully took the baby from Jason Varitek (without swooning as she was a dyed-in-the-wool professional), she asked the EMTs if anyone had alerted the police. But the two guys had been so flustered at the prospect of entering the Red Sox clubhouse— the regular men would be at the second game—they had never gotten to the point of connecting the abandonment of a baby with criminal activity. First they looked at each other and then to Varitek, who had become teary when he'd passed the baby off to the nurse. One of them said, "Police?"

As the nurse dashed past into the emergency unit, she called over her shoulder, "Do it."

The nurse didn't know that sixty Boston police officers were assigned to Fenway Park on game day, except when the Yankees were in town, and the number jumped to eighty. At the time the baby was left, a dozen had arrived, and would be joined by the rest thirty minutes before the gates opened. Another contingent was outside the park handling traffic and crowd control.

The first cop to get to the clubhouse had noticed commotion in the press box from his vantage point next to the dugout. Incredibly, the press box seemed to be emptying out. He ran up there, grabbed the guy from the *Hartford Courant*, and asked him where the hell everyone was going just as his cell phone rang.

The reporter said, "Stuff is going down in the clubhouse," at the same time that a dispatcher shouted into the cop's ear, "Somebody abandoned a baby at the Park. I'm hearin'—*in the clubhouse*! I don't know what kind of shit this is, but you'd better get over there."

As the cop took off, he experienced a chill in his spine though the day was growing warmer by the minute.

Babies abandoned usually expire before anyone finds them. Most often a garbage collector, who spots them the morning after they're born. The cop could only hope this baby was alive. He assumed the infant was a newborn. Almost everyone who heard the news assumed the same, and tried to put aside fleeting images of a bloody umbilical cord.

The cop's cell rang again. He opened it up while he ran. The dispatcher was still in shout-mode. "We're sending over CAC. It's true."

CAC stood for Crimes Against Children.

The cop kept running. The first problem he had to deal with was Amalie Benjamin, chomping at the bit and blocking the door, which the cop was about to open when the boy wonder General Manager, Theo Epstein, opened it for him. He referred to the clubhouse as "*My* clubhouse." He let the cop in and then assured Amalie in his calm and steady voice that she could still do her usual interviews after the game, but there would be no clubhouse report.

"What's going on in there?" she asked. "Some kind of debauchery?"

He said, "I wish." She was taken with his expression.

"Listen, Theo, are the guys all right?" The question reflected a genuine concern; absent was her usual journalistic aggressiveness.

"Yes. They are."

Right then, the two CAC cops arrived. One of them said, "Hey, Amalie."

She didn't know who he was, but everyone knew her. She couldn't sit in a restaurant without at least one guy yelling, "Marry me, Amalie!"

While the police officers went about their drill, notebook and pens out, firing questions, Theo said to Tito, "At least you didn't have to worry about batting practice."

Tito sighed. "Yeah. Now I only have to worry about not shooting myself."

Theo patted his shoulder.

Know-it-alls expound on how players are professionals and, therefore, undeterred by upheaval. But Tito knew exactly how emotional they could be, how an incident could demoralize them in a second, and how an event like the one unfolding meant a new concern for him—seeing to the team concentrating on the game at hand.

Once Varitek was on the way with his tiny charge, Tito called the team together, told them they had a game to play, and besides that, they would have to start all over again tonight. Then he directed them to repeat the words, "No comment," to everyone who asked about the baby until they were told to do otherwise. Big Papi said to his Hispanic comrades, "*En otras palabras*: Fuck you."

The two Japanese pitchers smiled. Their English was improving with each day, though not nearly as quickly as their Spanish. And *Fuck You*, of course, was a universal term.

Then Theo told all gathered he'd take the hit. Explain to the press that the police didn't want them to say anything yet. He said, "After all, this incident is a crime."

The players' eyes riveted into his. Theo was no dummy, which was why he'd been named General Manager at twenty-seven years old. He could sense the depth of seriousness playing out, and he knew how to take care of anything inflammatory. Knowing the advantage of swift action came naturally to him.

The police questioned the staff, the players, the manager— everyone who was in the clubhouse when the baby was found. And then the officers turned their attention to security, ticket takers, ushers, as well as Amalie, who groused to them that she should have been the first to know, not the last.

But nobody had seen anyone wandering around with a baby. When the cop held up the backpack, no one recognized it. Later, the guard on temporary duty, who had waved the phony sportswriter through Gate D got to see it. He told the cop it looked like any other backpack. He had no recollection of the man he'd let in. He was so astonished at what was going down he had no recollection of anything at all prior to the sounds of the siren.

Two of the three Red Sox owners—Larry Lucchino and John Henry—still hadn't arrived at the park. The third, Tom Werner, was rushed to the clubhouse along with a couple of higher-ups, by security the minute he pulled in. He was flabbergasted by the story of what had transpired. That is until Tito mentioned that Jason Varitek had accompanied the baby to the hospital. Then his eyes narrowed. He didn't like that part at all.

But Theo assured him, "Good public relations, Tom. You

get to tell Larry and John that Tek's action will honor the brand."

Tom's fears were eased. Tito caught the wink Theo aimed at him.

As the fans poured into Fenway Park, a crescendo of cell phone ringtones erupted, the majority sounding off with the first bars of "Dirty Water." The expanding rumor about a baby found at Fenway Park had apparently been fueled by a Sox blogger. Amalie Benjamin turned to a colleague from the *Globe* and said, "Remember when *we* got the scoops? Shit."

And her colleague said, "Who the hell is this guy? How did he know about this baby before we did?"

"Good question."

"It sure as hell is."

⚾

Up in the NESN booth, after the Red Sox had finished batting in the fourth, the news of the baby officially reached the two announcers, Jerry Remy and Don Orsillo. They'd been aware of the fearful rumors flying, but they'd had a job to do, wouldn't think about a baby possibly born in the club-house last night, left there to die. Between innings, Remy was sucking in as much Marlboro smoke as he could pull into his lungs before going back on the air, and Orsillo was making his way through a box of *Dunkin' Donuts*. Remy was told the rumors were true, and that he had to make the first televised announcement of this extraordinary piece of news, which was entirely acceptable to Orsillo. Though a superb announcer, he knew his place. Remy was a former player, a fan favorite, and now did a first-rate job as the team's color analyst, except when he lapsed into one of his fairly frequent laugh attacks. That's when his chain-smoking habit betrayed itself—his laughter would transcend into an uncontrollable coughing fit.

After the commercial ended, Remy said very seriously so no one would think it was a joke, "A newborn baby was found in the clubhouse this morning, just prior to the game." With that first line, the mindset of the 200,000 viewers throughout all of New England—except for Fairfield County in western Connecticut, considered by Major League Baseball to be part of New York rather than New England and therefore deprived of NESN—imagined Baby Ted Williams as just a few hours old.

Remy's producer slipped a piece of paper to him. He looked at it and reminded himself to get to his optometrist real soon to increase the effectiveness of his stupid reading glasses. He squinted as he read.

"The abandoned baby was first mentioned on a fan's blog, but the episode has been confirmed by Amalie Benjamin from the *Globe* who happened to be outside the clubhouse shortly after the baby was found. We don't know yet. . .how the baby's doing."

Then Remy, still imagining the worst, got choked up. Orsillo took over. He said solemnly, "We will let everyone know as soon as there's word of the baby's condition."

During the top of the seventh inning, Amalie appeared in the booth with Remy and Orsillo. She gave NESN's viewers what little she knew.

She said, "Whenever there's something so shocking happening, rumors fly, but I know from being around the players that the baby was a boy and that he was in a weakened condition."

She didn't want to add that the baby might have been drugged until it was confirmed. What she was thinking was that if it turned out that the fucking blogger knew about that, then he was a player, or a clubbie, or Tito himself. There wasn't a single thing Amalie could say that hadn't already been related on the blog. She was tempted to bring up the blogger's post, but damned if she was going to give one of those weirdos the time of day, let alone a plug. She's sure *she* was there! And besides, she had her own blog.

But when she wrote her story for the next morning's *Globe*, she did mention the blog, and noted that whoever wrote it had to have been on the scene. Her editor killed that part of the story, said to her, "You don't stir up shit, Amalie."

She said, "I'm not stirring up shit. I've already *stepped* in it."

"No, you smelled it. If you'd gotten into that clubhouse while the baby was there. . . *That* would be stepping in it."

She took her medicine, but she was thinking, *Dickhead*.

THE NUMBER ONE PLACE
Monday, 2:20 AM

What a couple of games and what a day. The Captain comes back from the hospital, pinch-hits for Mirabelli in the ninth, and hits a walk-off homer into the bleachers. And in game two, in front of a national audience, Dice-K with a great start, Oki with the hold, and Pap with the save. A formula we want to become very familiar with over the next few seasons.

Good to see J.D. Drew get out of his slump. Maybe this time it's for good. And the kid Jacoby Ellsbury, man, wow. Talk about speed. Whenever I see a (really) wild pitch with a guy on second, I always end up yelling at the TV (a common occurrence at my house) for the guy to just keep running all the way home. It's like some of these guys think you're only allowed to move up one base at a time. Not

Jacoby—he pulled off the feat today. Pitch gets away, he takes off from second, doesn't even think about stopping as he wheels around third, and scores easily.

But that wasn't the only rare thing to happen at Fenway today, as we know. The baby is a little boy, and he's okay. They're already calling him Teddy Williams. I guess "Baby Ruth" was too obvious. At least they didn't call him "Grady Little." Not a lot is known besides that, except this: that baby was drugged. This wasn't some teenage mom dropping her unwanted infant off on a doorstep.

And what about our Jerry Remy? Suddenly, he's a news reporter. Did you see the look on his face reporting on the clubhouse baby? It's always interesting to observe sportscasters talking about any non-sports topic. One minute they're explaining the safety squeeze and the next they're philosophizing about Shakespeare or something—but it'll always sound like sports. "You can't drink poison when there's a chance Juliet's still alive and there's a lefty on the mound! Terrible job!" But RemDawg and Amalie did fine, considering the seriousness of the event.

We all love Jerry Remy. And rightfully so. After hearing his authentic New England accented antics on Sox telecasts for the last 20 years, he almost feels like a crazy uncle who's always talking about the Red Sox between coughing/laughing fits. Only this crazy uncle gets paid for it. And got to play for the team, too. The weird thing is, he almost became the

living legend he is today before his announcing
career even began.

Anyone who knows the history of the 1978 one-
game playoff between the Red Sox and Yankees
knows that Remy, then our second baseman,
would've been the hero had it not been for a stroke
of Yankee luck. No, not the Bucky Dent homer that
gave him the middle name, *Fuckin'*. That wasn't
luck, just a "special" bat, wink-wink. I'm referring to
the play in the ninth inning when Remy stepped to
the plate with the tying run on first. He hits a hard
line drive to right field. It bounces in front of Lou
Piniella, who's standing there clueless with his arms
out, blinded by the late-day sun. A split-second
before the ball cruises past him, Piniella catches
sight of it, lunges desperately to his left, and snags
the back half of the baseball with his glove. The
runner at first has to put on the brakes at second,
and Remy is held to a mere single.

Had Piniella spotted the ball any later, or had the
ball been one damn inch further to his left, or, shit,
had Piniella not been positioned in that exact spot
in the first place, the ball would have rolled all the
way to the outfield wall, and Remy might *still* be
running. A walk-off, two-run, inside-the-park home
run, and, as Peter Gammons once pointed out,
Jerry Remy might have become the fourth-most
famous Red Sox player of all time. Ted Williams,
Yaz, Cy Young, and the little second baseman who
beat the Yanks and helped end what was then a 60-
year drought. Had it happened, even if the Sox

hadn't gone on to win the World Series that year (as the Yanks did) it would've changed the culture of Red Sox Nation. Instead, Remy continued to be just another ballplayer, his career petering out, thanks to a recurring knee injury.

Incredibly, via the broadcast booth all these years later, he's become one of the most famous personalities in Red Sox history anyway.

COMMENTS:

KGNumber5 said: And when we won in 2004, he finally got that World Series ring, too. He was born in Fall River, and I'm from New Bedford. If you're a Simpsons fan, they're kind of the Shelbyville to our Springfield. But you gotta love the guy. Cracks me up.

Mighty Quinn said: Nobody ever remembers that it was the Red Sox who made the more impressive comeback in '78. Sure, the Yanks were down 14 games and came all the way back over a period of months, but the Sox then went down 3.5 games, with 14 left. And they won twelve of those games to force the tie-breaker.

AJM said: Good call, Quinn. I remember that season well. That was the first team to make me cry. '86 was the second. '03 was the third. But the tears of joy in '04 made up for all of it. This century, fortune is smiling upon the Sox, not the Yanks. My thoughts now are with that baby, though.

CHAPTER

4

The extended family of Arturo Sanchez assembled that same evening at eight-thirty, in the last light of day, in the kitchen of the matriarch, Alicia Sanchez Palacios, on 5 Edgerly Road, near the Boston Conservatory, a half-mile east of Fenway Park on the other side of the fens.

Alicia and her two brothers-in-law had left Mexico for the United States forty-two years earlier. Her four children were all born in Boston. Alicia's late husband, Arturo, had emigrated from a small poverty-stricken village outside the town of Hidalgo del Parral, three hundred miles south of Ciudad Juarez, on foot. It had taken him six weeks to reach the city. He then walked across the Rio Grande to El Paso surrounded by a group of hotel workers—cleaning people and kitchen help. All but Arturo held temporary work papers allowing them to go back and forth between Mexico and Texas on a daily basis. Early that morning, someone had procured an expired paper for Arturo, but the border guards chose not to notice. Without undocumented workers, all the hotels and restaurants in El Paso would be forced to close, and the mayor's children would have no nanny.

Arturo's goal in life was to become an American so that his children would have opportunities to better the lot in life that they would face in the village, where the infant mortality rate was sixty percent. He wanted to go far from Mexico and never return; his own parents had died when he was a child, and then his older brothers and sisters all left their village to become migrant crop workers. They sent a little money back to him with promises to return, but they never did. Arturo no longer felt ties to his village, only to his two younger brothers who were ten and twelve when he left, and his wife Alicia, who he adored. She encouraged his quest with the promise that she would take good care of his little brothers and follow him as soon as he found a way for the three of them to do so.

She told him, "I will depend upon the trust we have for each other, Arturo. There is nothing else for me to depend upon though I will pray to God to stay by your side." The last thing she said to Arturo was spoken in a whisper while she watched him become smaller and smaller, trudging across the barren land spreading out to the horizon: "*Te amo, mi vida.*"

Arturo was not interested in the sort of temporary work available in El Paso. So he made his way to Oklahoma City, to Omaha, to Detroit, to New York, picking up various skills as he moved. Finally, he ended up in Boston, where he immediately found work as a housepainter with a company run by a fireman. The fireman was planning ahead for his retirement. Having such a business was illegal for the fireman, so he was only able to hire help on an equally illegal basis. He got mostly Irish guys, who could find no worthwhile work in Ireland, which was undergoing a serious recession. The painting company thrived, and then the fireman couldn't find enough Irish help.

He did hear about a couple of Mexican day laborers—including Arturo—working at a construction site, and apparently their multitude of abilities included house-painting. The

fireman scurried over there and hired them on the spot at
twice what they were making mixing cement. Arturo loved
painting because, aside from watery whitewash, he'd never
seen a coat of paint up close except for the statues in the big
church in the town nearest his village. He somehow attributed
the colors of the statues to the hand of God. To transform the
white of plaster to a new color felt productive to him. He'd
created something new. In his village, there had never been
anything new.

Now the fireman offered him a whole new expanded feeling of production. To transform the wood of a house from an
old, peeling, shabby gray to blue, or yellow, or green was a
spiritual experience for him.

Arturo learned a great deal of English as a painter because
the fireman and his Irish workers loved to talk and Arturo
loved to listen. So the fireman learned a little Spanish too, and
he opened savings accounts for his Mexican painters in his
own name to avoid any legal complications for them. And for
him. In this way, over the course of two years, Arturo was able
to save enough money to bring his wife and younger brothers
across the border as soon as he could figure out how.

Arturo kept his ears open. He heard about a group of nuns
whose mission was to bring together the families of men who
had managed to survive the near-impossible struggle to get to
the United States, find work, and by God's miracle, acquire an
affordable place for their families to live. The donation the
nuns required for Alicia was fourteen hundred dollars, and for
the two boys, five hundred dollars each.

Like his wife, Arturo had depended on trust. He trusted
the fireman and he trusted the nuns. In trying to thank the
fireman, he was waved off with the explanation that
Bostonians used to put signs in all their businesses that read,
Irish need not apply.

Soon Alicia and Arturo's little brothers were with him again. The fireman ended up hiring Arturo's wife too, who painted while the boys were in school. She stopped painting when she became pregnant with twins—also boys—who were automatically American citizens upon their birth. She would have two more children, boys as well, within the next five years. When the two youngest were in high school, the fireman sold his painting business to Alicia and Arturo, and every summer the couple hired his college-age children to paint houses. The fireman's sons would go on to be successful businessmen, while the girl went off to law school. And Arturo's younger brothers would become dedicated firemen. The former owner of Arturo's business attended the graduation ceremony in full dress uniform, proud to pin their badges on their new blue jackets.

Years passed, and the three oldest Sanchez children scattered to whatever places, jobs and marriages took them. The youngest son, George, would remain in Boston, a realtor who especially enjoyed selling houses his father had painted.

Now, at the family's Sunday evening meeting in the four-story home on Edgerly Road—a house Arturo and Alicia bought in 1966 for $32,000 and which was now worth two million—sat the matriarch, her two brothers-in-law and their families, including a couple of grandchildren presently asleep on the beds. Arturo had lived just long enough to welcome the first of his own grandchildren into the world. Finally, there was George, who lived with his wife of one year in the building's basement apartment. George's horrific crisis was the reason they were all at the table.

George's new wife was from Brooklyn, New York. Her parents had left the war and the killing fields of El Salvador behind, had ridden in a dilapidated truck to a US border somewhere in Arizona. She was just a child, and any details she remembered, she'd been warned never to speak of.

Her name was Cinthia Vega, and she had given birth to a son, Arturo and Alicia's sixth grandchild almost one month earlier, another bona fide American. He was to be christened Arturo in a few days, following the American tradition of naming a child after an elder, rather than the saint whose feast day was celebrated on the date of his birth. Cinthia insisted. She'd heard so much of the late Arturo, and she felt grateful to him—her son would not exist were it not for Arturo's courage and determination.

On this Sunday morning, right after breakfast, Cinthia decided to take the baby for a walk in his new stroller. She would check the family's vegetable plot on the edge of the Back Bay fens a few blocks away. There were dozens of plots there, called Victory Gardens when they were first planted during World War II: Victory Gardens had been created in almost every city back then, a time when it was not just necessary for soldiers' wives to man rivet guns, but also to augment the dinner table, what with all the food shortages. Boston's Victory Gardens, taking up half the fens' fourteen square acres, still thrived. The plots were watered and enriched by the Muddy River, which flowed in from a spring-fed pond three miles away, until it joined with the Charles directly opposite MIT.

Developers cringed at the sight of the gardens; if only they could snap up that land. But who knew? Who wanted to own a swamp? Now, the DEP prevented any such possibility. The fens provided food and shelter for forty-two species of migrating birds and many more water animals. The only fish in the Muddy River were large, slow-moving carp. Carp didn't require more than the limited amount of oxygen the sluggish river supplied.

When Cinthia was getting dressed into a shirt and shorts—

pleased that she could now button the shorts with ease—Alicia suggested she wait the full month since giving birth before venturing out on her own, wait till the baby's baptism in a few days as was the custom. But Cinthia reminded her husband's mother that this was America; she was feeling fine; and it was a glorious day; and that she had made several forays to the playground on the corner. Besides, she was worried about the plants not getting enough water on these hot August days. And she missed the friends she'd made at the Gardens, couldn't wait any longer to show off her adorable baby boy. She would spend the morning there.

Alicia sighed, and helped Cinthia dress the baby in a little yellow onesie and booties. They bundled him into his new stroller, tucked him into a white blanket crocheted by Cinthia's best friend back in Brooklyn who had recently married Cinthia's brother, Carlos. Cinthia stuck a few Pampers into the stroller's rear basket, and a bottle of water for herself. George walked with them to the corner of Haviland, then headed off to Mass Ave, and on toward the T station. It was a Sunday, a realtor's biggest day. He planned to go in for a few hours to catch up on some odds and ends and let the other agents handle the walk-ins. This decision was based on the badge of new fatherhood—utter exhaustion.

Cinthia and George would both be home by twelve; Sunday dinner was planned for two o'clock.

Cinthia headed in the opposite direction George took, toward Boylston and the Victory Gardens. But she never reached the Victory Gardens, never returned from her walk.

⚾

George and the rest of the family went out looking for Cinthia at the hour they had planned to sit down to dinner. The folks tending the Victory Gardens at first smiled broadly when they saw the Sanchezes, ready to shake hands, offer hugs and kisses, and extend their congratulations on the arrival of the newest child. Their merry smiles were soon transformed into frowns of worry. No, Cinthia hadn't been by. They hadn't seen her at all. The gardeners dropped what they were doing to offer aid and comfort, and to help look for her. Some of the gardeners were well-to-do women from Beacon Hill, some were immigrants, and the rest were in-between. The first group grew prize begonias, the in-betweens, cutting flowers like zinnias and also vegetables—squash and radishes and kale. The immigrants grew beans and chiles, explaining to their fellow gardeners that there were over forty varieties of chiles. The one plant in common to all the groups was the tomato, vines trained onto strong sticks or expensive trellises.

Cinthia and the baby seemed to have disappeared off the face of the earth.

The family now gathered together on Edgerly Road at Alicia's kitchen table argued about whether or not to take the advice of their gardening neighbors, and go to the police. But Cinthia was in the country illegally, even though in Massachusetts, everyone is entitled to public services, including police protection, whether they are citizens or not. George was afraid members of his own family might be placed in suspicion, or even detained, though they were first and second generation Americans. It happened. He did not want to be deterred from finding Cinthia, which he'd been trying to do so fruitlessly all day.

But this reasoning made no sense to his desperate uncles who asked George, "Is there something you have not told us?"

George looked into their eyes and said, "Yes." Then: "We had a fight last night."

As it turned out, the neighbors heard. Cinthia and George had been standing on the sidewalk and the building's windows were open. George felt his wife should respect his mother's desire to wait a month before going off on her own. He was the most religious of the brothers. He was worried something might happen to little Arturo before he was baptized. To his family, he brought up the spectacle of such a catastrophe, how the baby would end up in limbo.

"And what did Cinthia say to that?" his uncle asked him.

"She said limbo was a dance, and that we'd all do the limbo at Arturo's christening party in a few days. I didn't find that was funny."

Alicia, with the merest trace of an accent, said, "But it was funny to Cinthia. It is why we love her."

The older of the children, supposedly sleeping in the nearby bedroom, was behind the kitchen door eavesdropping. She wanted to help so she came in and said, "Uncle George, I learned in catechism that there is no such thing as limbo anymore. The Pope says."

The child was put back to bed, and the adults continued their argument, understanding now George's reluctance to go to the police. The mother of the little catechism student suggested that maybe Cinthia was upset, that she probably missed her family, and being of a certain temperament she'd never hesitated to let be known, had probably gone back to her home in New York to get away from all the in-laws for a few days. George's aunt said, "It is hard to be away from your own mother when you have your first child."

This was their last hope. And so they called Cinthia's family. Cinthia's father immediately called the Boston PD, and then he and Cinthia's brothers set out from Brooklyn.

The police officer who took the call did not connect the missing Brooklyn woman—who he understood to be still living in Brooklyn—and her son with the Fenway Park baby.

Like everyone else, the officer was under the impression that
the abandoned baby was a newborn. The baby these men
described was just shy of a month old, and besides, both the
mother and child were missing together. The desk duty officer assured the caller that nothing had come in about a mother and child.

At 2 AM, Cinthia's father and two brothers, along with
George and one of his uncles, arrived at the District 4 area
precinct serving the neighborhood that included Fenway Park
and the Back Bay. The cops, whose hectic weekend was finally slowing down, suggested Cinthia went to stay with a friend
while she got over the snit she was in with her husband. Or
maybe, one of them added, she had a boyfriend. With that, all
hell broke loose and the cops were forced to make a couple of
arrests—George, and Cinthia's brother Carlos—before the
rest of the two families retreated to plan a further search for
her and the baby, and to find a lawyer for her husband and
brother.

During the same late hour when Cinthia's family were
with the police, two teenage boys, prostitutes, were taking up
their spots just beyond the Victory Gardens in the fens, in an
area referred to as *the reeds*. The growth so described was not
actually any kind of reeds, but rather an invasive and wide-
spread species of phragmites choking the oxygen out of the
Muddy River. A john was already waiting—the spot was list-
ed on at least a dozen websites. He paid one of them, and he
and the boy disappeared into the high, thick, dank growth.
This john was a new one, nervous, and insisted on going
deeper into the reeds closer to the margin of the river, slug-
gishly flowing past, its edge so undefined that it couldn't real-

ly be considered a riverbank. The waters blended in with the swampy fens floor before it widened enough to create a pond, twenty-five yards further on.

The john trudged through the reeds, his eyes darting nervously all around, while the boy wisely kept his own eyes to the ground so as not to step into the sludgy mud.

The boy suddenly stopped. The john started to turn just as the boy screamed, a shriek so extended and unearthly, that the horrific noise of it glued the john and the boy, too, in place. Then they both ran, the boy crashing his way toward the Victory Gardens, the john mistakenly heading toward the innards of the fens, stumbling and sinking into the muck before getting a hold of himself, and taking advantage of the towering Fenway Park left field stanchion, using it as a guidepost. The lights had gone off after the day's second game, but the tall structure was eerily silhouetted against the star-filled night sky. The john never saw the body that had so freaked the boy.

An anonymous call came into 911.

The call was taken at the D-4 precinct and the desk duty officer groaned at the thought of his fellow law enforcers spending the rest of the night sloshing through that wet gunk. In fact, he mumbled to himself, "Poor bastards," after he said to the missing persons desk, "Break out the waders. You guys have a fishing trip ahead of you."

The desk duty officer had not seen the report on George and Carlos, now in custody, and even if he had wouldn't have connected a possible missing wife and child with a body in the reeds, most certainly that of a man living an alternative lifestyle.

THE NUMBER ONE PLACE
Monday, 8:05 AM

Last night after game two I met up with a friend who
had been at both games. He's been at every game
this season. Every game for the past *several* seasons, actually. We hung out at the BeerWorks for a
while, watching the tourists roll in—undoubtedly
turned away from a packed Cask'n Flagon, which
they'd checked off their list of sites to visit after seeing their first Fenway game. Which means they
bought tickets from a scalper, thinking they'd made
a sweet deal, only to find it's quite hard to follow a
baseball game when there's a steel girder between
your seat and home plate.

Was good to hear my friend's perspective on the
wild day at the park. He said by the fourth inning
there was a "Yankee game buzz" to the crowd. On
our way out of there, we walked down Yawkey
Way—there's something very cool about walking
down that street when it's not jammed with people—
toward the Back Bay fens. That swampland over
there, you know, that big untapped area that's
bound to be bought by the Red Sox and turned into
some kind of baseball Disneyland, was crawling
with the police. It looked like some kind of casting
call for cop extras. I swear one of them was Ricky
Gervais. Could it be they finally did a sting on the
area, notorious for young male hookers? From what
I always heard, those guys and the cops pretty
much had an understanding. "We have sex in these

reeds and you guys look the other way. . ." Something like that. Maybe the understanding was off.

COMMENTS:

KGNumber5 said: I wondered what was going on there. The legendary homeless guy, Mr. Butch, just died and I know memorials have been planned. Maybe they had one over there and the cops showed up or something.

PatG said: Nah, the Mr. Butch memorial is in Allston. Too bad about that guy. I'll never forget seeing him every time I'd go to a show at the Rat in Kenmore Square.

Empy said: I can see the fens from my apartment window. Things got quiet later on last night, but this morning the cops are all over the place. What's the story?

CHAPTER

5

At ten on Monday morning, a FedEx envelope arrived in the mailroom at the corporate headquarters and news bureau studios of ESPN in Bristol, Connecticut. It was addressed to Michael Kim, a smart, popular and poised sports news anchor. The letter was marked *Personal*, no return address.

Kim picked it up. He could have deemed it suspicious and sent it to security, but after holding it to his ear and giving it a shake, he detected no sounds of swishing powder. He said to his producer, "I'm taking the odds that it's not anthrax." He opened it.

Inside the envelope he found a picture of a young woman—pretty, curly hair, tanned—and a brief note which read: *This is the mother of the baby found in Fenway Park.*

Kim and his producer called the Boston police and were advised to send a jpeg photo right away. Then the two men decided, since they hadn't been told not to (*and* since this was a breaking news story), that when Kim went on the air, he should hold the picture up to the camera, and implore anyone who knew the woman to contact Boston PD.

In Portland, Maine, several members of the Sea Dogs squad—the Red Sox Double-A team—were watching *ESPNews*. They were all from the Caribbean or Central America, plus one from Japan, and were doing their homework. Their language coach was actually a former ESL high school teacher/Red Sox fan who, on a lark, had offered his services to teach English to the Japanese players, and to the Hispanic players if need be. He was delirious not only to be hired, but to receive the designation, *Coach*. He immediately assigned his students to watch *ESPNews*, particularly Michael Kim. Kim spoke in a clear, refined manner reflecting his roots in the American Midwest where some argued that English was spoken accent-less. And of course, the Sea Dogs, being professional athletes, could absorb a great deal of the broadcast aided by their extensive knowledge of sports terminology adapted and woven into their own language, *beísbol*, the prime example.

When Kim held up the picture of the anonymous young woman, something very strange happened. At the rear of the group of players was a shy, nineteen-year-old Dominican named Luis Sanseverra, who could throw an unhittable fastball with pinpoint control. He'd been brought up via the powerful Jack Lagunas, a superagent based in California, who specialized in Hispanic players. Luis stared at the picture of the pretty girl while the other players made comments as to her fine looks, and he suddenly became stricken. He leaped to his feet and shouted, "*No!*" which meant the same in thing in both English and Spanish. He then let loose a string of more words than he'd spoken in the six months since he'd been sold to Portland by his brilliant agent, who seemed to produce players out of the clear blue sky.

During the first few days Luis had spent in Portland after arriving from the Dominican, the other players wondered if he was deaf rather than shy. They'd say, "Hey, Luis!" and he wouldn't even look at them.

When the players shifted their gaze from the television to Luis, they were shocked when his blathering was overtaken by uncontrollable crying. They practically had to hog-tie him, he was so hysterical. They couldn't make anything out of what he was babbling until, in such a plaintive wail, he sobbed, "*Mi corazón.*"

The trainer ended up stabbing him with a syringe full of Ativan, while the manager called Jack Lagunas—the kid's superagent. Instead of speaking to his client, young Luis, Lagunas surprisingly said, "I'll be on a plane to Boston in an hour," and he hung up.

But before Lagunas even arrived at LAX, the Sea Dogs manager was turning his attention to another major event of that day, officially welcoming David Ortiz to the clubhouse. Big Papi was there to help promote the Sea Dogs by taping a commercial asking the people of Portland to continue to show their enthusiastic support for their local team as the Eastern League early-September playoffs approached. Papi was told about Luis Sanseverra, his countryman, who was now lying half-conscious on the massage table in the trainer's room.

Papi, a giant teddy bear of a man, was not only adored by the fans but by the players and coaches, too. His easy-going manner was infectious, the power of his bat inspired all. When an interviewer once mentioned his great size, clearly alluding to the possible influence of bulk-enhancing steroids—or perhaps human growth hormones—Papi never grew the least bit testy. Instead, he responded to the interviewer's significant pause by saying, "I'm a big guy. They testing my urine after every damn game. Always they finding the same thing—rice and beans, rice and beans, rice and beans."

Now, he spent a good half hour with Luis, comforting him

and trying to find out what had caused him to lose his marbles. No one bothered the two players—one so brawny, the other a beanpole—but the Hispanic players hovered by the door of the trainer's room. Papi got up and slammed it shut. He didn't slam it in annoyance, but because he was so strong. Just a touch on the door sent it flying. When Papi opened it again, he filled the doorframe. He turned once more to Luis, who was now sitting up on the edge of the table. He nodded at him in a conspiratorial way, and went back to give him one more reassuring Big Papi-style hug.

Then Papi explained to the manager, "He say some girl whose picture is just on television is his girlfrien'. She suppose to be the mother of the baby we foun' yesterday."

"The picture was of his *girlfriend?*"

"Yeah. But Luis say the girlfrien' didn't have no baby. She a virgin. He say, Him too. I tell him to settle down and I fin' out about his girlfrien'. I call his family to see if she all right, you know? I fin' out, then I come back and see him."

The manager said, "I really appreciate this, Papi. He seems like such a nice kid. Shy. He doesn't say much. Not even to the Spanish guys. Stays to himself. They can't get to him."

"Yeah, well, I going to get to him. Keep quiet about the whole thing. Till I figure out what the hell is going on."

"Okay, Papi."

"And by the way. . . Spanish guys? They from Madrid. Us guys. . ." He stuck his thumb into his chest ". . .Hispanic."

David Ortiz put on his sunglasses, shook everyone's hand, and left. The Sea Dogs couldn't help but note that there was no Big Papi smile on his face.

So perhaps it was the players who eavesdropped, or maybe one of the camera team there to make the tape heard something, but somebody told somebody that the girl whose picture was on *ESPNews* was Luis's girlfriend.

An hour later, two police officers arrived at the clubhouse. They wanted to ask Luis about the girl, about the baby. Luis, once more, went nuts, became aggressive, and tried to run out. The cops cuffed him and brought him to the stationhouse.

①

Rocky Patel is a Boston Homicide Detective First Grade. The detectives knighted with that appellation are the best of the best: they understand the word of law; they share brain cells with coroners; they are intimately familiar with the workings of the crime lab; they put in training stints in Quantico; they do not make mistakes. Consequently, they boast an extraordinarily high success rate insofar as arresting some really bad dude. More important, they are able to set the stage for convictions based on evidence, as opposed to faulty eye-witnesses or coerced confessions.

It is said in Boston that there are fewer detectives first grade in the world than there are cardinals in the Church.

They answer directly to the chief.

By afternoon, Rocky Patel had received briefings from four departments: his own; missing persons; CAC; and Public Safety, now known as Homeland Security—the folks who remain desperate to make sure no one converts any more planes leaving Logan into weapons. At CAC, he spoke to the man in charge, Lt. Marcus Chan, who told him he was actually on the way to the game on Sunday, when he got word of the abandoned baby.

"My girlfriend got us tickets. Paid some illegal internet crook a week's salary for field boxes. Spent the game in the clubhouse and then at the hospital. Never saw a single pitch. Incredible, isn't it, Rocky?"

"Yes, Lieutenant." Rocky would never call a superior by his first name.

"You're not going to ask me if I noticed anything unusual?"

"No Lieutenant. If you had, I would have heard from you."

"That's right. You go to any games, Rock?"

"I am ashamed to say I have not been to a single one. I try to see the games on TV. But my wife took me to the Rolling Rally in 2004."

"Omigod."

Rocky laughed. "I enjoyed it. I found it quite spiritual."

Lieutenant Chan said, "Man, if I was a Chinese immigrant instead of fourth generation American, maybe I'd see something spiritual there. So go to a game, Rock, you'll love it. And this year we'll all go to the Rally, how's that sound?"

"You are presuming another championship?"

"Last year we had heart palpitations and cancer. This year, just stupid things like a strained oblique, whatever the hell that is. We're goin' all the way, Rock. Again."

The array of photographs, files and notes filling up Rocky's laptop screen, beginning with the details of an abandoned baby found at Fenway Park, required all his concentration. In addition, there was also the morning's discovery of an unidentified dead woman in the fens—murdered, according to the medical examiner. There was the photo of a girl that an anonymous individual had FedExed to ESPN claiming she was the mother of the abandoned baby. Also, a loner, Double A player now being held in Portland who claimed to be the boyfriend of the woman in the ESPN photograph. Two more things: a promise to help the player from David Ortiz, the Red Sox designated hitter, who had initially seen to the Portland kid's distress; and finally the words of an anonymous blogger who knew, as Rocky put it, a number of substantiated facts that he shouldn't have known unless he was inside. Inside baseball, inside the media—maybe even inside the police department—though no one wanted to go there just yet. That connection remained to be seen.

Minutes after all the unconnected dots had been gathered together on the chief's desk, he'd assigned Rocky Patel to connect them. He needed someone who was not only brilliant, but who wouldn't be dazzled by the involvement of the Boston Red Sox, which eliminated 99.9 percent of the force. He also needed someone with a particular mindset, who could take such an array of disparate elements confronting the chief and find the pattern necessary to move forward. The chief recalled a visit from an FBI agent on assignment to Boston for an especially dicey case involving a judge and his politically connected family—much like this case, a nightmare because of the high profile of those involved. He recalled the agent because of the acclaimed reputation that preceded her, and because he couldn't get over how much she looked like Nicole Kidman.

She'd said to him, "I knew this would be interesting when I met with your detective. Patel. He told me he had Jesus in his heart but Shiva in his blood."

The chief's response to this observation was: "Well, I sure as hell've heard of Jesus, but who's this Shiva?"

And she'd said quite patiently, "One of the Hindu trinity. The god of destruction and reproduction. Quite the juxtaposition. An entity seeing to the Phoenix rising from the ashes, wouldn't you say?"

The Nicole Kidman look-alike FBI agent had even seen to finding out who the rest of the trinity incorporated: Brahma and Vishnu. The chief really didn't care to know; he had enough trouble with the Father, Son and Holy Ghost. One trinity was plenty. And he never understood that Phoenix-rising thing.

He only knew that Rocky Patel was this agent's man.

Rocky stared at the pieces of paper on his desk—there would always be paper-people—and he mentally shifted about the pieces not knowing if any number of them might not even fit into this particular puzzle. After twenty minutes of staring, not moving a muscle, barely flickering his thick eyelashes shadowing his large dark eyes, he went to his laptop and clicked on the blogger's address. The banner at the top of the page had the familiar pair of red socks, and the title—*The Number One Place*. Rocky read the last few days' posts. This blogger, called Jay, knew what went on in the clubhouse which meant he was there, or else someone had filled him in. He also knew the baby was drugged, and it was Rocky's understanding that all those present in the clubhouse were asked not to mention that to anyone. But there are always leaks. And then, incredibly, the blogger happened to be walking by the fens when the police were in there looking for a body.

For *now*, the blogger served as a provocative piece of the puzzle. He would be dealt with later.

The detective went back to his statue-like demeanor. He not only needed the time to search the puzzle pieces, as well as his soul, he mostly needed to decompress after the burdensome hours he'd just spent alongside the medical examiner in the fens, and later with him again at the morgue.

The officers who had been sent out into the fens at 2 AM, gave up after about twenty minutes. Even with their flashlights they kept tripping over the web of roots lurking beneath the mud. Instead, they focused on talking to the denizens of the reeds, many known to them having been arrested for prostitution, though most of the arrests the cops made there were for vagrancy. The reeds were a place more popular with closeted gay men than male prostitutes, lonely guys wanting to hook up with each other for a few minutes of anonymous sex. It was not unlike that bathroom in the Minneapolis airport. Not worthy of the Boston PD's time. When the cops found underage prostitutes, though, they called in someone from CAC.

One of the boys the cops fingered said to them, "I ain't tellin' who told me, but Mikey. . .you know Mikey, right?"

"Right."

"Mikey was somewheres in there." He pointed past the gardens. "The guy that picked him up wanted to go farther in—stupid dork. Guy was stressed. Mikey is the one we heard screamin'—like some kind of banshee. Who called 911? It sure wasn't me."

"Maybe it was Mikey who was stressed."

"He's stressed *now*, that's for sure."

"Yeah? So where is Mikey?"

"I don't know. But from what I hear, he ain't comin' back any time soon. I mean, would you, if you saw some dead body?"

The officers could surely identify with Mikey's state of mind.

"Meanwhile," the boy said, "we ain't got no more customers tonight. And I'm outta here."

The kid knew the drill. He allowed the officer to try to convince him to take advantage of available help, and counseling, and guidance, before taking off ahead of CAC's arriving. The kid responded, "Those CAC guys will send me back to my father, and I really ain't too crazy about how he burns me with cigarettes when I'm sleepin', ya know?"

The officers told him he could go, and they watched him drift away into the night. One said to the other, "Tough."

"Yeah."

They talked to some of the other teenagers, now gathered together on Agassiz Road. They stood around the water utility building just off the little brick bridge traversing that portion of the Muddy River dividing the fens down the middle. Because Mikey was a pretty straightforward kid, all of them believed he really did see a body in the reeds.

In the light of dawn, a more extensive search party was sent out, and within a fairly short time, they'd come upon the body that Mikey and the john had nearly tripped over. A woman.

The medical examiner waited there for Rocky who he knew was on his way. He wouldn't turn the face-down body over until he first discussed his initial findings with the detective. Rocky arrived in minutes, and squatted down next to him.

The woman was wearing a pink tank top and denim shorts. A flip-flop lay nearby. Her long black hair was in a pony tail. From her splayed-out position, it was clear that she'd been unconscious or dead when dropped to the ground. Her right arm was bent under her body, and her left arm was flung out over her head. She wore a wedding ring and a gold bracelet. It was a trendy Pandora bracelet hung with several charms.

"Forensics teams are pretty much finished up. Only thing they found. . .the shoe prints of the person who dropped her here. Only prints that are deeper on the way into the reeds, and more shallow on the way out. Trouble is, they became sullied when the water seeped into them, filling them up. Muddy River's tidal, compliments of the Charles and our beautiful harbor.

"Body temperature. . .rigor. . . She's been dead for a day, my guess. And no one's come up with the other flip-flop. Probably still where she died."

Rocky wrote these details in his notebook. If he wrote something down, he had another piece to help put together the jigsaw puzzle.

The time came to turn her.

The techs were exquisitely gentle with her, lifting her shoulders and hips, cradling the back of her head to hold it steady as they rolled her onto her back. Wet mud covered the entire front of her body and her face. There was nothing more to find out from her there at the scene.

The examiner placed plastic bags over her hands, securing them with rubber bands. Then he said, "Let's get this poor girl out of here. When I've cleaned her, when I've taken care of the basics, I'll get back to you, Rock."

"How long?"

The examiner did not intend to waste any time.

"Give me three hours."

Rocky looked at his watch. "I'll be there."

⬤

Shoulder to shoulder with the coroner, Rocky watched as he removed the sheet from her body. Her clothes and jewelry and shoe had been bagged, and the mud washed off.

The first jarring detail Rocky could not help but notice—the incisions he expected—before registering anything else beyond the tragedy of one so young being dead, were the strange smears across the woman's swollen breasts.

The examiner said, "Breast milk. Lactation continues after death."

And Rocky experienced a sharp pain in his core. He was the father of a six-month-old child. He'd recently calculated that his wife spent at least ten times the amount of time nursing their baby as she did feeding herself. Rocky was continually offering her glasses of water crammed with slices of oranges, lemons and limes, or bowls of sliced peaches suspended in fresh yogurt. His wife, Lucy, was half Irish on her father's side. That side of her family kept plying her with Guinness Stout to increase her supply of milk for the baby. Lucy's mother was Italian; her family had owned one of the most popular restaurants in the North End for several generations. Lucy was the chef, at present on maternity leave. Her mother filled the fridge with Saran-wrapped plates of braciole, gnocchi and fish covered with sauces made from olive oil, butter, and garlic—all to be heated up when Lucy was not nursing the baby, which seemed to be all the time. Lucy often read while she nursed. When Rocky would point out that the baby had fallen asleep, she would look down, whisper, "See ya later," and ease him over to Rocky who would put him in his crib.

The baby grew to be the size of a moose. Lucy's grandfather began calling him Bronko Nagurski, which Rocky learned was the name of a legendary football player of yore.

The few times that Rocky and Lucy went out, she would pump what seemed to Rocky like a quart of milk from her breasts. Then there was milk smeared across them, so she'd have to take a shower before they could actually leave.

The examiner interrupted Rocky's thoughts. "She gave birth very recently. About a month ago, no more. No less either. Could tell by the condition of her uterus.

"She was hit twice. Left cheek with the palm of a right hand, right cheek with the back of the same hand. Hit so hard the blows caused her neck muscles to bleed and her brain to concuss when it whiplashed in her skull. On her right cheek—you see that cut, Rocky?—the perp wore a heavy ring."

"Such blows still would not have killed her."

"That's right. She wasn't dead when the perp dragged her

into the fens to hide her. He just threw her to the ground and she ended up face down. She was unconscious, of course. She suffocated in the wet bog out there."

Another pain shot through Rocky. Then he asked, "Sexual assault?"

"Not raped, no sexual injuries."

Rocky said, "I suspect that will be some small relief to her loved ones. . ."

The examiner's eyes met Rocky's. He could only hope the same. Rocky had the greatest respect for this examiner. The man referred to victims as his patients, not as bodies. He considered his physical exams—and seeing to the testing of specimens—as no different from what any doctor does whose patients are alive. He would point out to people who found his manner eccentric that there were many patients who couldn't convey what happened to them—babies and children, or the mentally disabled, or foreigners who can't speak the language, or those who are afraid to speak at all.

He said to Rocky in his advocation of his patient: "I know you'll fight for this girl, Rock."

Rocky gazed down at the body lying in front of him. He could see that she must have been quite lovely despite the injury to her face. He swore to himself that he would find the perpetrator who had ended this poor woman's life and left a child desolate. He vowed to see justice served.

He nodded to the examiner who took up the sheet, and covered her.

When Rocky was back at his desk, he'd removed those horrific images from his brain and went on to considering his time with the young ballplayer from Portland, who had been brought to the D-4 precinct in Boston that included the area where the crime had taken place. Rocky was now in charge of a task force of hand-picked officers—hand-picked by Rocky—given temporary space at D-4. Rocky could have assembled them where he worked at headquarters, but he wanted to be in the neighborhood.

He'd planned to question the player when he arrived, but decided to wait. The kid hadn't slept and he wouldn't eat either. The last thing Rocky needed was for Luis Sanseverra to go hysterical again. So he'd tried, through an interpreter, just to get the player to tell him how they could reach his girl-friend. But Luis wouldn't speak to him or anyone else until he heard back from David Ortiz, who had promised to help him. Luis had not been arrested, but was being held as a person of interest. He was advised to contact a lawyer. He said he did not need a lawyer; he just needed to wait until Big Papi could come to help him.

Rocky and the examiner had the lab move the dead woman's specimens to the front of the line; Boston's modern headquarters were state of the art with an in-house DNA lab—testing capacity, limitless and swift. And Rocky had a public case. They would find out if the abandoned baby's DNA matched hers very soon. Rocky noted that whenever this baby was mentioned, no one referred to him any longer as the abandoned baby. Most everyone was calling him, "Baby Ted Williams."

Rocky had lived in Boston from the time he'd arrived from the Gujerat at age ten. He would never really get used to the ways of the people of Boston though he loved their ways very much and, in fact, had married one of them, much to the dis-may of his parents. But they'd come to adore Lucy. Rocky's mother and her daughter-in-law started teaching each other to cook their own cultural delicacies; Lucy's mother came to introduce a new dish at the family's restaurant—Pasta

Gujerat, angel-hair pasta with white bèchemel sauce, only half yogurt, and sprinkled with finely crushed cashews rather than parmesian cheese. Then with the arrival of Bronko, Lucy's mother and Rocky's couldn't stop hugging each other whenever they gazed upon their first grandchild.

Sargeant Marty Flanagan, Rocky's partner, opened the office door and peeked in. "Luis Sanseverra's agent is here. He's got a lawyer with him." Marty told Rocky the name of the lawyer and Rocky rolled his eyes. He knew that tens of thousands of dollars had already been placed into the lawyer's checking account, something the fellow required before he so much as spoke to a client on the phone.

"Allow the lawyer to see Mr. Sanseverra, Marty, but keep Lagunas with us. If he wants to see the detective in charge. . ."

"Oh, he certainly does. . ."

". . .tell him I'm busy at the moment."

Marty smiled and left, and then he was back.

"Says he's going to sue us, big surprise. I'll tell ya, Rock, this Lagunas guy ain't lookin' too good."

"What do you mean?"

"He's, like, wicked antsy. If he keeps bitin' his nails like he's doin', he'll end up lookin' like Venus de Milo."

Rocky's curiosity was roused. He went out into the outer office teeming with activity. His half-dozen officers on the case were all on their phones or studying their computer screens, calling back and forth to each other. Lagunas sat in a corner where there were a couple of upholstered chairs for outsiders to sit until one of the cops could get to them. Lagunas was clearly antsy, but he was also steaming with fury.

Rocky walked over to him and held out his hand. "Detective Rocky Patel. I have detained Mr. Sanseverra."

The superagent stood up. He was the same height as Rocky, around five-nine, black wavy hair, skin the color of *café au lait*, and as handsome as a movie star. He lapsed into a diatribe having to do with his rights being denied. His language was accented which told Rocky he'd learned to speak English after the age of twelve. It was Rocky's experience that when the language was learned prior to that age, there was no accent, just a touch of the first language's idiosyncratic grammatical usage. Rocky himself spoke English without an accent, but once in a while reverted to the gerund form of a verb which he did now.

"I am thinking that you are rightly upset, Mr. Lagunas. But I cannot let anyone other than his lawyer see the young man till I have had a chance to speak to him myself. Presently, he will speak to no one until a gentleman who has promised to advise him arrives."

"Advise him? And who the hell would that be?"

"A fellow ballplayer."

"*What* fellow ballplayer?"

Rocky looked down at his notebook and rifled through the pages. "Let me see. . . Ah, here it is. David Ortiz. Now if you'll excuse me. . ."

Rocky walked away as the man shouted, "*David Ortiz?* What the fuck has Ortiz got to do with anything?"

But then the lawyer appeared, and he and the agent began yelling at each other. Rocky disappeared into his office.

A few minutes later, Sargeant Flanagan peeked through the door again. Rocky waved him in. Marty plopped down in the chair on the other side of Rocky's desk. "Shit, how I love it. The kid told Mr. High-Priced Lawyer the same thing he told us, just keeps saying he promised Big Papi he wouldn't say anything to anyone. Papi promised he'd come back. Course the lawyer can't speak Spanish so he has no clue what the kid is goin' on about. He asked us for an interpreter. Told him all of ours were busy. Get your own."

He laughed.

Rocky said, "Now this Papi. That would be David Ortiz? The player?"

"Yeah, Rock. That's who he'd be."

"Get him."

"Get who?"

"Get Mr. Ortiz."

Rocky noted Sargeant Flanagan's expanded glee. The man couldn't contain his excitement as he dashed off. And Rocky had no idea of knowing that his partner was damned grateful that the Red Sox had won the second game of yesterday's doubleheader and that Big Papi had knocked in three runs.

THE NUMBER ONE PLACE
Monday, 5:10 PM

An off-day for the Red Sox today, but not for Big Papi. Ortiz was up in Portland, filming a TV spot for the Sea Dogs. But a more serious matter was at hand up there, as the young Dominican phenom pitcher Luis Sanseverra turned out to be right in the middle of this baby situation. I had *ESPNews* on today when Michael Kim showed the picture that was supposedly the mother of Baby Ted. Apparently, she's the girlfriend of Luis. Papi, a country-man of Luis, was able to console the kid.

Another interesting thing is that a look at the Dominican League stats over the last few years shows no player named "Luis Sanseverra." The latest stats of Luis on the minor league websites all show his high school numbers, which can't be completely verified anyway. One thing we do know, this kid's rookie card might actually be worth something someday. Of course, I said that about a lot of cards when I was little.

Think about it: Our parents' generation treated their baseball cards like rectangular ragdolls, flipping them around on the floor, throwing darts at them, and—that age-old classic—putting them in the spokes of their bicycle wheels. Then their parents threw the cards away when they left home—only to find out years later that the collection would've been worth a fortune.

Our generation, on the other hand, treated baseball cards like they were gold, immediately sliding them into protective plastic or glass sleeves, careful not to bend their corners or scuff their faces. Our parents dutifully held on to our collections when we moved out. But now that we're adults, we've discovered 99% of our cards are worth nothing. . . .

But the fate of the real Luis, not the cardboard one, is what's important right now. He's fortunate to have a friend like Big Papi.

COMMENTS:

SamCat said: Indeed. This sounds like a mess. I just hope Yankee fans don't start acting like they're better than us because we've got this controversy going on right now.

Red Sox Chick said: What do you mean "*start* acting

like they're better than us?" As long as A-Rod's on
their team, I don't think they can say anything, with
all the crap he gets into. Besides, this doesn't say
anything bad about our organization. It's not like the
team is hiding anything.

MattySox said: *Our generation treated baseball cards
like they were gold*? Speak for yourself, man. I used
to turn my Yankee cards into little ashtrays. Graig
Nettles made a *great* ashtray.

Jay said: Bill Lee would be proud, Matty.

ConnecticutSoxFan said: I'm glad Michael Kim got
this story first. In a sports world where anchors care
more about catch phrases than stories, he's a
breath of fresh air. You were talking about how
sports people don't usually know how to talk about
"real" news—he's one guy that does.

Marshall said: I was skeptical when ESPN decided to
start their "news" channel. But I agree—their
reporters do a nice job.

CHAPTER

6

David Ortiz was on his way to the D-4 precinct early that evening. His red Mercedes, with a hand-built engine that could have him charge forth from zero to 60 mph in less than four seconds, would cross paths with Marty's unmarked cop car as it headed toward his house ten miles west of Fenway Park. Since he'd gotten home from Portland, Papi spent the rest of the day on the phone making, what seemed to his wife, a hundred calls. She wanted to know what was going on, and he said, "I tell you after dinner, Che."

She loved how he called her *Che*, his little revolutionary, the college girl from Wisconsin he'd met when he played for the Twins. He got a kick out of the whole New England Patriots thing, but he rooted with her for Green Bay, too.

"Okay, Papi."

During dinner, a phone call came for Papi. He didn't take phone calls during dinner because he enjoyed chattering with his children in Spanish. He loved this time with them—he and his wife wanted them to be fluent in both languages. The housekeeper quietly took the call at the opposite end of the huge kitchen. Papi made exceptions for emergencies.

She said, "Excuse me, Mr. Ortiz. It's the manager of the Sea Dogs. He says it's an emergency."

Papi went out into the living room and picked up the phone. He listened and then he said, "*What?*" so loudly that the children came running from the table to him, eyes as big as saucers. He shooed them back to the kitchen. His wife stood in the doorway and he told her he'd be right there.

A minute later he was back standing at the kitchen door. He said, "Che, I need to talk to you a minute." He said to the children, "Eat your dinner. *Déjame hablar con Mami. ¿Estamos?*"

His wife gave the kids a look that said, *Do what Dad says or else*, and went out to him.

"I gotta go. They arrest that kid from Portland."

Now his wife said, "*What?*" just as forcefully as her husband had, but the children stayed put under the threatening gaze of the housekeeper.

Yesterday had been a long day. After the doubleheader, Papi did not follow the usual post-game routine. He was physically exhausted and the experience with the baby had wrung him out. He did plant kisses upon his own babies, gently so as not to wake them, but he didn't take a soak in the tub; didn't have a second dinner (he'd had a first before leaving for the park revolving around massive portions of rice and beans); no TV or movie; no relaxed calls to relatives in his home town of Haina; no making love. Just a few husband-and-wife-whispers before he fell asleep.

Now he said, "The kid, he's in Boston. I got the precinct address. I tell you everythin' when I get back, okay?" He kissed her and got his keys out again.

She asked him, "Do you want me to go with you, Papi?"

He smiled. "No, Che. You go tell the kids, I see them when I come home. We go to Dairy Queen."

He kissed her again, and the minute he was out the door,

she got on the Red Sox wives' email and phone trees where they shared their lives and their husbands' lives with each other until fall, when they could return to their permanent homes. A band of sisters connected by six countries, Puerto Rico and twenty-two of the fifty United States from California, to Texas, to Florida, to New York.

On this day, they had made their way to Children's Hospital and cooed together over Baby Ted Williams who'd been moved from the neonatal ICU, and put in the transition unit. He was crying. They were surprised to see how big he was. They'd expected to see a one-day-old infant. Once that realization sunk in, Manny Ramirez's wife broke down. She said, "He must miss his mother." The staff at Deaconess offered Kleenex and comfort to all of them.

Each and every one would have adopted the child in two minutes if she could. Without saying as much, they instinctively took on a guardianship role just as their husbands had—they grilled doctors, nurses and aides, demanding what the baby's unknown mother would have demanded: How is he? When will he get better? When can he leave the hospital?

The staff told them he'd been dehydrated—not severely, but he'd required a glucose drip. Now he was on the road to wellness and his prognosis excellent, but of course the staff would have to remain cautious and watchful with such a young patient, whose medical history was unknown.

Jonathan Papelbon, the best closer in baseball, had gotten married two years earlier. His wife, though without children of her own, asked the charge nurse if anyone was rocking the baby in a rocking chair and if not, she'd like to volunteer to do that. The young woman had been inspired by the relationship between her new friends and their children. As it happened, Children's Hospital had in place a program whereby volunteers were utilized to do just what she'd wondered about—rock babies who'd been born with crack cocaine in their systems. Nothing else could calm them.

Since Baby Ted Williams was, in fact, recovering from a barbituate in his system, it was determined that Papelbon's wife could certainly rock this infant.

As she was led off to wash her hands and don pink scrubs, she turned and said to the women, "I hope I don't drop him."

They assured her she wouldn't.

The newest Red Sox wife was soon ensconced in a rocking chair, Baby Ted Williams in her arms. She got into a rhythm and then began singing, "Hush Little Baby, Don't You Cry." He finally fell asleep after twenty minutes. She'd become worried because her lullaby repertoire ran out fairly soon. She just kept singing, and in the middle of "Sweet Caroline," a Fenway staple, Arturo conked out.

Before the women left the hospital, they assured their latest compatriot that she did a great job, though they told her that a baby didn't require such an extensive variety of songs. Mike Timlin's wife said, "But I think he especially responded to 'On Top of Old Smoky.'" They all had to laugh. Jonathan Papelbon's wife laughed too, and then she said, "That's what my Dad used to sing to me."

The wives discussed another matter that was on their minds: David Ortiz's overbearing concern for a Double A player. None of the wives could guess what was going down with Papi. His wife swore to them she was clueless.

When Papi arrived at police headquarters, Rocky Patel intuited that he should keep the superagent away from David Ortiz. All cops appreciated that any kibitzing between possible persons of interest had to be prevented at all costs. Once

an artificial story was constructed that seemed to make
sense—and often made no sense—juries would cling to it like
newborn possums to their mother's underside. *Kibitz* was one
of Rocky's favorite words. He'd thought it was an Italian word
till his wife straightened him out, failing at an attempt not to
laugh.

Ortiz was brought directly to Rocky's office. The ballplayer seemed to take up the entire space, a phenomenon not simply due to Ortiz's size, but to his grand and magnetic aura.

The first thing Rocky said to him after introductions were
made was, "Do you want an interpreter?"

Papi said to him, "Not unless you do, man."

Rocky apologized. Ortiz shrugged.

Then Rocky said, "I'm afraid I've just sent someone to your
home to ask you to come in. My partner, Sargeant Flanagan.
I was not sure if Luis Sanseverra could be trusted to know
whether or not your promise to speak to him was genuine. I've
learned from Sargeant Flanagan that he arrived at your house
just a few minutes after you'd left. He apologized to your wife
for disturbing her. And I apologize to you—again it seems—
but it had become necessary for me to speak with you right
away. You may call her if you like, before I bring you in to see
Mr. Sanseverra."

First, Papi took him up on his offer. David Ortiz and
Rocky Patel were two men whose wives came first. Papi took
out his cell phone without first protesting the discomfort his
wife may have been subject to. He reached her, and after she
assured him the officer was a gentleman, he asked her again
not to worry about him. And again, he would explain what
was happening as soon as he got home. Before he hung up, he
said, "*Te amo. . .Che.*"

This time the "Che" didn't quite soften her up. After hearing her husband's news she saw to it that every other Red Sox

wife heard it too. She knew none of them would sleep till they did. She promised they'd have an email by morning.

Now, in Rocky's office, Papi expressed his fury. Rocky had wondered how that fury would manifest itself, and he waited while Papi exploded and let loose a long string of expletives— Spanish ones and English too. Two cops took a couple of steps toward him, but Rocky put up his hand like a traffic cop stopping a line of cars. When Papi took a breath, Rocky offered him a bottle of water which he drank in one gulp. The water served to put out the fire. The big ballplayer composed himself.

Rocky himself was an athlete, a former semi-professional boxer.

He said, "I understand your anger, Mr. Ortiz."

And Papi—controlling his voice so that it was back to its usual calm tenor—said, "You doin' your job, man. I sorry myself."

Rocky, right then, appreciated Papi's good will.

"You came to speak to the young man from Portland, Mr. Ortiz?"

"Yeah, I did."

"Before I can let you do that, I must tell you what you don't know. Please sit down."

Papi was glad to sit down. His knee was giving him a lot of trouble. He'd been keeping the pain a secret as a competitive ballplayer of his caliber was wont to do.

Rocky gazed at him from across the table. "A woman's body was found early this morning not far from Fenway Park. She died under suspicious circumstances. She recently gave birth. She may well be the mother of the baby you and your teammates found at Fenway Park."

Rocky gave Papi a few seconds to let that sink in. Once

Papi's eyes were locked into his again, he said, "We are testing her DNA to see if it matches the baby's. Also, she may or may not be the woman in the picture shown to the public on *ESPNews*. We're working on that, too. Luis Sanseverra has said that the woman in the picture is his girlfriend, but he will not answer our questions so that we can determine if that is true. He refuses to identify her by name. He will not cooperate with us.

"And so, we hold him based on the rule of law that allows me to determine if he is a person of interest. If so, I can choose to detain him. He is a person of interest." Rocky gave himself a small moment to consider exactly what he wanted to say next, and then went on. "I need to arrest him, Mr. Ortiz, so that he will be forced to talk to us. I can feel free to do that because he now has legal representation which, most fortunately, will give us as much protection—perhaps more—than it will give him. But your knowledge of what the young man's connection is in all this may mean my not arresting him."

Papi's elbow was on Rocky's desk, supporting his chin. At first, Papi said nothing. That was because English was his second language, so he decided to think for a moment in order to explain things as clearly as he would like. Rocky empathized; he'd just done the same thing. Rocky's empathy was grounded in not having mastered English himself until he was in a Boston middle school that offered an ESL program. Understanding the second language had come fairly quickly. Expressing himself in the new language required more concentration. So Rocky waited patiently.

Papi was well aware that this was not simply an interview with a TV reporter. When he was ready, he sat up straight and said, "The woman in that picture is Luis girlfrien'. She's at home and she fine. She never had no baby. Luis say when he saw her last time, six month ago, she a virgin. Him too. He love her. She love him. They kids, ya know? *Kids.* See, I got to tell Luis all this before he have a fuckin' heart attack. I sorry about the dead lady. I sorry if that baby belong to the dead lady. Very, very sorry. But it got nothing to do with Luis."

Of course, it had everything to do with Luis, but Rocky understood Papi's point of view. Rocky leaned back in his chair and said calmly, "Mr. Sanseverra asked you, in particular, to find out this information for him. Obviously, he could have done it himself. I do not believe his choosing to depend on you was because of a language difficulty. He could have asked the translator in Portland to do it for him. Or could have called his agent and asked him. But it would seem he wants no part of his agent. So why you, Mr. Ortiz?"

Papi would not beat around the bush. "Because he need to trust somebody. He feel he can trust me. The young guys, they look up to me." Papi leaned in toward Rocky and lowered his voice. "Listen to me, Detective. He got a big problem. He ain't Dominican."

"Where is he from then?"

"He Cuban, man. He's afraid. So I find out from my connection. . . In the Dominican you go back and for' to Cuba any time you want. I find out about his family. His girlfriend. All of them okay. They all fine. In Cuba."

Interestingly, when Papi introduced this piece of information, Rocky had learned just a short time earlier via Marty that the superagent, Jack Lagunas, specialized in Cuban players who managed to jump ship during tournament or exhibition play outside of Cuba. Lagunas helped them gain asylum and then represented them. He had made an extraordinary fortune, and the cop who found out this information for Marty pointed out to him that all the players this agent represented happened to be of the highest caliber of talent.

Marty had said to Rocky, "The guy goes around like he's some kind of humanitarian, like he deserves the goddamn Nobel Peace Prize. It's all bullshit. He's found himself a gold mine."

Rocky needed to assure David Ortiz that Luis would be treated fairly. Immigration problems were not within Rocky's purview. If the young ballplayer was pretending to be Dominican when he was actually from Cuba, then immigration could handle any possible violations to Unites States law. When and if they found out about it.

Though tempted to ask Sanseverra's real name, for the moment Rocky needed to cut to the chase. "Mr. Ortiz, we need a DNA sample from Mr. Sanseverra. We need to swab the inside of Luis Sanseverra's cheek with a Q-tip. It will take five seconds. If he agrees to do this, I will let him go. Then if his DNA does match the baby's, he will be under suspicion, subject to arrest. I will then bring him back for questioning.

"He needs you, but *I* need you, as well. I need you to convince him to consent to the cheek swab. His lawyer will be present."

"But. . ."

"I don't care where he's from, Mr. Ortiz, or how he came to be in this country. It is not within my duty to the Commonwealth of Massachusetts to question any action concerning undocumented immigrants."

Papi trusted his instincts. He sensed he could believe this Indian detective, too. "Listen, Detective. . . That kid. He got another problem. An' I think I gonna make it my problem."

"What would that be?"

"The kid, he seventeen. Not nineteen. Seventeen. He suppose' to be in high school."

Rocky never skipped a beat. "In due respect, sir. That makes him my problem. He is now—and I mean right now—under protective custody."

Ortiz said, "Okay. Good. So now. . . His lawyer speakin' English?"

"I don't think so."

"Good. His agent got to be there when I talk to him?"

"I will not allow it."

Papi smiled his famous broad grin. "I fix everything."

"Thank you."

"*Nada.*"

At the office door, Papi asked Rocky one more thing. "You goin' to put a cop in there when I talk to Luis?"

"Yes."

"He speakin' Spanish?"

"Yes."

Papi shrugged. "Like I say, you doin' your job."

Rocky respected Papi's determination to be careful. If there was more to all this, it was of a personal nature. Papi would prefer not to betray Luis Sanseverra, but he also knew you can't always get everything you want. He'd made his choice.

The big man lumbered down the corridor accompanied by a bilingual police officer who'd held out his notebook and asked for—and received—an autograph ". . .for my son." He didn't have a son.

Later the cop reported to Rocky. "First, Papi goes in to see the kid. . ."

"Mr. Sanseverra?"

"Yeah. The kid takes one look at him, starts crying and right away Papi tells him to do what he says. He tells him about the cheek swab. He tells him, 'You need to show that you're not the father of the baby.' Then Papi asks him if he knows about DNA. Kid said he was always in honors science class. Kid says he'll do anything Papi wants. He's agreed to the cheek swab, no problem there, Rock."

"Who's in there with him?"

"Ryan. I made sure Ryan got on the horn to the lab like you said. He's doin' it. Then Papi and me leave, but Papi wants to talk to Lagunas for a minute. I told him it was okay, so. . ."

"You told him what?"

"It's *Big Papi!*"

Rocky sighed. "Go ahead."

"The minute Lagunas sees Papi, he takes a major shit. Screams at Papi that's he's not only Luis's agent, he's his legal guardian, and he's the only one who should be talking to him, not Papi. So Papi lets him finish and then tells the guy to go fuck himself. Papi says to him, 'If you're going to keep on stealing players, you should wait till they're old enough to shave.' The kid. . ."

"Steal?"

"Yeah. That's just how Papi put it. *Robar.* To Papi I guess it's sort of like robbing the cradle. But here's the problem. The kid wants to go home."

"To Cuba?"

"Cuba?" The officer looked at Rocky as if he were demented. "He's Dominican. Luis wants to see his girlfriend. He wants to see his mother, too. He wants to go back to the team he used to pitch for before he came here. Basically, he's real immature, he's young, and he's homesick."

"Did he mention the name of the team?"

More looks from the cop wondering if Rocky is suffering from something worse than dementia. "Uh. . . No."

Rocky dismissed the officer. He snagged Marty, filled him in, and told him to find out from David Ortiz what

Sanseverra's real name was and what team he played for in Cuba.

He had to wait for Marty's reaction to the surprising news before he could go on.

"You said Cuba, right Rock?"

"That's right."

Being a cop, it didn't take long for Marty's surprise to dissipate. "The plot has thickened."

"Yes. Tell Mr. Ortiz we need to verify his story, but that we will keep the information confidential."

"We will?"

"Yes."

Marty went off to intercept to Big Papi before he signed out of the precinct, a feat that would turn out to be a long process what with the onslaught of requests for autographs.

Rocky found Jack Lagunas. The minute Lagunas laid eyes on him he went into another tirade. He gave Rocky the same dressing down he gave Papi, saying he was the boy's guardian. Rocky now knew this not to be the case. It had taken minutes to learn that Luis had no legal guardian. Well he had one now. The boy's green card stated he was Dominican, a document that also falsified his age.

Just as Shiva had risen from Papi's bloodstream without Papi knowing it, Shiva was rising again from Rocky's, and Rocky could feel the god's power. This awareness allowed him to control the way his anger would manifest itself, a lowering, deepening of Rocky's voice, and an ever darkening cast to his large eyes. He said to the agent, "You are but a fiduciary, nothing more. A concern has presented itself wherein there is some question as to whether or not Mr. Sanseverra is from the Dominican Republic, and whether or not he is in this country legally. And there is some question as to whether he's a minor. I am putting him under protective custody. And rest assured he will not throw another baseball until I say so."

All the color left Jack Lagunas's face. Rocky said, "But you may speak to him."

He led the fiduciary to the interrogation room where Luis had been sitting. The room was empty except for Officer Ryan. Ryan looked up at Rocky and said, "The kid's in the can."

Rocky noted the pile of Kleenex on the table.

"Did the young man use those Kleenex?"

Officer Ryan couldn't fathom such a question, but it was Rocky asking it. "Yeah, Rock. He was cryin'. Blew his nose, too."

Rocky ran to the men's room. But as he'd already guessed, Luis was not inside. Luis was gone.

Rocky came back into the interrogation room, where the complacent cop was rocking his chair onto its back legs, while he listened absent-mindedly to Lagunas's continuing rant. Lagunas was invisible to Rocky. He said to Officer Ryan, pointing at the pile of Kleenex on the desk, "*Do not touch those Kleenex.*"

Ryan looked down at the pile. "Sure."

The superagent got into Rocky's face. "Where the fuck is he?"

But Rocky was too busy to answer. He'd grabbed the phone on the wall to confirm that someone from the lab was already on the way down. He then replaced the phone. He was very relieved that Luis Sanseverra had left him a sample of his DNA at the behest of David Ortiz.

Rocky told the officer and the superagent, both staring at him, "Mr. Sanseverra has chosen to leave." To the officer—his eyes now grown wide—he directed one more remark. "Officer Ryan, Mr. Sanseverra was free to leave as he is no longer under suspicion. You are to guard those Kleenex. Do not let anyone touch them except the technician who will arrive shortly from the lab. Use your weapon if necessary. Do you understand?"

Officer Ryan's jaw fell open.

Rocky thundered, "*I asked if you understood me, Ryan?*"

"Yeah, I sure do."

Lagunas's face turned such a deep, dark, purple-red that Rocky thought his eyes would pop out. The detective turned his back on him, went out the door, and ran down a flight of stairs to reception. There was a lot of commotion in progress. Phones were ringing and no one seemed to be in any rush to pick them up. Officers and secretaries were comparing autographs.

Rocky buzzed himself out but then stood there in the doorway between reception and the waiting room. Everyone looked up, took in the glare of shiva, and went back to business—far too late to stop Luis Sanseverra from walking into the night.

Next Rocky called Immigration and Customs Enforcement for advice. The ICE guy told him what he already knew: "If you fly all ten million Cubans to Oshkosh, they stay. No questions asked. Can't do anything for ya, Detective."

THE NUMBER ONE PLACE
Monday, 11:00 PM

I've been checking websites all night. The *Globe*, the *Herald*, ESPN—nobody's mentioning anything further on the kid, Sanseverra. Last they seem to know is how Papi was up in Portland consoling him

But Luis is outta there. Was taken to see the boys in blue right here in Boston. Interesting.

We've got the rotation set up nicely for the Yankee series starting tomorrow. Lester, Beckett, and Schilling. You know how hard it is to get Yankee tickets—but I did manage to score a single obstruct-ed-view for tomorrow night by calling the ticket office when they opened this morning. Sometimes you get lucky that way. Of course, while all the other people near my seat are craning their necks to see around the section 6 pole, I'll be in the standing room area atop the grandstand behind the Sox dugout. One of the best views in baseball, as long as you don't mind standing for three hours. Oh, wait, the Yanks are in town. *Five* hours.

COMMENTS:

Leg It Out said: You're lucky to get Yankee-game tick-ets. I remember back around '65, walking to Fenway on game day, getting a bleacher seat for free after the third inning, and verbally tearing Mickey Mantle a new one from the front row in cen-ter. Now I'm lookin' at a second mortgage if I wanna bring the family to the ballpark.

I'mMovingToCanada said: Ah, the '60s. Glad I'm not the only geezer who reads this blog. You hear a lot about how the '67 Red Sox changed the whole cul-ture of baseball around here—and it's absolutely

true. Yaz could do anything he wanted that year.
The skyrocketing ticket and beer prices, the packed
houses, everything that came after—all worth it
when I think back to that magical summer 40 years
ago. And that magical autumn three years ago!
Gotta take two out of three from those Yankee jerks
this week.

MattySox said: I heard A-Rod tried to console Luis,
too, but failed. The guy can't console in the clutch.

LouisianaLightnin' said: As a Yankee fan, I'd like to
take a shot at you for going to the well a little too
often on the A-Rod "clutch" jokes. But honestly,
you're probably right.

CHAPTER

7

Late Monday night, Rocky and his wife sat together at the kitchen table drinking spice tea. Sitting opposite her husband once again, tea cup lifted, she saw the pain in his face that he no longer needed to hide.

"Rocky. . . What?"

"There is news. . .about the baby."

"Tell me."

And he did. He always shared his work with her. She was so often able to give him the peace necessary to clear his mind for the kind of logic that was required.

"A baby abandoned. . ." He sipped his tea...twice. . . "Lucy, any situation that revolves around the abandonment of a baby is full of sentimentality. Dreams of the poor desperate mother. . . People offering to help, to adopt the infant. . . Fantasies of a scene where the woman is tearfully re-united with her child. . ."

He became lost in the thought of knowing such fantasies were not to be.

Lucy said, "Go ahead, Rocky. It's okay."

He knew it was okay. Better than okay. To go over events with Lucy would give him new insight. He said, "At this stage we are spared the emotionally charged atmosphere that would surround a child-snatching. Always such a volatile situation."

He looked up into his wife's eyes. "We are about to release the news that the mother of this baby was murdered."

"Oh, no."

"We should have the DNA results first thing tomorrow. But I suspect we have her. And I have seen her body."

Lucy got up, went around the table, and squeezed into her husband's lap. She put her arms around his neck. She would help get him through the next moments of all that was going through his mind. Rocky, what with the array of Hindu gods residing in his blood, was able to absorb strength from the solidity of Lucy's body.

They were suddenly distracted; Bronko, in his crib, was making noises at his Pooh bear. Soon he would make new noises meant for his mother.

Lucy sighed. "Will he ever get over his need for a mid-night snack?"

Rocky smiled. "We never have. I'll bring him to you and I'll warm up some *chana pindi* for us."

While Rocky went for the baby, Lucy moved to the rock-ing chair in the corner of the kitchen, by the window. Then, while she nursed him and Rocky was at the stove, he described his time with the medical examiner. Then they had their snack, put the baby in his crib, and went to bed. In each other's arms, Lucy said, "Let's count our blessings, Rock."

The next morning, Rocky picked up the *Globe* on his doorstep. A picture of Baby Ted Williams was on the front page. Rocky could sense the despair in the infant's solemn eyes.

In the kitchen, he ate a bowl of cereal. His phone rang.

DNA strands of the dead woman and those of Baby Ted Williams were all but identical. None of the DNA extracted from the samples left at the precinct by Luis Sanseverra matched the infant's.

Rocky called Sargeant Flanagan with the news, told him he would see him at headquarters shortly.

Within minutes, Marty called him back just as Rocky was putting his gun in its holster, under his jacket.

"Rocky, get over to Children's. A big family of Mexicans are there claiming Baby Ted Williams is theirs. They're the same people who were at D-4 last night reporting a woman and her child missing."

"A woman and child reported missing? How is it I never heard about this?"

"That's what I wanted to know." Marty had said to the desk duty officer, "What the fuck are you talkin' about?" Now he said to Rocky, "The guys on duty last night didn't make any connection. Everyone is still under the impression that Baby Ted is a newborn. You believe what you want to believe, I tell ya."

"What exactly happened?"

"Seems things got out of hand. Two men arrested. The family is claiming that one of the men is Baby Ted's father, and the other his uncle."

"Arrested?"

"Yeah."

"Are the men here illegally? There'll be no getting around that now."

"The guy who's supposed to be the father was born here."

"Then he's American, not Mexican."

"Shit, Rocky. Do I call myself American?"

No, he didn't. He claimed to be Irish, though it was his grandfather who emigrated from Cork, not him.

"Never mind, Marty. What about the second man?"

He told them he was the missing woman's brother. He's

not a Mexican, he's from El Salvador. But he got his citizenship papers a few years ago. So we're good. These people heard about Baby Ted Williams but the picture on ESPN—well it wasn't their baby's mother. And—here we go again—their baby was almost a month old. The word was still out that the baby at Fenway Park had just been born and abandoned. *Jesus.*"

"Has a social worker been sent over to the hospital?"

"The hospital's full of social workers, Rock."

"I believe it best to send one of ours. That family must be treated gently. They must be given privacy and calm. They've lost their baby, now he's been found. They are undoubtedly beside themselves about the child's mother, and they're about to find out that she has met a violent end."

"I'll see to a social worker."

"Good. It is best that I call the chief."

Rocky reached his superior and condensed the conversation he'd just had with Sargeant Flanagan. He introduced the conversation though, with a prelude: "Chief, that body found in the fens last night was the mother of the baby. . . of Baby Ted Williams." Then he told him the rest. Finally: "Sir, as you know so well, this is a public event. I think it best if you to go to the hospital and speak to the reporters who might have already gathered. See the family. Tell them our aim is to help them. And I would include Mayor Menino in all of it."

The chief was having a difficult time believing his ears. He hadn't had his coffee yet. But he suddenly felt wide awake. "Rocky, listen. Before we. . ."

"I'm going over to D-4 now. Someone in authority must deal with the two men who were arrested. I need to ask them a lot of questions. And one of them will have to ID her. It will be good that the husband has his wife's brother with him. And our social worker must be kept apprised so that she can give the news as it comes to the rest of the baby's family. I will see to that here."

"Rocky, listen. . . There's no mistake? It's for sure that the baby. . ."

"It's for sure, Chief."

"Okay. You got what you want. I'm calling the mayor now."

He hung up before he got a chance to hear Rocky say, "Thank you sir."

Before heading out the door, Rocky peeked in on his sleeping wife. Then he peeked into Bronko's room. The baby was on his stomach, lifting his upper body with his strong arms, trying to focus on the puppies and kittens imprinted on his sheet. He was concentrating so hard, he didn't notice his father. Rocky tip-toed away so as not to disturb his boy's little business at hand.

In his car, Rocky tried to concentrate on the traffic rather than the emotional and tragic hours that were about to unfold; a grieving father was about to be reunited with his son and will then have to face an unspeakable loss.

George Sanchez and Cinthia's brother, Carlos Vega, both utterly disheveled, sat in an interrogation room at D-4 listening to Rocky, who sat across from them at a small wood table. He apologized for their difficulties. There were three officers in the interrogation room, one a woman who sat next to Rocky. The other two stood on either side of the door.

Rocky's initial question was directed at George Sanchez: "Do you have a picture of your wife and son?"

"Yes. In my wallet."

The wallet was brought from the evidence pen.

George took out a snapshot of Cinthia holding Arturo. It was taken a week earlier when Cinthia had been to the beauty parlor for a new hairstyle. She'd called it her anti-postpar-tum-depression look. Her smile was bright. Rocky recognized her. A pain shot through his heart.

Rocky said to George. "Your baby is in a healthy condi-tion. I will see to your being reunited with him shortly."

Both men sat up, as if jolted by a bolt of electricity. Then they looked to each other. George put his hand on Carlos's arm. They waited. But Rocky did not continue. They knew what the silence meant. Rocky was giving them the time they needed to steel themselves, helped by the news that the baby was found and was well. But George instinctively put off what would come from Rocky. He asked, "Where is the baby?"

"At Children's Hospital."

Both men took in breath.

Rocky said. "Again. He is fine. He is there for observation and will soon be ready to go home. Your family is at the hospital."

Alas, Rocky knew as soon as he said the words, that he'd given the men a false shred of hope. Quickly, he went on to what had to come next. "Mr. Sanchez, I'm so sorry to tell you that even though your son is well, I also have very bad news for you." He looked to the other man at the table. "And for you, sir."

George had felt a spring of hope when he heard Rocky's words, that their family was at the hospital. With those words came a fleeting image of Cinthia telling everyone within her range to let her have her baby. Now he knew that he would never hear a description of such a beautiful picture. Next to him, Carlos trembled.

Rocky had been holding something in his left hand. Now he put his hand out, palm up. Lying there was the gold bracelet that had been removed from Cinthia's body. George reached over and took it. He held it to his face, pressed the Pandora bracelet into his cheek, closed his eyes. He'd bought the gift for his wife, to thank her for her labors in giving birth to their baby. It was strung with four charms and there would never be another. He brought the bracelet down so that Carlos could see it, and fingered each charm: Cinthia's birthstone, an amethyst, set in a heart; the baby's birthstone, a ruby, in the tummy of a teddy bear; a cube imprinted with the letter C; and a rose. Cinthia had insisted on growing roses in their Victory Garden plot, even though George's mother had chided her: "If you want to grow roses, Cinthia, you must move to England." It was Alicia who insisted on buying her daughter-in-law the rose—a little joke between them.

George forced himself to look back up at Rocky, who spoke very quietly. "Your wife is dead, Mr. Sanchez. We don't know the circumstances but she was a victim of homicide. You have my profound sympathy."

Carlos Vega took his brother-in-law into his arms, and he said to Rocky, "You have her then?"

"Yes."

"Did she suffer?"

"She was hit and rendered unconscious. She died a short time later."

George said to Rocky, "I want to see her."

"You will."

George's shoulders were heaving. Carlos spoke again, destitute. "She was my little sister. I decided to wait for the baptism before coming up. I couldn't find the time to come and see her new baby. I told her I would wait till the baptism."

"I'm sorry. I'm truly sorry. For you both. But I need you, Mr. Vega, or you, Mr. Sanchez, to identify her."

Carlos said to his brother-in-law, "Do you want me to do this for you George? For her?"

George said, "No. We will see her together. I need to get to Arturo."

The Boston PD chief announced to the wall of cameras and microphones that Baby Ted Williams had been identified, and that the body of his mother was found Sunday night, a victim of homicide. She had been identified three hours earlier by her husband George Sanchez, a Boston resident, and her brother, Carlos Vega, from Brooklyn.

"Her name is Cinthia Sanchez."

The chief did not take questions, but before he introduced Mayor Menino, he described a hotline that had been set up to take any information from citizens who might have information. He gave the number twice.

The mayor had seen to George Sanchez's and Carlos Vega's release. He determined that Baby Ted Williams should be handed over to Mr. Sanchez as soon as humanly possible. Several years earlier the mayor had been appalled when the Cuban child, Elian Gonzalez, was not returned to his surviving parent immediately upon the authorities learning of his identity, that they made the poor boy wait. He had just been present at Children's Hospital when the baby's grandmother placed the infant in George's arms.

A hush fell over the crowd of reporters and camera crews; no one wanted to miss what he had to say. Menino, a loving grandfather himself, described the scene. "The eyes of the father and son met. The little baby smiled. The father did his best to smile back. It was heartbreaking. *Heartbreaking!*"

He took out a handkerchief, wiped his eyes, and composed himself. "I have been assured by the Police Commissioner that all the force, and effort, and manpower we have available will be devoted to finding the killer of Baby Ted's mother. . ." He paused. "Excuse me. The baby's name is Arturo. Arturo Sanchez. He was named after his grandfather, a citizen of Boston, who many of us knew, a man who saw to raising a fine family in our city."

The mayor had to wipe his eyes again. That gave the reporters the edge they needed to start firing questions at him. The questions were typical of an aggressive young press corps; ninety per cent of their queries began with the same numbskull phrase having to do with feelings.

"How did you feel when you first heard about the abandoned baby?"

"How did Terry Francona feel when he learned Baby Ted's mother had been murdered?"

"How did the police feel when they realized they'd arrested Baby Ted's father."

The mayor told the reporters he felt terrible when he heard about the baby, but that he had no knowledge of Terry Francona's feelings, or the feelings of the police. Then he said, "The baby's name is Arturo."

Scanning the reporters Menino spotted Amalie Benjamin amidst the milling throng.

Relieved, the mayor said, "Miss Benjamin, please."

The young *Globe* reporter asked, "Have you any idea as to motivation? Why would anyone snatch a baby, kill his mother, and then leave the baby in the Red Sox clubhouse?"

The mayor put his handkerchief back in his pocket. He said, "This case is under the direction of Boston Homicide Detective First Grade, Rocky Patel. Detective Patel will answer those questions as soon as he has the answer and as he can take a moment of time from his investigation. Thank you very much. I must now offer the Sanchez family whatever the city of Boston can do to help them with their funeral arrangements."

The conference was over. Reporters flipped open their cells. Detective Patel was not in his office. The desk duty officer responded to the query he was to hear over and over again that day: "When can we speak to him?" And they all got the same answer: "He is investigating the murder of Cinthia Sanchez, and the endangerment to her child. I don't know when he'll be available." And when Red Sox players called, which they did regularly, wanting to find out how the baby was doing, the officer told them that Arturo was well and was serving as a great comfort to his family.

⚾

Before Rocky left for home late that afternoon, Marty checked in with him at D-4 one last time.

"About that blogger, Rock."

"Yes."

"You've checked the blog out, right?"

"Briefly."

"He still hasn't been tracked down."

"How is that?"

"We called in some tech guys. . . Ever notice how all the tech guys are named Gary?"

"I hadn't."

"Well, this one Gary told me he talked to the hosting site, and they said anyone who uses their service is allowed to do so anonymously and privately. Until they see a warrant. Little early for that, right?"

"Right."

Marty collapsed into a chair. They were all sleep-deprived. "Anyway, Rock, if you click on the blogger's profile, he's got one name—Jay—he says he lives in the Boston area, he's a fourth-generation Sox fan, his immigrant great-grandfather learned to speak English listening to Red Sox radio, and he's got two cats. I'll bet you don't want to know the names of his cats."

Rocky said nothing.

"A lot of people read that blog, Rock. Guy's got a real loyal following ever since somebody pointed out that the day the Sox got Dave Roberts, the blogger referred to the trade as *a steal.*"

Rocky said, "Dave Roberts. Now that would be. . ."

"See, Rock. 2004. Playoff game with the Yankees. The whole series does a one-eighty when Roberts steals. . . Never mind. The main thing is. . ."

Marty stopped speaking because Rocky was staring with great intensity at nothing. Then his gaze returned to his partner, and he said, "Of course, Posada's play could in no way be faulted, which showcased further the brilliant reflexes and speed of Roberts."

Marty blinked. Then he doubled over with laughter.

Rocky said, "Do you know what I've decided to do about Jay, the blogger?"

"No, Rocky, I don't."

"I'm going to leave a comment on his blog, and ask him to get in touch with me. It never hurts to ask, does it?"

There was a knock at the door. Officer Ryan opened it a crack and peeked in. He was desperate to get out of the dog-house.

"What is it?"

Ryan opened the door a little wider. "Look at what just came in via a delivery boy." There was a brown envelope in his hand.

Rocky couldn't help but notice that the rest of his team had gathered in a bunch behind Ryan. Now what? "All of you, please. . . Get in here."

They did, and Ryan put the envelope on Rocky's desk. The outside of it read, COMPLIMENTS OF DAVID ORTIZ. Rocky opened it and six tickets for that night's game fell out. Inside was a note Big Papi had scribbled. Rocky read it aloud:

Detective Patel, I would like you and your family to
enjoy tonight's game.

His men's faces fell. He said, "You are my family too." But
they all knew Rocky's wife, knew what a die-hard Sox fan she
was. First they insisted Rocky go—enjoy the game with her,
and then there followed a discussion on whether such a gesture could be accepted to begin with. The men concluded that
the Boston PD received complimentary tickets to Red Sox
games every year. A cultural tradition of good will and nothing more.

"Go for it, Rocky," was the sentiment. "It's been a long
day."

Later, out of earshot, another sentiment prevailed: *The*
Yankees! Lucky bastard.

Officer Ryan had hung back. "Uh. . . Rock?"

Rocky sighed. "Yes, Ryan."

"Did Papi sign that note? Cuz if he did, I was wondering
if I could have it."

Marty picked up a paperweight from Rocky's desk, an
award for one public service or another, and threw it at Ryan,
who just managed to get himself back out the door before he
got beaned.

Rocky arrived home at four o'clock. He hugged Lucy. She
told him she needed an ambulance what with the shock of
seeing him at that hour.

He said, "Where's Bronko?"

"He's watching TV."

He stared at her.

"I'm kidding. My mother took him out in his carriage. *I'm*
watching TV."

"I am glad you have found some moments of relaxation."

Lucy's eyes often welled with tears because Rocky would express his love for her so unexpectedly. Then she would have to blink them back so he wouldn't become concerned.

She said, "I love how I'm always in your head, Rock."

"And in my loins."

She swatted him, she laughed, and then she draped her arms around him. "We're all alone, cutie."

He kissed her. Then he said, "But I have a surprise for you."

"Oh, goody. What?"

He disentangled himself, took the envelope out of his inside pocket, removed the tickets and held them out for her to see.

Lucy stared down at the tickets and then clapped her hand over her mouth so she wouldn't scream—the kind of thing that tended to freak Rocky out.

She took a few breaths and said, "Where did you get them?"

He took Big Papi's note out of the envelope and handed it to her. With that, she couldn't help herself. But Rocky had prepared himself for the scream.

When things calmed, she asked, "Can we all go?"

"All?" Rocky was secretly hoping she would want to take her friends. He had so much thinking that needed to be done.

"Yes. My mom and dad, yours, and us. Oh, Rocky, can you somehow come?" She looked at the tickets again. "Omigod. Section 21." Her eyes returned to Rocky's. "These seats are incredible! They're in the first row of the grandstand. Right behind home plate!"

Then she said, "*Rocky*! Bronko gets to go to his first Sox game! *Against the freakin' Yankees*. Can you believe it?"

Rocky said, "I do believe it. I am planning to go."

"You are?"

"Yes."

She threw her arms around him. "I really do need an ambulance. *Your* first game too, Rocky! I never thought I'd see the day. I'm so glad you can do this. So, so glad."

Off she went to the kitchen phone to panic first her father, then her mother walking the baby and desperately trying to make out what her daughter was saying through the static on her cell phone, and then Rocky's mother. None of them had been able to calm down until they understood the reason for her hysteria. Rocky's father had taken the phone from his wife, asked Lucy if he could speak to his son. Rocky assured the senior Patel that everyone was fine, and that yes, he would feel out of place, but that they should do it for the baby. When the round-robin of Lucy's calls were over, it had been agreed—they would all attend the game.

Lucy pulled her shirt over her head and yanked off her jeans. She and Rocky made fast love since her mother would be back any minute.

◉

Bronko fell asleep in the third inning, and stayed asleep until eleven-thirty when he was placed in his crib, covered with his new Red Sox baby blanket.

THE NUMBER ONE PLACE
Tuesday, 11:55 PM

Jay-haters, stop reading now. You can't have a better baseball day than I just had.

I had a single ticket for Red Sox-Yanks tonight.

Drove to Fenway right from work, and ended up in a perfect metered spot on Comm Ave. To get quarters, I go into the convenience store next to that sex shop that use to advertise "adult cakes" in the window, and buy the cheapest thing I can find, a Mrs. Fields cookie. I fill the meter and head over to the park.

Then I see former Brooklyn Dodger fan turned Sox freak Doris Kearns Goodwin walking around. You always get a good showing of celebs when the Yanks are in town (although I've seen Doris at "regular" games, too.) Also saw El Tiante driving his Lincoln Navigator toward the park. Renee Russo was in the house, too, as was the ageless New York sports reporter, Warner Wolf. During the game, from my standing room perch, I saw Affleck in his usual spot by the Sox dugout with Garner. No Matt Damon, though. And next to the Yankee dugout in the front row was Penny Marshall, Rosie O'Donnell, and Rosie's friend from "Nip/Tuck" who the girl next to me said plays the anesthesiologist, Liz Cruz. And in the players' guests section, that detective who's in charge of the Fenway baby case. He was there with his wife who the guy on the other side of me told me is the chef at the best Italian restaurant on Hanover Street. In fact, he wondered who was holding down the fort because it looked like her parents were there. They own the restaurant. The detective's mother was there too, and was wearing a red sari, cool. And they had this baby they were passing back and forth until he fell asleep. The "Nip/Tuck" girl told me that she knew this cop who told her that the detective was going crazy trying to find who killed the Fenway baby's mother because he had a baby of his own. Amazing.

But my goal tonight was to get a baseball. You gotta understand, before I was "blogger" guy, I was "try to get a ball" guy. In fact, sometimes I curse the existence of cameras, as I go to a lot of games, but am always too busy taking photos to try for balls in batting practice. So, today, I ditched the camera and decided balls were the top priority. Your best chance for a BP ball at Fenway is in right field, beyond Pesky's Pole. Any ball hit down that way will roll along the curved fence. Everyone will lean down, but the ball should stay just out of their reach until the point where the fence is low enough. You find that magic spot, and you should nab a souvenir. But that's too easy. I had a different plan.

With Papi's group of hitters coming up, I opted to go to straight away right field, about 20 rows up the bleachers. This gave me a good view, and lots of space to work with, as most people stand down in the front by the bullpens. Papi proceeds to launch one right toward me. I'm right in an aisle, of course, and I see it's gonna land in the section to my right (41), a little in front of me. I start trotting down the steps, carefully watching the ball, despite the tough 5:00 sun. It clunks into the empty seats, and I'm sprinting down the uneven steps. I make sure to go down beyond the row I've estimated it's sitting in, because it could roll down, and because my only competition is coming from below. I choose my row and bolt into it, manically thinking, "Don't mess this up." I'm running along the row, looking to my right, hoping I see the ball. If I don't, I have to guess whether it's a row above or a row below, and start jumping over seats. At that point, others will have gathered and it's a free-for-all. That's a game you don't wanna play. Fortunately, I see the ball, right there in the row above me. Sweet. I know it's mine. I reach over and grab it. David Ortiz, dude. David Ortiz. Ball. My fifth lifetime, all scored in batting practice. It's not like getting a game ball, but it'll do.

At this point, I'm thinking nothing can go wrong. Jon Lester, fresh off his recovery from cancer, gives up an early homer, but I'm still confident. The Sox tie it, and later take the lead. I get to see the return of Youk and Manny, both having missed time with injuries. We all go nuts for both of them as they're announced.

Then Joe Torre decides to walk Varitek to pitch to Ellsbury. He gets a hit to basically put the game away—although Papi's blast into the bleachers (same spot as the BP one I'd gotten earlier) cements it. Oh, and tonight's "Sweet Caroline" was as perfect as it gets. The final bit of the song faded out right before a chorus, so we did the "self-sing" for a *full* chorus, which is really the holy grail of Sweet Carolines.

The game, exciting as it was, became enough of a blowout in that last inning that I got to run down to the field boxes where my buddy sits to watch the ninth from the empty seat next to him. We win it, and I head out to the car. In all the excitement, I forgot to get food at the game. I'm starving. But I reach into my pocket to find. . .a Mrs. Fields cookie!

I make it home in about 15 minutes; no static on Storrow Drive at all. All this is happening on about the most beautiful night you could imagine. Even in summer, you *always* bring a sweatshirt to Fenway at night. It was so nice tonight, though, I made the call to go with just a T-shirt. Was totally comfortable all night—the perfect night at Fenway. If you'll excuse me, I'm gonna go pan the Mystic River. We can all split up the gold later.

I get home and listen to this one—Luis Sanseverra, that player from the Sea Dogs? His agent—superagent—Jack Lagunas is in town from LA. He's looking for him! Luis was last seen at a Boston PD station, as I mentioned before, and now he's gone.

COMMENTS:

Peter said: Sounds like you had a great time. Wish I'd been able to score tix for this series. . .

It's a Jellyfish said: Me too. The only celebrities I saw last night were the Robert Redford guy and the blazer guy—from my living room.

MattySox said: Oh, yeah, Redford was going nuts tonight. And he did his usual "run away to beat the traffic" as soon as the third strike was called on Jeter to end the game. News flash! Jeter thought the pitch wasn't a strike—how could it be when he didn't swing at it?? Heheheh.

Melanie said: Wait, Matty. You weren't at the game but you saw Robert Redford? Can somebody fill me in here?

Red Sox Chick said: I'll field this one. Some of us are a little obsessed with the fellows that you see on TV during Fenway games. They're right behind the plate so you can't help but notice their movements and reactions to every single pitch. One looks like Robert Redford, another wears a blazer, etc.

Melanie said: Okay, now that you mention it, I have seen those guys. Although I always called the one guy "Jerry Springer." I guess that's your "Redford." Who are those guys? Why do *they* get such sweet seats??

Red Sox Chick said: One's a lawyer, I think, one's a Red Sox higher-up, and one runs that local glass company—you've heard the jingle. I think it's hilarious when his own company's ad shows up on the fence in front of him as he sits in his front row spot.

Amy said: Springer, Redford. . .did anybody watch the *game*??

Rocky Patel said: I AM A BOSTON POLICE DETECTIVE. I NEED WHATEVER HELP YOU HAVE TO

OFFER. PLEASE TELL ME HOW WE CAN BEST
COMMUNICATE.

Jay said: Okay, Detective, I'll call the hotline.

Nooey said: I was the girl next to you. I got Rosie and
Liz Cruz's autographs. Liz wrote her real name,
Roma Maffia. Couldn't get anywhere near Affleck.
Hope you can help the cops, Jay.

CHAPTER

8

The next day, Rocky and Sargeant Flanagan were standing on the east end of the Boylston Street bridge. They leaned on the ornate granite balustrade above the Muddy River and looked down into the water just where it narrowed down from a large pond. Behind them, the river flowed under Boylston, then under Ipswich, beneath the train tracks where it had been diverted underground via a massive concrete pipe, under the Mass Pike, and then beneath Comm Ave, Beacon Street, and Storrow Drive, whereupon it flowed into the Charles. The distance from the Boylston Street bridge to the Charles River was a third of a mile.

The green-gray water was being worked by large, fat, lazy carp eating the flora of the river bottom, riling everything up and contributing to the muddiness of the aptly named river. A few people actually fished the river even though carp took on the flavor of where they fed; these carp tasted like mud.

This humid vista lying before the police officers was as thick with wet, heavy foliage as the Amazon. It brought back flashes of memories to Detective Patel, of the Gujerati land of his childhood, just after the cessation of the monsoons.

A couple of yards from Rocky and the sargeant, at the other end of the bridge, was an artist, his easel up against the balustrade. He was tall, wizened, white-haired—just in the process of packing up his paints and cleaning his brushes when he noticed the detective and his partner. He called, "You guys lost?" The artist was used to tourists who couldn't figure out where they were, and how there could be such a vast swamp smack in the middle of Boston.

Rocky went over to him. "Thank you, we're not. We're police officers." He showed the artist his badge. "Detective Patel. This is Sargeant Flanagan."

The man smiled. "Thought I might run into a few cops sooner rather than later. After the last couple of days."

"Were you here by any chance on Sunday morning?" Rocky asked him.

"Yep. Can't take a day off or I'm set back a mile."

Rocky knew exactly what the man was talking about. He watched him methodically rinse his brushes in turpentine.

"So I must ask you if you noticed anything unusual."

"Yeah, I guess I did."

Marty took out his notebook and opened it. "What was that?"

"Heard a car's wheels screech. In the distance. A car takin' off real fast, ya know? Unusual because it was a Sunday mornin'. No traffic."

"This screech. . .was it definitely a screech as opposed to the noise when a driver slams his brakes?"

"That's right."

"Could you tell me the direction this distant screech came from?"

The artist used a brush to point east over Rocky's shoulder, the opposite direction from Fenway Park, a quarter-mile behind him. "I guessed that way. Over behind Hemenway Street, around there."

"You can't see that far from here."

"No. But I could tell."

"How is that?"

"I live back there myself. In the artists' co-op. Lucky me. Qualified back in 1973. Started out payin' eighty bucks a month for my room. Gone up a thousand percent in twenty-five years. Still a helluva bargain. And I like the. . ."

"Can you say what time it was you heard the screech?"

"What time?"

"Yes."

"Well. . .early. Not too early. Never wear a watch. It was a Sunday doubleheader, Detective. You get to see the fans all delirious when they get those free parkin' spots back there. Don't blame them. Highway robbery, what these guys get just to park your damn car. I don't own a car. Lucky me again. Keep it simple."

"Did you see anything on your walk, then? Besides happy fans finding their free Sunday spots?"

"Not much."

"Not much? That response is not the same as nothing."

The artist began placing the brushes into a case. "Didn't think about it at the time. Saw this baby stroller right in the middle of the sidewalk. Looked brand new. A minute later a kid came along, college kid I'd say, walked off with it. He'll probably get five bucks for it. As if five bucks'll make a dent in the cost of a textbook. I hear a book today is goin' for. . ."

"Could you show me exactly where you saw this stroller?"

"Don't know if I could. In that neighborhood behind Hemenway. . . About where Hemenway meets up with one of the public alleys. It's all little twists and turns. Maybe further back. Edgerly."

Sargeant Flanagan darted a look to Rocky. Rocky felt the look. He asked the artist, "Have you not connected that stroller with the baby found at the park? With the woman who was murdered?"

The man began blinking. "I can't really connect things too good."

"Your name sir?"

"Woody Guthrie."

Without skipping a beat, Marty asked, "Would that be Woodrow?"

The artist smiled. "Yeah, I guess it would."

Marty wrote in his notebook: *Nut job.*

Rocky said to the artist, "If we went over there together, followed the steps of your walk. . . would that refresh your memory?"

"Uh. . . No. I try to avoid reality. Came directly here from Nam. I had enough of reality. I tend not to commit things to memory, ya know?"

Rocky did not know. But he understood how the unwillingness to take in reality had presented itself in the artist's work. On his canvas were shades of green, a little blue, a touch of yellow. No forms. It would seem he was trying to capture the tangle of color below him. The man had succeeded in the presentation of the scene without the reality of individual leaves, and trunks, and stems. No ripples of water, either, nor the fish making the ripples.

Rocky said, "If any reality forces itself in, will you contact me?" He handed the artist his card.

"Sure. Will do."

As Rocky and Sargeant Flanagan walked across the bridge, and then onto the path leading into the Victory Garden, Marty whispered to Rocky, "That guy took a few too many hits of Agent Orange."

Rocky suspected it could be so.

The pair spent some time questioning the Victory Gardeners. None of them heard any tires screeching, but sound is obscured down in the fens.

Then they walked back over the bridge along Boylston Street; crossed the winding avenue that had been named Fenway before there was a ball park; a right into Hemenway; and then a left on Haviland Street. It was just a few steps down Haviland to the corner of Edgerly Road. They gazed down the line of lovely, 19th century, row houses. The Sanchez's lived in the third one, number 5. At the corner where they stood was a postage stamp sized park. A small plaque on the fence read: *Mothers Rest Playground.* A couple of moms chatted while they pushed their toddlers on the swings.

Rocky stepped over to the women, introduced himself and showed them his badge.

"I am investigating the homicide of Cinthia Sanchez."

Pain crossed their faces instantly.

"Tell me. Did she bring the baby here?"

One of them said, "Yes. All the time."

"The last time I saw Cinthia was the day before she died. I held Arturo while she pushed Sam."

Sam was her two-year-old in the swing.

Both of the women had tears in their eyes. One pulled a couple of Kleenex out of her pocket and passed one to her friend.

Rocky said, "We're sorry to have to disturb you."

Sam's mother said, "Please find who did this."

Marty said, "We will."

In the rear corner, up against the fence, along with some debris, Marty saw a dirty rag that looked as though it might once have been white. He and Rocky walked over as the women and the two children watched, and picked up Arturo's crocheted baby blanket. They were careful not to handle it any more than they had to. There was no choice but to return to the women who were now sitting on a bench while their little ones played in the sandbox.

Detective Patel squatted down so that he wouldn't hover over them. "I'm sorry. Could this blanket have been Arturo's? I would ask you not to touch it."

The women looked at the filthy, crumpled blanket in Rocky's hands. First, they recoiled. Then they bent over their blanket, heads almost touching. One of them reached toward it and Rocky had to pull it back. She looked up into Rocky's eyes.

"Yes. Cinthia told us her girlfriend made it."

And the other. "Her girlfriend was her sister-in-law."

"Are you sure?"

They needed more Kleenex. They were sure.

The detective and his sargeant went to their car, and Marty pulled a plastic bag out of the trunk. He put the blanket inside. They surmised that the blanket was blown along the street, and then through the playground where it came to rest against the fence. Or perhaps some kids had played with it, and then thrown it there.

Neither the detective nor his partner spotted Cinthia's other flip-flop in the gutter where Hemenway crossed Public Alley 909. The detail they were about to send out would find it as well, and the stroller, too, in a nearby pawn shop.

Rocky and Marty sat down across from each other at Rocky's desk, and discussed the likelihood that Cinthia and George had been watched. Minutes after they'd parted company—George heading toward Mass Ave and Cinthia going in the opposite direction—someone grabbed her.

"The question, Marty, is why? Why does someone grab a woman and her baby, beat her up, throw her in the fens, and leave the baby at Fenway Park? And secondarily, why Cinthia? Random. . .or perhaps not."

"And how the hell is it connected to someone else sending a picture of another woman in Cuba to a TV station, and saying she's the mother of Arturo?"

Rocky did not answer. Marty rolled his eyes and prepared to wait. If he knew the elementary rudiments of Yoga, which he did not, he would have recognized the position Rocky had assumed. *Namaste.* His palms were together in the position of Christian prayer. His forehead bent to touch his fingertips. What Marty did know was that Rocky wouldn't be back from the mother ship for a minute or so. If the phone rang, he'd get it because Rocky wouldn't hear it.

He took out his nail clippers while he waited.

Rocky took his hands from his forehead and looked up. Marty put the nail clippers back in his pocket.

Rocky said, "We don't know. But I fear a connection."

"Yeah. Me, too."

One of the officers knocked on the door and came into the office. He said, "I've got a turnstile guy at Fenway on the phone. Says we should talk to some sportswriter. . .a guy who came to the park early on Sunday. Ask him if he saw anybody."

"We questioned all the media, didn't we?"

"Exactly. There wasn't a one of them who got to Fenway before ten-thirty. Most of them said they were lucky they got there in time for the game."

Rocky said, "Get the..."

". . .turnstile guy?"

"Yes."

Jimmy Gorman was past retirement age, had sold his hardware store in Quincy five years earlier, moved to Florida with his wife, and moved back three months later.

He said to Rocky, "I missed everything. I missed my friends, I missed my house. I missed everything. Realized how many friends I had. Didn't miss the hardware store, have to say. Not with fuckin' Home Depot crawlin' up my ass. Never intended to come back in a million years—wanted to be warm, ya know? But I got eight grandchildren. Rather put up with the snow than miss the birthday parties. So I came back and soon as I get back this one friend—fellow Hibernian— says he can get me in with the Sox. Stead of sittin' around Spring Training with all the other Q-tips, I'm suddenly in with the Red Sox. I mean, *I am fuckin' in!*"

He slapped his knee.

Marty had to explain to Rocky later, the Q-tip reference— "White hair and white sneakers, Rock." Rocky had said, "An amusing image."

Jimmy Gorman went on to tell his story: "I'm rackin' my brain, ya know? See, the Dunbar truck is about to arrive with the money so we got to go into a full court press. Us guys who man the turnstiles are kind of minor security. The gates are all closed except for D so that's where they send me. How I'm supposed to stop an armed robbery, I sure as hell don't know, but I'm there mainly for the employees who'll be comin' in. Check their IDs and stuff like that."

He paused, not sure if he was performing adequately for the police.

Rocky said, "I see. And so you saw someone you think might be able to help us."

"That's right. The first wave had come through—the laundry guys and such. Cochran was already there, course. Manny, too. I saw his car—first one in the players' lot. Took his gold Hummer that day."

Marty held his breath, hoping Rocky wouldn't say, *That would be Manny Ramirez?* He didn't.

What Rocky did say was, "And then?"

"Well, it would be a little quiet till the next wave. . .the vendors, those guys. The money is set to come during the gap."

"How long is that gap?"

"Around ten minutes, fifteen most. But that's when the sportswriter came in."

"And I understand you didn't recognize him."

"Never seen 'im before. But they come and go. Some have three-day passes, two-day, some one-day."

"How exactly did you know he was a sportswriter?"

"Pass was blue. And he looked it."

"Did you check the pass? Beyond just recognizing the color?"

Jimmy Gorman scratched his head. "See, there's no time to check the passes. We got about 40 million employees at Fenway. Just have to make sure the color's right. And like I said, he had the right look."

"You had a feel for him, you might say."

"Yeah. Ya gotta use your instincts. He was a good-lookin' guy. Sharp. Spanish guy. Sunglasses."

"Was he carrying a bag?"

"Nope. Backpack. They all got backpacks." Then Jimmy started biting his nails. Rocky waited. He looked up again. "After I called you guys. . . Ya know, to tell ya the guy might be of help, I got to thinkin'. I kind of looked for him at last night's game. Went pokin' around. Didn't see him. Talked to Jeff—he's the *Courant* guy. Told me he didn't know about no new Spanish guy on Sunday.

"So I'm chewin' the fat with Johnny Pesky—he's the only guy in the organization older than me—said he was hangin' around early Sunday in the weight room when they found the baby. He says there's no Spanish guy he don't know. He knows everybody. The guy I told him about? He says there's no such guy."

Rocky flicked his glance toward Marty. George Sanchez's alibi had been gone through with a fine-tooth comb. Three real estate agents who worked with him all placed him at the office Sunday morning, and then twenty minutes after he'd left for the T, neighborhood Victory Gardeners remember him running toward them, his frantic words. There was no time for him to knock his wife unconscious, leave her in the fens, and then put his baby in Fenway Park. Marty showed Jimmy Gorman a copy of George Sanchez's mug shot.

"Do you recognize this man?"

Benny studied it. "Sure. He was in the paper this morning. The baby's father."

"Does he look anything like the sportswriter you saw?"

First Jimmy said, "What?" Then: "You gotta be kiddin', right?"

"Please look at the picture again."

Jimmy did. Then he gazed back up at the detective. "The guy I saw was slick." He handed the picture back. "Looked absolutely nothing like this poor devil."

Jimmy was dismissed with the request to keep thinking about the sportswriter and to call if he came up with anything else.

When he left, Marty said, "George could look slick."

"He probably did before the world shook beneath his feet."

"And if he's the one who shook the world. . ."

"We must not dismiss such a possibility yet."

"That's right."

THE NUMBER ONE PLACE
Thursday, 3:30 AM

I had to go down to NYC for work today. Yes, I have an actual job when I'm not writing about the Sox— and yes, they wish I put in the same effort for them as I do on this blog. . .

Took the 3rd Avenue Bridge to avoid tolls. Sox hats were everywhere, as usual in New York. Think about it, we're the third-most popular team there. Second, some years. I love spotting that B on the street and giving the nod—like we're a secret society. It's no secret at the Red Sox bar, Professor Thom's, though. Next time you're in New York, and the Sox are playing, head over to Thom's, 2nd Ave and 13th Street. It's so great to be in a place where every single person in the room is there for one reason: to root for the Red Sox. You don't always get that, even in Boston, since there are bound to be some people in any establishment that just happen to walk in not even knowing there's a game on. But at a New York Sox bar, you're going there to be with "your kind." You think it was tough being a Red Sox fan in Boston during the 86-year drought? Imagine if you were one in New York. Those people went through some shit.

But they've always had their safe havens right there in the Big Apple. Former Red Sox player Jerry Casale, not to be confused with Devo's Gerry Casale, ran the restaurant Pino's from the 1970s until a few years ago. There's also the Hairy Monk. And I watched game six of the 2004 ALCS at the Riviera—the game where A-Rod slapped the ball out of Bronson Arroyo's hand, and the Sox won a nailbiter to force game seven. Man, what a wild scene, all of us spilling out of the bar that could barely contain us, into the streets after the game, whooping it up like it was New Year's Eve. (It kinda

was, if ya know what I'm sayin'.) Any baseball-clue-
less tourist walking by at that moment surely
thought the local team had just won. Nope. It was
their bitter rival.

Thom's is the place to be now, though, and I
watched along with hundreds of Sox fans, including
several BLOHARDS, as the Red Sox kicked Yankee
butt. Stuck with the Yankee announcers, the sound
was turned off, and people got up two by two and
announced an inning over a loudspeaker, as is the
tradition there. So much better than having to hear
Michael Kay.

Manny with two mega-dongs tonight, one into the
Monster Seats, and one over them. And Josh
Beckett is finally pitching the way we knew he
could. Good thing the Marlins "threw in" Mike Lowell
in the Beckett trade, too, as he collected two more
doubles tonight. Another step closer to taking this
division for the first time since '95. And people say
the team isn't as loose as the '04 team with Damon
and Pedro and Millar. But come on, this is a fun,
wacky bunch! Manny, Papi, Papelbon. . .and
Tavarez and Lugo are total nutcases, too. I once got
to a game early and saw Tavarez eating chicken
that a fan was feeding him from the front row. And
during batting practice, Lugo will wear other guys'
jerseys, and bow to the crowd when his name's
announced. I love these guys. What other team's
pitchers has a percussion band going in the
bullpen? It's a bonus when your team wins and has
a ball doing it.

I would've loved to have partied with the guys and gals of Thom's deep into the night, but I had a four-hour drive ahead of me. Made it back to Boston before 3 AM. If you were wondering, Yes, both 95 and the Pike had construction going on. Go to sleep, guys!

Still waiting on Baby Ted Williams news. I did get a message while driving that Luis Sanseverra is still missing, and superagent Jack Lagunas who was staying at the Copley Plaza, left this afternoon and hasn't been seen since. I'll be calling that Detective soon as I get a little sleep.

COMMENTS:

Pweezil said: One more win, and it's a sweep.

Candletoast said: The Yanks are gonna need a bigger boat. . .

Surviving Grady said: Speaking of Sox bars, you gotta go to Sonny McLean's in Cali when you're out there. Great place.

SoSock said: Nic & Dino's when you're in Chicago. . .
DC in DC said: The 4 Courts in DC.

KGNumber5 said: When I went to Florida last year, we found this place called Boston's. Red Sox stuff all over that joint. Somewhere between Boca and West Palm.

Zed'sDead said: The Lompoc here in Portland shows every Sox game. Not Maine—Oregon!

Humpty Tim said: Sluggo's out here in Arizona.

AustinFlyGirl said: There are plenty of Soxcentric places in Texas. Come on down!

Jay said: It is truly Red Sox Nation. Thanks, everybody. And I like to reiterate this every chance I get—lots of these places have been around for years. This isn't a "oh, they won, now everyone likes them" deal. Whenever I see the Sox on the road, all the Sox fans I meet seem to be other migrating New Englanders, not local bandwagoners. Just listen to the chant—even in visitors' parks, it sounds like "let's go Red Sawx."

Kara12 said: Did you wake up? It's morning. Have you talked to that cop yet?

CHAPTER

9

The next morning, when Lt. Flanagan came into the office with coffee for himself and tea for Rocky, he said, "Did you by any chance read the blog while you were walking the floor with Bronko last night?

"I didn't, Marty."

"Says he's going to call you. Heard anything yet?"

"No."

"Well, it's early. And he was out late." Marty went around the desk to Rocky's computer. "May I?"

"You may."

Lt. Flanagan logged onto *The Number One Place*. Rocky read the post. He mused, "I wonder where this blogger's interest lies."

"Gotta be some reporter. They go nuts, those guys. Can't print anything unless it's verified. So they have their blogs and print whatever the hell they want. Wonder if Lagunas really is at the Copley Plaza.

"You haven't found out?"

"Found out what?"

"If it's true what the blogger says about Lagunas? I surely don't need to speak to him to find out that much."

"Jesus, Rock. I just walked in the goddamn door."

As Rocky returned his gaze to the computer screen, he asked, "And are you now settled in to the point where you are able to call the Copley Plaza?"

After Sargeant Flanagan spoke to the manager of the Copley Plaza Hotel, he was back. He said, "Lagunas is registered there, and the manager is going to call back after he checks to see if he's in the room. Meanwhile, this blogger thing . . . I mean, Rock, it's embarrassing. If the guy is right— like he's been right about everything else he says—he isn't playing guessing games. He's some kind of fucking fly on the wall."

"Yes. He is inside. He might have a psychopathic need to be found out, and thence, infamous. But I like to think he's inside baseball, possibly on a low level, with no hope of rising any higher."

"Do you know what I think?"

"Yes, Marty, I do. You think he's one of us."

"Yeah. On a low level with no hope of rising any higher."

Rocky smiled sadly. "It is usually our worst fears that drive us. But we know that most of our worst fears are not reality. We will do what needs to be done—search out the trail between the blogger and us."

"But if this guy is our worst fear, heaven help the son of a bitch."

"By *heaven*, Marty, are you meaning a compassionate Jesus?"

The citizens of Boston love to talk sports, politics and religion. But Sargeant Flanagan did his utmost to avoid talking religion with his boss because he couldn't dope out the Hindu stuff. Just too damn foreign. He'd said to his fellow officers once, "Call me an atheist, but I just can't make heads or tails out of this *Hare Krishna* boogie-woogie." Now he said to Rocky, "It's just an expression."

"All right, then. To move along, what exactly do we know

of Mr. Lagunas's recent behavior that the blogger does not?"

"Well, here's something—the day Lagunas left LA, he took a hundred grand out of one of his accounts. Cash." Marty sighed. "Geeze, Rocky, I wonder what it would be like to do that? Walk into Sovereign Bank around the corner and say to the chick, 'Honey, I need a little cash to tide me over. Could you slip me, like, nine-hundred-and-ninety-nine C-notes and just throw in a couple of fifties for. . .' "

"You are saying the opportunity has arisen where we can follow the money."

"Yeah. It has arisen. Our guys just found that out. So why would he need so much cash?" Marty answered his own question. "*A, he needs to bribe somebody; B, he owes someone a bundle; or C. . .*"

". . .Mr. Lagunas is planning to appease a blackmailer."

Detective Patel often finished Sargeant Flanagan's sentences, not because the two men weren't necessarily of the same mind, but because Rocky sometimes lost patience with the lieutenant's creative linguistic style, just as Marty sometimes lost patience with Rocky's deliberate cadence.

Rocky said, "Or perhaps he is seeing to a disgruntled employee. An employee he had to let go. Or maybe he cheated a business partner and feels guilty. Or. . ."

"But we're going with blackmail, right?"

"The only option that so often leads to a perp's ever-expanding criminal behavior. I wonder if his enemies number highly."

"He's a fucking sports agent, Rock. His enemies number *wicked* highly. They include the owners of all the major league baseball teams for starters. To say nothing of a kazillion fans who don't like an agent cuttin' a deal so that their favorite player ends up in pinstripes."

"Becomes a rival Yankee?"

"Yeah. Especially right after he says he'll never play for the Yanks. Rest in peace, caveman."

The phone rang. Rocky picked up, listened, and then he said, "Very good," and hung up.

"The hotel manager. The blogger was right about the movements of Mr. Lagunas. I want you to go to Los Angeles and find out what you can about his recent dealings."

"You do?"

"Yes."

"Uh, right away?" Sergeant Flanagan was afraid of flying.

"Yes. While I see to his movements here." Rocky looked at his watch to make a point.

Marty stood up. "What do you say the odds are that the guy is on the receiving end of foul play? I mean, like, now. As we speak."

"Sergeant. If his body shows up before your flight, I will *still* need you to take care of business in Los Angeles. Meanwhile, we will try to find him. If he doesn't turn up, you can tell me what you think the odds are of his possible demise once you've completed your scoping of Los Angeles."

My *scoping of Los Angeles*. Marty would never laugh out loud at the things Rocky came out with, unlike Lucy who couldn't help herself. He headed for the door. He turned back once to say, "Hey. Good luck, Rock."

"And you, Marty."

As it turned out, Lt. Flanagan had the less challenging task. He was in LA by late afternoon, one o'clock, Boston time.

Jack Lagunas's office was in Newport Beach so Marty had to drive the forty-odd miles from LAX. He would be there by two.

The office sat on the same bluff overlooking the Pacific as Scott Boras's, tucked between the Big Canyon and the

Newport Beach Country Clubs. *Office* was not quite the word Marty would use. He took in the 12,000 square foot building—actually half the size of Boras's—and approached the massive stainless steel door. A matching steel plaque on the wall, just to the left, read *WorldWide Baseball*. The rest of the building seemed to be made entirely of glass. Black glass. Marty touched a button and the stainless steel soundlessly opened in, the kind of door that made Marty want to say to the first person he encountered, "My name is Bond. James Bond."

The reception area of WorldWide Baseball spread out in all directions, a view to the sea on one side, the canyon to the other. There were a few pieces of sleek furniture—a few sofas, tables and a curving desk. A sleek receptionist sporting a few kilos of gold chains around her neck sat behind it, studiously ignoring Marty. On the walls were handsomely framed blow-ups of ballplayers' photographs anchored by one of Ted Williams taken in 1939, Ted's rookie year, when he would turn twenty-one. The photo had been enlarged to five by seven feet. Sargeant Flanagan was able to date the photograph because he could make out the patch on Ted's sleeve, which commemorated the 100th birthday of baseball. That birth year—1839—was an arbitrary date based on a bogus letter a fellow from Cooperstown wrote to a friend. He claimed another friend, Abner Doubleday, had just invented this really interesting game he was calling Base Ball. The playing field would be a square set on one of its points—a diamond. And so, the need to demonstrate that baseball was a homegrown American game and not some poor sister to the British game, rounders, was fulfilled.

Marty himself owned one of those patches; he'd had it framed, and hung it on his own wall of player photographs in his living room.

He noted that all the players pictured on the walls were Hispanic, all of them represented by Jack Lagunas except Ted.

Marty allowed the incredibly gorgeous receptionist to ignore him. He didn't mind because he got to enjoy the life-size image of the young Ted Williams. Ted really was built like a splinter, and in this photograph, his face was raised in profile as he gazed out into the distance where the baseball he'd just crushed was still airborne four hundred feet away. The photo was in color. Marty figured maybe it had been colorized, this being LA.

The receptionist didn't like being ignored by someone she was ignoring so she condescended to saying, "Did you have an appointment?"

Still looking at Ted, Marty asked, "It that picture colorized?" though the James Bond line tempted him sorely.

She turned her perfect face with a sweep of her caramel hair, which was almost the exact shade of her flawless skin, and looked at the photograph. She turned back to Sargeant Flanagan, who was now gazing at her instead of the picture. "I wouldn't know. And is there anything else arousing your . . .curiosity?"

"Yeah, there is. How come Ted's up there? He's the only. . . uh. . .white guy."

She smiled. "He is half Mexican, I'm told."

"Hey, you're shittin' me. I never knew that." But Sargeant Flanagan did know that. He said to her, "I'm told he was an atheist."

That proved disconcerting. She tilted her head to study this stranger more carefully. Upon an initial encounter, Marty liked to make people think he was an idiot, and then he liked to mess with their heads.

Marty took out his badge. "Sargeant Marty Flanagan.

Boston Police. I'd like to talk to whoever's in charge here when Lagunas isn't around."

The receptionist took in the badge. She said, "Then your officer ID number is 1630?"

"Nope. That's the year the Boston Police Department was founded."

"There was a Boston in 1630?"

"Yes."

"But not a country."

"Just our little bay colony."

She smiled at him—the contrast between her pearl-white teeth and her drop-dead red lipstick—enticing. "Mr. Lagunas happens to be in Boston. Isn't that an amazing coincidence?"

"Which is why I didn't ask to speak to him." Under his breath, he added, *Ditz.*

Just then a young, but rather stodgily dressed man emerged from the door to the left of the big photograph of the Splendid Splinter. Marty wondered at his wing tips, a style of shoe not known to proliferate in LA. The man strode to the receptionist's desk without taking note of Marty. "Gloria, I need everything we've got on. . ."

Gloria interrupted him. "Mr. Byington, do you know if this is a genuine color photograph?" She pointed her Montblanc over her shoulder at Ted.

"What?"

"This gentleman from the Boston Police Department would like to know."

She flashed the enticing smile at Sargeant Flanagan again, who smiled back. Maybe not a ditz after all. Marty took his badge out again for the pleasure of Mr. Byington.

Rather than question the meaning of the number, 1630, the man said, "Oh shit." And then, "Come into my office."

Marty couldn't help but wink at Gloria before he followed this no-first-name fellow. Gloria rolled her eyes, but in a good-natured way.

Mr. Byington invited Marty to sit down while he went around to his big leather rolling chair behind his cherry desk topped with more black glass. Hey, maybe you can't get clear glass in California is what Marty figured. After all, you couldn't get Thomas's English Muffins until they'd been in Massachusetts grocery stores for twenty years. First time in LA, he'd ordered them for breakfast. The waitress had said, "*What* kind of muffin?" Marty clarified what kind and she'd said, "I got corn, bran and blueberry."

It was always fortunate for a police officer when the person he needs to question, in turn, needs to vent. All Marty had to do was sit back and listen to no-first-name Byington.

His words flowed out in a stream. "Jack carried things too far. He's *greedy*. Well, we're all greedy in this business, but you take care not to cross people. I mean, of course you cross people, but you'd better know where to draw the line."

Ditz is what Marty thought once again, only this time he was pretty sure of it.

The man kept talking. "Who you go to when you need to get something done, for example. You can't get your hands dirty. Well Jack has allowed dirt into our business, and now we've got the Feds poking around. Then he goes to Boston without even letting me know, and now *I*—not *him*—*I've* got some fucking Boston cop here—no offense—harassing *me*."

As sympathetically as could be, Sargeant Flanagan asked, "No offense taken. But, wow, what do the Feds want with you guys?"

"Hey, we specialize in Cuban players."

"Feet on the ground, no problem though, right?"

"Yeah, but that's not always so easy. We've been. . ." And

suddenly the sports agent named Byington seemed to realize that he was talking to a cop, not an old friend. And he knew a cop was a cop, whether representing a town, city, state or the Federal Justice Department. He stared at Marty sitting comfortably in front of him. "What exactly do you want?"

Marty straightened his back, leaned forward, and said, "Listen, pal, I want the same fucking thing you want. I want Luis Sanseverra."

Byington gulped. Then he straightened his back. "That's just it, isn't it? Where in God's name is he?"

"I'm guessing you heard from your employer as to. . ."

"My *partner*."

"Excuse me. Partner."

"No, I haven't heard from him. He's looking for the ballplayer. Sans. . .uh. . ."

"Sanseverra."

"Yes."

"Where's he looking?"

The agent's lips formed a tight line.

"We'll find out without your help, but we'd appreciate anything you can do to simplify things. What with the involvement of the FBI. . . . You guys have all learned that you can lie to ballplayers, to owners. . .you can make up all the shit you want. But when you lie to the Feds, you'd better follow up with a jingle to Martha Stewart and ask her advice on what to pack."

Marty shifted in his seat so that Byington would get a glimpse of his .40-caliber Glock.

The glimpse worked. Byington's face flushed. "Listen, this is all a lot of garbage that has nothing to do with me. Jack. . ."

"Thought you were partners."

"We are. But he likes keeping his little secrets. And now I've got to deal with the FBI and some cop." He waved his hand as if Marty were a fly. "Beautiful."

"I'd like you to deal further, Byington."

The gun was still in view. Byington returned to his vent mode. "This whole thing has always been a train wreck waiting to happen. These morons who. . .who acquire Cuban players for us. . . . I mean they used to be, like, diplomats or something. Now we're screwing around with a bunch of. . .gangs!"

Marty was intrigued. Time to pull this guy's chain again, only a little harder. "Listen, I want your boss. I need to. . ."

"My *partner.*"

"Whatever. Where is he?"

"I don't know."

"Did he owe someone money? Like a whole lot of money?"

Every muscle in the man's face went slack.

Marty asked, "So had he decided recently not to pay the morons you spoke of? The *gang*? Not to pay them the money he perhaps *owes* them? Did you go along with that? Schnauzering a gang member? I mean, you being the partner and all?"

The man stuck his jaw out. "Listen to me. Jack has some people who *think* they're owed money. They fucked up. They don't get paid. We don't owe them a goddamn fucking thing. That's the name of the game."

Marty slouched again, and asked in a more conspiratorial way, "Do you consider these fuck-ups—who maybe have a different name for their game than you do—are. . .uh. . .dangerous?"

The jaw retreated.

"See Byington, here is what I need to know. Who exactly are these fuck-ups? I want their names so I can call on them and see if they're hosting a young ballplayer. Or maybe even your partner."

Byington re-composed. He looked down at his big watch.

Then back to Sargeant Flanagan. "They're temporary employees. They're nobodies. Scum. I doubt they're even on record. I mean, this is California. Half the people here are illegals. All I know is, right now, I've got to take a meeting. So if you'll. . ."

Sargeant Flanagan stood up. He handed Byington his card. "Call me as soon as you want to give me the names of the nobody, scummy, fucked-up employees. Before your partner realizes he's too big for his britches. Because when he does realize it, maybe it'll be a little too late."

The guy stared at the card, but then he took it. Marty turned on his heel, crossed the expanse of carpet, and opened the door. Byington stumbled around his desk. "Wait!"

Marty didn't bother turning back.

"Shit. I'm a *front*. I've never been part of Jack's decisions. I don't know what the hell these damn spics think they're doing because. . ."

But Sargeant Flanagan was out Byington's door, and as he passed Gloria's desk, Gloria—having heard the remark made by her boss—said to Marty in a low voice, "He's an asshole."

Marty looked at her, made a gun with his thumb and index finger, aimed it at her, and said, "I'd love to chat with you, Cuba. How bout I give you a call?"

"Sure. You do that. Irish."

Out in the hallway, Marty was entirely pleased with himself. Good call, he thought. He filed Gloria's face in the folder in his brain under G—for *gorgeous*, not *Gloria*. Now there were three faces in that file; the other two had red stripes stamped across them, which was Sargeant Flanagan's code for serving time. If Gloria avoided the red stripe and he was ever back in LA, he'd look her up. Probably not much chance of that all coming together, but it was worth a few prayers. He started with, "*O Lord I am not worthy, that thou shouldst come to me, but. . .*"

Before he was even out of the building, Marty had Rocky on his cell.

"WorldWide Baseball is slightly bigger than the Taj Mahal, but I've only seen a tenth of it, plus a killer reception-ist, and a token white guy partner who is considerably freaked out. Make that scared shitless, and I don't know what he'll be if Lagunas runs into more trouble than he's apparently already in. This guy is way out of his league, no pun intended. The Feds have been to visit, Rock."

"Have they?"

"Rocky, when you get a couple of Cuban athletes jumping ship during Olympic trials in, say, Montreal—whatever—and they're looking for asylum. . ."

"I know about defections. And Cubans. . . . Why would there be a problem?"

"Anybody illegal who gets caught, gets detained and sent back. But yeah, you're right. Cubans—not so fast. If their feet are dry—meaning they've made it to ground—the US just takes 'em in, no questions asked. If they got wet feet, like wet from the waters of the Straits of Florida slogging around in the bottom of their boat, back they go. And don't ask me who the screwball politician was who came up with that shit-for-brains inspiration because I sure as hell wouldn't know."

Rocky was silent.

"Rock, tell me you don't know. . . . I mean, like, who the politicians are."

"I don't, actually. But I will find out."

Then he was silent again. Marty waited for him to finish thinking. This allowed Marty to say one of his own brand of prayer, rather than relying on a hymn from when his mother forced him to join the church choir. A prayer for a hopeless cause. Marty knew there was a saint officially available for hopeless causes, but he could never keep his saints straight. He stuck with "God." *Please, God, have him tell me I should stay here.*

Rocky spoke. "I will reach out to the very excellent source I have at the FBI and see what's going on here. In the meantime, you will need more leverage. You'll have to stay in LA. At least until tomorrow."

Rocky imagined exactly how the sargeant was pumping his fist. As soon as Rocky had heard *killer receptionist. . . .* Well, Marty always loved a challenge.

In a most professional tone, Marty responded, "All right, Rocky, whatever it takes."

"It takes more details which you will need to uncover as soon as possible. Get us the names. You need to find out who it was Lagunas came to see in Boston. And then, perhaps I will be able to find Lagunas himself."

"You got anything yet?"

He had, but he didn't have time to go into it. "I'll fill you in when you get home. I've met with our blogger. Very interesting." With that, he hung up before Marty could ask, "Was he dressed in blue?"

⚾

That night, Gloria took Marty to Dodger Stadium to see the Dodgers play the Mets. At the start of the game, Gloria, who was wearing the clingiest of tank tops and not a damn thing under it or what would be the point, gestured toward the lines of players standing at attention for the Star-Spangled Banner. Her index finger moved along the lines as the music played. She said, "Ours, ours and ours. Ours. Ours . . ."

Marty leaned into her hair and whispered, "We don't talk during the national anthem."

"Well if that girl knew how to *sing*. . ."

Marty recognized that his not judging Gloria's irreverent behavior unfavorably wasn't fair to people who weren't gorgeous, but—what the hell.

Between innings, Marty went to the men's room and made a point to stop by the home team's dugout. He shouted down, "How ya doin', Nomah?"

Nomar gave a nod, as he always did when he recognized a true Boston-accent rather than a tired, mocking one.

Three innings later, Marty went to the concession stand, and on the way back made a detour to the visitors' dugout. He held out two beers. "Hey, Pedro. I got a coupla nice cold ones for ya."

Pedro grinned his grin and flipped Marty a double bird.

During the game, Marty learned from Gloria that on the first floor of WorldWide Baseball, in a giant room tucked away behind reception, were forty computers running twenty-four hours a day. On the second floor, fifty flat-screen TVs, monitored for every bit of international news from Tokyo to San Pedro de Macoris to come down the pike. And in the basement, ten XM satellite receivers with information that usually beat out anything from the TVs with the exception of whatever news Michael Kim was breaking.

Gloria said, "In this business, you can never have too much information. If you get a flash to Jack before anyone else—I mean if your information is first—you win a prize. The amount of the prize is determined by the ramifications of your information. The WWB's version of end-of-year bonuses."

Marty said, "And to think. . .I was told it was all about how fast you could throw, how hard you could hit and how you could manage to run, jump and catch all at the same time."

Gloria said, "It's all about money."

"So do you get to know any of the ball players?"

"I wish. I get to know the press. Sometimes they're actually pounding on the door when I get to work. I have to tell them what they already know—that Jack decides who to see and when to see them. Command performances only."

At the 7th inning stretch, the fans began leaving. The score was tied, three to three.

Marty looked around and said, "Where the hell are these people going?"

"They're done."

"*Done?*"

She said, "They think the game's over. People are standing up, they figure it's time to go."

"It's the *seventh inning!*"

Gloria shrugged her creamy bare shoulders. "This is LA. We're still learning."

"The game is *fucking tied!*"

"Actually, the fans are faking it. They want to get in some beach-time. There's a great concert on the Santa Monica pier tonight."

Marty sputtered some more and Gloria laughed. Her teeth were so polished Marty thought they looked like beads rather than teeth. Her red and glistening lips made him so crazy he had to look away from her—like looking into the sun. She comforted him by placing her hand on his thigh. Pat, pat, pat. On the third pat, she left her hand in place.

He said, "You wanna cut outta here, Cuba?"

"Yeah, Irish, I do."

In the hours before Rocky spoke to Marty again, he had been driving across Boston, first to the Copley Plaza where the manager confirmed the blogger's post that Jack Lagunas had left the day before. No one had seen Lagunas since. The concierge remembered Mr. Lagunas because he'd needed a car and directions. He left around two in the afternoon.

The manager said to Rocky, "He didn't spend last night in his suite."

The concierge pointed down at the huge ledger opened in front of him. "He's in my log. He was pretty insistent that he needed a car. I don't remember where it was he wanted to go, but it couldn't have been far because I was able to talk him into taking a taxi instead. So much simpler since there are no empty parking spaces in Boston."

As Rocky and the manager walked away from the concierge desk, Rocky took out a search warrant. The manager, entirely nonplussed, went to a computer and then led Rocky to Lagunas's suite, $970 a night.

In the bedroom closet hung a yellow linen blazer, a yellow shirt and yellow pants. Three different shades of yellow, the shirt the brightest. Gleaming pale tan loafers were on the floor of the closet. Lagunas had chosen not to dress up when he went out. Either that or he had another city casual outfit, Los Angeles the city that fit his style though. Not Boston.

His small bag contained two polo shirts, a pair of jeans and underwear, a silk robe, no pajamas. The only other pair of shoes he'd brought was on his feet. He wasn't planning on staying in Boston very long. Either that, or he was one of those people who always traveled light, and then bought what he needed when he arrived at his destination. He'd been in a hurry though; he'd forgotten socks.

Lagunas hadn't bothered to take the time to put the contents of the bag into a drawer.

A case of toiletries, also unpacked, was in the bathroom. The hotel's complimentary shampoo, soap, etc. were untouched. He hadn't taken the time to shower. He'd traveled first class—maybe he'd chosen to tidy up in the VIP lounge at Logan.

On the desk, on the top page of a neat stack of notepaper in a leather holder, was the impression of what had been written on the piece of paper that previously sat atop of the stack.

Rocky held the paper at an angle to the lamp. It was easy to read because the five-star hotel offered their guests pens of substance and 20 lb. notepaper—very cushy stationary. The impression read: Kelly's Diner, 674 Broadway, Summerville.

The superagent didn't know Boston. The paper should have read, Somerville. Rocky wondered how the man could imagine people in Massachusetts would name a town Summerville.

Rocky knew of Kelly's Diner. It was a block from the Somerville fire house. A couple of firemen from the gym where he boxed—when he had the chance—worked at the station, and they always seemed to be planning to meet at Kelly's Diner.

Rocky left the hotel, assuring the manager, "Yes, you've been very helpful, thank you," and went to his car.

Boston suburbs are more neighborhoods than suburbs, closer to what Washington Heights is to Manhattan, than what Malibu is to LA. The towns with their different names all ran into each other; Somerville adjoined that section of Boston by Mystic River, and its back end butted up against Cambridge. Where one town started and another began was impossible to tell.

Somerville, once home mainly to working stiffs, as factory employees had called themselves, was gentrifying quickly, its squares becoming homes to art spaces and hot clubs. Kelly's Diner was a classic '50s train car, an authentic one, at that. Displayed prominently on a shelf holding a row of coffee mugs was a pink and black, two-toned '56 Ford Fairlane. A statue of Elvis singing to a hound dog was on one side of the Ford, and a photograph of James Dean on the other.

Rocky sat down at the counter. Immediately, the waitress grabbed the pot of coffee, approached him, and before she could ask, "Coffee?" he showed her his badge.

"My name is Patel. I need to disturb you, Ma'am. I have a few questions I must ask."

She glanced down at the badge and then into Rocky's face. "What are you? An Arab, or something?"

"I was born in India."

"Hey, no kiddin'? I never been, but I love that curry stuff you guys eat."

Rocky smiled. "I remember little of India myself, but I can recall the fragrance of curry spices drifting about the air."

"That's nice. So you want some coffee? This pot is getting' a little heavy here."

"I would love a cup of tea." Rocky read her name tag. "Clare."

"Sure. You got it. . .uh. . ." She raised an eyebrow.

"Detective."

"Detective. Thought so."

She put the coffee back, and brought Rocky a cup of hot water and a tea bag. "Cream and sugar?"

"Please."

She reached over and slid the sugar jar closer to him, took two creamers out of her pocket and plunked them down. Then she looked at the picture Rocky held out to her. He asked her, "Have you seen this man before?"

She didn't hesitate. "Yeah. I seen him. Yesterday. Three guys came in. He was one of 'em. They spoke Spanish."

Rocky dunked his tea bag.

"Came in around two-thirty. We close at three so I figured, hell, I'm going to have to make them understand they got a half hour, period. I figured at five of three, I'd go over, point at my watch, and say, *Hasta la vista*, the only Spanish I know besides *abierto*. Learned that thirty years ago. . .*abierto* . . ." she rolled the *r* dramatically, ". . .on 'Sesame Street.' Don't remember what the hell it means though. Anywho, the problem didn't arise. They only had the coffee, and then they were out."

Rocky said, "*Abierto* means *open*. The first Spanish word I learned on 'Sesame Street' was *agua*."

"Hey. . . Yeah! *Agua*. *Water*, right?"

"Right."

"I'm smarter than I give myself credit for."

"I'm sure you are, Clare. So you know nothing of their conversation."

"Well, I know they were arguing. I mean, *really* arguing. Ya know when ya got people hissin' in each other's faces? The guy in your picture there? Class act. The other two? As my mother woulda put it. . .goons."

"And how would you define *goons*?"

"A goon is a guy you hope you never meet in a dark alley. But the classy guy? Came in a taxi, a rarity. He left with the other two."

"Did you happen to see them get into a car?"

"You're in luck, Detective. People know when we close. Two guys got the prime spot right in front of my door." She pointed. Rocky turned and looked.

When he turned back she was smirking. "I don't know one suburban assault vehicle from another, but this was a big one. Real big."

"Color?"

"Black."

Rocky had one last sip of tea, and then he took out his wallet.

"On me, Detective."

"I insist. How much do I owe you?"

"Put a buck in here."

She reached down the counter again and plunked the Jimmy Fund container in front of him. She said, "You guys watch our backs, ya know? And the kids need this more than I do."

"You're a generous woman, Clare."

"No I ain't."

"And one more thing." Rocky took out another picture, the picture of George Sanchez. He laid it on the counter. "Does he look like one of the men you saw?"

She picked it up. Her chest rose and fell as she took in an extra gulp of air, just like everyone did when they thought about the baby, Arturo. She handed the picture back.

"You're barkin' up the wrong tree there, Detective. The guys I saw were twenty years older than that poor little baby's dad, God bless."

Back in his office, Rocky called a number from his file; the FBI agent he'd worked with once. He got her assistant. They exchanged pleasantries. She said, "Glad you found out who that baby belonged to Detective."

"And we are glad, too."

"He's okay then?"

"He is."

The message Rocky left for Agent Poppy Rice was: *Why is the FBI investigating Jack Lagunas?*

Rocky glanced at his watch. Almost noon. When the blogger called the hotline right after Marty had left for his flight to LA, Rocky arranged to meet him during his lunch break. Jay chose the Trident Café, a hip place on Newbury Street, just a couple of blocks from Edgerly.

Rocky went to the café directly from Somerville. The blogger was waiting outside the door. Jay looked just as Rocky imagined he would look: young, jeans, sneakers, black shirt and a Red Sox hat, though Rocky hadn't imagined that the hat would be so old that little strings hung down from the frayed edges of the brim.

Rocky put his hand out. "You are Jay?"

"Yeah, I am. Hi."

They shook hands. Rocky followed the blogger inside. The café was also a bookstore. Jay had secured a little round table at the far side of the bar. His laptop sat on the table alongside his drink, a Mango Tango smoothie, and his veggie burger. Rocky though it looked good and ordered the same—they had something in common, both vegetarians.

Rocky always cut to the charge. "How do you know what you know?"

The blogger cut right back. "My father's college roommate works for the Red Sox."

Rocky kept his gaze steady, directly into the blogger's eyes. He said, "The man is obviously supportive of your work."

Jay couldn't believe his ears. A man of a certain age considering his blog, work. He said, "Yes."

"He and your father have remained close then?"

"Yeah. I call him *Uncle* like I did when I was little. But he's my friend."

"Uncle what?"

"Do I have to tell you his name?"

Rocky did not want to spook the young blogger. "Not at this time. Tell me instead, how your uncle knew Jack Lagunas was at the Copley Plaza, had left, and hadn't returned."

"He'd made an appointment to speak with him."

"How did he know he was even in Boston?"

"He keeps tabs on a lot of people."

"In his capacity as an employee of the Red Sox?"

The blogger paused. "Yes."

"I take it then, that your uncle gives you your information for reasons other than his fondness for you?"

"Yeah."

Rocky's burger came. The blogger sucked his smoothie up the straw. "Why exactly is he using you? Why does he want to bring Jack Lagunas's name before the public?"

"Because the papers are chickenshit."

"And what does your uncle feel the newspapers should be reporting on?"

"Hold on a sec." The blogger dug his vibrating cell out of his pocket, looked at who was calling, shut it off, and put it back. "Sorry. See, my uncle's got this bug up his ass."

"What nature of bug would that be?"

"You ever heard of the Pestano Pipeline?"

No period of *namaste* could help Rocky on this one. Jay proceded to tell him a most intriguing story while they downed their burgers, grey-green vegetable fluid dripping down onto their plates every time they took a bite.

THE NUMBER ONE PLACE
Thursday, 11:30 PM

Lagunas still hasn't shown up back in Boston. Maybe he's with his client, Luis Sanseverra. Wherever that might be. I meet up with Detective Patel today. I'm just telling him stuff I know. Stuff about Jack Lagunas, for example.

In 1990, Yader Pestano, a Cuban pitcher, became the first ballplayer to defect. He needed an agent, and Juan Lagunas, a mob guy in Miami, contacted some agents to see if any of them would represent Pestano, but none of them wanted to get mixed up in any immigration shit. So Juan Lagunas changes his first name to Jack, moves to LA, starts an agency that he calls WorldWide Baseball, and ends up representing Pestano. (Wish I'd thought of that, ha.) In less than a week, he negotiates a huge contract with a major league team for a ton of money. I heard Lagunas was going around bragging it was the easiest money he ever made in his life. He'd say, "It beats robbing banks."

So for the next twenty years, not only is Lagunas representing a bunch of players, but guess what? He comes up with a dozen Cuban players. None of their defection stories can be verified. Lagunas is maybe *smuggling* players out of Cuba. Now I'm wondering about Luis Sanseverra. I'm gonna look into that guy.

Major League Baseball has successfully suppressed this phenomenon now commonly referred to as The Pestano Pipeline. The media, except for a paragraph or two in a very few newspapers, as well as Major League Baseball, have chosen to ignore it, same as drugs, until Jose Canseco stuffed their faces in it.

Now, Lagunas is missing and some serious shit is about to hit the fan. More to come.
Getting back to normal: I finally got to hear Remy's take on this Yankee series, after watching the last

two games from Fenway and 2nd Avenue respectively. "Respectively": The baseball announcer's best friend. Schilling pitched well tonight, but Gagne blew it as usual, and Andy Pettitte got the win. Giambi's broken-bat homer that snuck inside the Pesky Pole was the nail in our coffin. Just think, Jason, if you had hit a cheapie like that at home, the Yankee Stadium crowd would've asked for a curtain call. I understand Tino Martinez once was asked for a curtain call for tying his shoes correctly after only three tries.

But we took 2 out of 3, so the division still looks safe. Now the Orioles come to town for three this weekend, closing out the long homestand.

One more thing. Lugo and Cora were over at the family of Baby Ted today. They live right near Fenway, so I guess there's been a fairly steady stream of Red Sox guys visiting, bringing food and stuff. Every interview with a player seems to end with a "How's the baby doing?" or "How's the family doing?" Finally Cora today mentioned how they try to find a little time to get over there. He says it's really, really tough.

COMMENTS:

Canvas Alley said: I think that's great that the players are doing that. I can't imagine what that family must be going through.

Castigli-owned said: Jay, I never knew this about "the pipeline." You're right, obviously they've swept it under the rug.

LiveFreeOrDie said: You know, I kinda like Lagunas and Boras and these other tough agents. I'd want them representing my kid. They get the money that the players are worth.

AJM said: Be careful who you hitch your wagon to, man. Remember when Bobby Brady idolized Jesse James, and then one of James' old victims popped into the Brady house (come on, Joe Namath and Davy Jones found the place, it was clearly on a main thoroughfare), and told Bobby the truth about Jesse? And then Bobby had the dream that Jesse killed his whole family? Just a warning. . .

MattySox said: So how do you know what you know, Jay? I'm dyin' heah.

The next day, the FBI office in Boston delivered a confidential file to Rocky that had been faxed to them. The agent put it in Rocky's hands and said, "Hope it's what you need, Detective."

Rocky said, "I suspect it is."

"Considering its source, so do I."

There was a scribble across the top of the cover page: *Rocky—Here's your stuff. It's a working indictment. We need the means to acquire a search warrant to verify names. If you want to talk to the agent in charge of the case, his name is right on top. And big congrats on Rocky Jr.! Heard the news last week. Gift on the way. Love to Lucy.—Yrs, Poppy Rice.*

The document that arrived thanks to Agent Rice read:

THE CHARGE AGAINST JUAN "JACK" LAGUNAS

Jack Lagunas did knowingly and willfully combine, conspire, confederate and agree with other persons known and unknown to the Grand Jury, to commit offenses against the United States that is: to bring aliens to the United States, to transport aliens within the United States, to conceal these aliens within the United States, knowing and in reckless disregard of the law of the United

States for the purpose of commercial advantage
and private financial gain.

THE PURPOSE AND OBJECT OF THE CONSPIRACY

Jack Lagunas intended to enrich himself by
smuggling Cuban nationals who were prospective
major league baseball players into the United
States.

THE MANNER AND MEANS
TO ACCOMPLISH CONSPIRACY

Jack Lagunas hired others who owned and oper-
ated vessels to smuggle aliens. Jack Lagunas and
co-conspirators failed to disclose the location and
identities of the baseball players to the
Immigration and Customs Enforcement. Jack
Lagunas and co-conspirators transported baseball
players to California in a rental van. Jack
Lagunas and co-conspirators were responsible to
seeing to the training and conditioning of the
baseball players once they arrived in California.
Jack Lagunas was responsible for authorizing
payments for the housing, meals, equipment and
clothing of the aliens. Jack Lagunas financed the
smuggling ventures and distributed proceeds to
pay co-conspirators for their participation in the
scheme. Jack Lagunas caused wire transfers of
$840,000 on the account of a person known to
the Grand Jury as C. L. at Community Capitol
Bank to be distributed to the co-conspirators to
be charged with arming themselves with deadly
and dangerous weapons in the commission of
these illegal acts on the high seas.

The working document concluded with the line:

ALL IN VIOLATION OF TITLE 8,
UNITED STATES CODE 1324

At the bottom of the page was another scribble from Agent Rice: *Rocky—This indictment is about to sink your Beverly Hills superagent. He's claiming he performed humanitarian acts. But as we well know, his crime is identical to all illegal human trafficking—he put the lives of innocent people at risk through a smuggling operation where he would profit from their labors. There were kids on those boats too. Fuck him.—Poppy*

Rocky had to smile, and he thought, Agent Rice has a bug up her ass, too, identical to the one contained inside the blogger's surrogate uncle.

She'd added a PS: *We may not know all the names of the criminals who have maintained this operation—the Pestano Pipeline—and kept it alive for over ten years, but we've learned that the talent blockaded in Cuba is worth millions of dollars. There are a few politicians who'd better be able to explain this fiasco to me, how it's been kept under wraps all this time. Because as you might put it, Rocky, I intend to see to the rolling of heads.*

While the FBI worked on gathering enough evidence to search the office of WorldWide Baseball, and to confiscate files and computers, Sargeant Flanagan secured a warrant with no problem at all—with ease, in fact, what with the publicity surrounding the death of Baby Ted Williams's mother. So standing by as an LA police officer laid the warrant down on Gloria's desk, Marty shrugged at the look she gave him. He hadn't been able to detect any hint that Gloria had knowledge of the illegal shenanigans of her bosses. She was window dressing.

Gloria handed the officers keys, each clearly labeled as she was efficient as well as able to dress a window.

Flanagan watched, alongside Gloria, as the cops unlocked Lagunas's office door, and removed pretty much everything that wasn't nailed down to a van parked outside the great steel door. They even wheeled out an entire cabinet of CD's since CD cases made for great hiding places. All the perp had to remember was: *third row, eleventh from the left*, say, to get whatever secret information he had hidden away, or perhaps the funds for a rainy day.

Sargeant Flanagan was left in charge of Byington. Byington wouldn't know his name was on the warrant until LAPD finished with Lagunas's office. Marty could see that Byington was quite pleased with the reckless dismantling. He was reminded of Fredo in *The Godfather*, the older brother who always wanted to show that he was as clever and important as the kid brother. But maybe Byington would survive Lagunas, unlike poor Fredo, who didn't stand a rat's chance in hell against Michael Corleone.

When the time came to show the warrant to Byington, the LA officer waved it at him, tapping his fat, rough finger to Byington's own name. Then the police contingent headed into his office.

Marty took great pleasure in the predictable steps Byington followed the as he got caught red-handed with the goods. First, he was appalled. He sputtered to Sargeant Flanagan, "But I don't *understand!* Whatever my partner may have been up to, WWB is a first-rate, legitimate business in good standing, and might I add that I. . ." etc.

Second, he got all puffed up in reaction to Marty's face which appeared to be set in New England granite; Byington's sputtering stopped, and he attempted a threat: "I am calling

my lawyer now. *Right now.* This is a travesty and I intend to
. . ." etc.

Marty yawned and gazed out at the view of the Pacific.
Not as nice as Cape Cod. No lobster pots for starters.

Third, Byington switched to defense: "Now, listen, we may
have stepped on a few toes over the years, but believe me, anything illegal is something I would never have been. . ." etc.

Marty turned his gaze to the canyon. Didn't turn orange,
gold and red in the fall.

Fourth, Byington's head swiveled left and right. He moved
closer to Marty and attempted to ingratiate himself, "Ya
know, Officer..."

"Sargeant."

"Excuse me. *Sargeant.* I'm a partner on paper. I told you
already—I'm a *front.* I'm not Cuban. I'm not anything. Maybe
I know a little Spanish—I mean, *I have to*—but I'm actually a
silent partner. I've got the family name. I'm the token white
boy basically paid to. . ." etc.

That Step Four required Marty to finally make a remark
with words he had ready and waiting to let fly. He got into
into the silent partner's face: "Listen, token white boy, the
only thing you've said that makes sense to me is that you
intend to call a lawyer. I know I would if I was about to be
arrested."

Step Five was a biggie: "*Arrested?!?!?!* For what? I didn't *do*
anything! I never would have let that fucking Lagunas use my
name. . .my *stature*. . .if I dreamed there was anything illegal
going on."

Sargeant Flanagan said, "And when you get around to
reaching your lawyer, emphasize to him how much you want
to make a deal. Because if you testify, you get off. Also called
copping a plea."

And then, finally, with everything sinking in, Step Six, accompanied by tears: "*Testify?* Omigod. Oh, Jesus." He grabbed the phone on Gloria's desk. But he couldn't get an outside line without her. She pressed a button with exaggerated nonchalance. Sargeant Flanagan loved the sound of a grown man crying when he notices he's sinking into quicksand and there's no one holding a stick out to him. When, in fact, if anyone had a stick, they'd just wave it around and laugh.

Marty turned his attention to the best view in all of California—Gloria. She winked and stuck her tongue out at him.

Marty was now in love with Gloria.

By nightfall, even though a few desk guys at LAPD were still opening and shutting CDs, Sargeant Flanagan was on his way back to Boston with the names of certain employees of WorldWide Baseball who were not mentioned in the company's books. These employees earned a lot of money moonlighting whenever they could squeeze in the time between drug running jaunts from Columbia, to Puerto Rico, to Miami. Their names had been found in "Ramones Mania".

Marty had a few beers with a couple of LA officers before his plane took off.

One said, in reference to the team he rooted for, "What about our fucking first baseman? We still going to have him in the playoffs if this sting goes down?"

And Sargeant Flanagan explained the concept of wet feet, dry feet. Then he said, "So not to worry."

The cop said, "What a bunch of shit." He took a swallow of beer and then added, "But whatever works."

In Boston, David Ortiz heard from his sister who had, in turn, heard from Luis Sanseverra. He'd called from Havana, said to tell big Papi that he was home and fine, and to thank him. Tell his Sea Dog teammates the same thing. She assured Papi that he sounded happy.

Big Papi then called his manager. Tito told him he'd see to Red Sox management learning about Luis. He suggested to Papi he put it all behind him. Papi said he would except for one thing.

"Tito, call that detective for me. Tell him Luis is back in Cuba. Tell him he good."

Tito promised he would. And he decided that, the next day, before batting practice, he'd call a meeting, get the players together and give them a pep talk. Tell them they should feel good about themselves, not letting the events of the week keep them from playing so well. He told them he was proud of them, their concern for the Sanchez family important. But with the Yankee series over, he could see that his guys were drained. He would remind them that they would soon be together with their old buddy, Kevin Millar, and they'd all have a lot of laughs. Mainly, they needed to concentrate on beating Baltimore's butt.

THE NUMBER ONE PLACE
Friday, 11:30 PM

The Red Sox lost a rough one to the Orioles tonight. The usual let-down game after a Yanks series. Either that, or Kevin Millar slipped some sleeping pills into their Gatorade. Cowboy up! But the O's had an advantage—with all those Sox fans cheering against them at Fenway tonight, they must've felt right at home.

With the game going south for the Boston nine, the fans started in with the wave early tonight. Now, if you're not a Sox fan, you're looking at me like the McFlys, circa 1955, when Marty casually mentions his *two* television sets. It just can't be, right? Wrong. The "wave" arrived at Fenway in the 1980s. . .and it never left! And you thought the practice was officially discontinued in 1990. Nope. Every night at Fenway, you will see at least one wave. I think I know why.

As a card-carrying member of WaveBusters in the 80s, I've often been known to throw up a middle finger instead of standing up as the thing went by. I always thought it was dumb to go to a game and then pay attention to something other than what's going on in the field. But you have to realize, Fenway Park was built in 1912. I love the place but there are certain seats—no, entire sections—where watching the game will make you wake up the next morning with a stiff neck. Other locations give you a perfect view—of a pole. And while most seats in the tiny park are close to the field, some of the ones in the bleachers are well over 500 feet away. Out yonder, my friends, is where the wave starts.

Until the new ownership took over a few years ago, you could barely hear the PA from out there. Add that to the fact that the scoreboard is directly behind you, and the players are mere ants, and you get a few thousand people who are forced to make their own entertainment. We also lead the league with beach ball delays and spontaneous rhythmic clapping—hey, at least we don't let the scoreboard tell us when to cheer. Bronx, I'm looking in your direction. The wave is almost a way to unite the crowd, or at least remind the aristocracy that they're not alone. I usually sit out there, and I can tell you, it's a great feeling when the wave, usually after a few failed attempts that peter out in the dead zone along the right field foul line, finally reaches the box seats down by home plate. The bleacher folks go nuts, watching their creation take life, and knowing that they just coerced a whole lot of rich people to get out of their chairs from a tenth of a mile away. And before they know it, they have to do it again. And again and again, as the wave endlessly circles the park.

So, while I still cringe when some doofus is standing there, back to the field during a key rally, desperately trying to choreograph a wave, I think the thing does have its place at Fenway. Let's just keep it to one per game, though, eh? And you can tell me you hate it, but you know you do it.

Today, Jack Lagunas's partner was arrested in LA. Major League Baseball is looking at a huge problem, here, that to me is a lot worse than the whole steroids thing.

COMMENTS:

Anthony said: You're right, we all say we hate it, but
    we all obviously are doing it, or it wouldn't get
    around the park. The way I see it, 3 million people
    each year do the wave, yet if you interviewed each
    one, they'd say they hate it, almost to a person. It's
    all about peer pressure, I think.

Kara12 said: Wait, the analogy doesn't work because
    the McFlys thought Marty was kidding because no
    one had had two TV sets *yet*, while the Wave is
    something that *used* to happen but doesn't *any-
    more.*

Jay said: You may be right, but the two things still
    would muster a similar reaction.

RebGirl said: Shouldn't that be "McFlies"?

MattySox said: Hey, quit fighting over the 20-sided
    dice, guys!

Jay: Touché, Matty. But what makes you so sure base-
    ball geeks are higher on the totem pole than D&D
    geeks? We're all geeks, let's just live together in
    geeky harmony.

Pweezil said: Thats right, but more importantly, we
    need this stuff to take our minds off the Lagunas
    suituation.

CHAPTER

11

One man on the list of people Rocky now thought of as "co-conspirators" as opposed to "perps," was doing time. Rocky knew this to be a profound stroke of luck. The man's current abode was the Forrest City Federal Penitentiary in eastern Arkansas. He'd needed the luck because five of the other co-conspirators swore they'd never been to Boston in their lives, and there was nothing to show they had. Then there were two more, unnamed. The five co-conspirators seemed to have amnesia when it came to revealing the names of the other two. But prison life tended to jog a memory.

Rocky and Sargeant Flanagan met at a food court at Logan for breakfast, Marty just in on the red eye. They couldn't eat for another fifteen minutes when the breakfast place opened at seven. Rocky was booked on a 10 AM flight to Forrest City's nearest airport—Memphis—by way of Philadelphia, followed by Charlotte, North Carolina. The dispatcher who broke the news of his routing said to him, "Gotta love US Air."

But Rocky didn't mind. Unflappable was a word people often used to describe him. The detective gave credit for his ability to maintain a serene demeanor to Devi, the mother-goddess of us all. (There were a very few moments though, when Shiva would blast past her, usually with Jesus gripping his coattails for all he was worth, to keep Rocky from exploding.) Rocky enjoyed airports. He could blot out everything with ease as he'd learned the art of meditation from his human mother, who insisted the family meditate every evening between dinner and homework. His powers of concentration thrived, too, when he was making his way in an airplane from A to B, as he would this morning—A to B, then on to C, and then to D.

On the other hand Sargeant Flanagan exited his flight with eyes so red he looked like he had conjunctivitis. It was impossible for him to sleep on an airplane what with his life and death struggle to will four hundred tons of metal zipping through the sky at five-hundred miles per hour, thirty-four-thousand feet above the ground, all night. Clearly the machine was meant to stop the nonsense, and at any moment, drop like a hammer.

While Rocky and Marty stood in the just-forming breakfast line, Rocky told him about the meeting with Jay. Although Marty thought all he had to say was quite interesting, he was more curious about other elements. "Jeeze, Rocky, you should have made him tell you who the uncle is. Maybe it's Tom Werner."

"That would be one of the Red Sox owners."

"It would."

"If we need that information, we will get it. For now, I think we must avoid a public display. Let us take advantage of the uncle's information. Why scare him off? Worse, why arrest him? However, if Lagunas doesn't show up soon. . . Well then of course, we turn over every stone no matter who's sitting on it. We just flip them off."

They took their trays to a table. Marty said, "How about we turn off our cells, Rock? Just till I get though my bacon and eggs?"

This was a running joke. Every time their cells rang while

they were eating, Marty would say to Rocky, "I told ya we should have turned off our cells." Now, he stabbed at his sunny-side up yolk with his fork, and fantasized about what it would be like to sop it all up with his toast. Enjoy the puddle of sog before a phone rang. No dice. His first bite was in his mouth when Rocky's default AT&T ring sounded. Marty's own ring was the first three bars of "Shipping Up to Boston," the Dropkick Murphys' punk Irish jig, already ubiquitous before Jonathan Papelbon chose it as his warm-up music at Fenway Park, following "Wild Thing," which accompanied his journey from bullpen to mound when he'd come in to save a game.

He watched Rocky while he chewed and swallowed like a demon. Then Rocky closed the phone and stood up. Marty had managed to scarf down the eggs and toast telling himself the home fries and bacon weren't all that good for him anyway. And he'd never in a million years get used to whole wheat. Might as well chew on a piece of Styrofoam.

Rocky said, "Take your time, Marty. You will be the one to handle the prisoner. It would seem I have a new task right here. In addition to a crime, we are now going to have to work around what should prove to be a very public scandal. We are officially forced to turn over every stone no matter who sits on it."

"What the hell happened now?"

"I had been hoping the FBI and Immigration Enforcement would be the ones to deal with the professional baseball side of Jack Lagunas. But no. I have just learned that Lagunas is dead. He shot himself. He is all ours."

Marty did not actually register surprise. He just muttered, "Shit." He'd been a cop too long. He downed the last of his coffee. "Figures, doesn't it? When a steel vise is closing on your head, and you feel your skull getting crushed, you get a wicked fuckin' headache. Thing is, he won't be able to tell us if he ever ran across Sanseverra."

"Sanseverra no longer matters to us."

"He matters to the Sea Dogs."

Rocky ignored that. "No. I meant he no longer matters considering the message I got from Terry Francona."

"You got a message from Tito?"

"I'm afraid I haven't had a chance to get to that yet."

"So now you do."

"Not really. But the boy is home. He's back in Cuba."

"No kidding. How'd he get there?"

"Presumably, someone helped him."

"Who?"

Rocky went back to ignoring Marty's questions. "There's more. Concerning the suicide of Jack Lagunas."

"There is?"

"Yes. He chose to shoot himself at the very place in the fens where Cinthia Sanchez's body was found."

"What?"

"Yes. It's so."

"But Cinthia Sanchez wouldn't have any connection with that character."

"I shouldn't think. And if there were, I can't imagine him asking the concierge at the Copley Plaza where she'd died, and then going there to take his own life."

"You'd call that penance in my neighborhood. Lagunas didn't know from penance." Marty looked at his watch. "So now I have to leave you when you've got a big-time mess on your hands."

"An especially complicated mess. I'd thought I had one puzzle with a large section missing. And there is a second puzzle altogether, with no sign of a bridge that might connect the two. Could Cinthia have led a double life? Could she have worked for Jack Lagunas? And did he feel the need, as you say, to perform a fatal penance—take his own life at the exact same place where she lost hers? So unlikely, Marty, but there are times when we must consider the unlikely."

"As unlikely as that?"

Rocky first sighed, then said to his partner, "Have another cup of coffee, Sargeant, and then see to the ticket change."

Marty was already feeling his batteries re-charge. "Wait a minute, Rock. Going backward. . . Like, we had cops all over the fens."

"The crime scene investigation was closed yesterday. The tape had been removed."

"That was goddamn fast."

"This is the height of the tourist season. Yellow tape flying about at the edge of the Back Bay is not conducive to pleasure-seeking."

Marty said, "I hate this, Rock. The more complicated it gets, the longer it takes."

"We will try to work faster." Rocky handed him the airline confirmation. "There are two conspirators as yet unnamed. You will convince the prisoner to name them. A deal will be struck. Use your imagination. I will have someone from Justice ready to support you."

"Tell me this particular prisoner didn't murder someone."

"He didn't."

"Well at least there's that. I hate like hell getting a lighter sentence for some hitman who's whacked a hundred guys. So how many stops is this plane going to make?"

"It's US Air."

Marty had just a one-word response. He said it with such force that Rocky actually felt the physics of the word. And it started with the letters *ph* rather than *f.*

THE NUMBER ONE PLACE
Saturday, 9:30 AM

I got to meet Bill Lee last night. The Spaceman
was doing an appearance at a local VFW dinner—
I wasn't gonna miss that. I asked him what he
thought about Lagunas, etc., what with him being so
pro-Cuba. He didn't get into specifics, just reiterated
what he usually says about Cuba, an island he's
played plenty of baseball on: That the people there
play the game for all the right reasons. I happen to
agree with that. They don't play it to make a buck or
to sell T-shirts, they just love the game and they're
loyal to their hometowns. The whole embargo thing
is so ironic as far as baseball is concerned.

Cuba took to the American game of baseball in the
nineteenth century as a show of independence from
Spain.

Anyway, if you don't know anything about Bill Lee
other than he was the guy who sprinkled marijuana
on his pancakes, check out one of his books, or go
see him next time he does a public appearance.
Most ballplayers speak in clichés. Bill Lee speaks
his mind. Notice I didn't say "ex-ballplayer." His
major league career ended 25 years ago, but he
loves the game of baseball and still plays every
chance he gets. It's too bad the guy was underap-
preciated during his time with the Red Sox. He was
a smart, left-handed, free spirit pitcher who always
stepped up against the Yankees, and to this day
hates them as much as we do.

What more could a Sox fan want?

Oh, and he signed my ball, "Yankees Suck. Bill Lee."

COMMENTS:

ConnecticutSoxFan said: I love Bill Lee! My favorite
story he tells is the one where he's pitching in the
'75 World Series, and there's a rain delay. Johnny
Bench is interviewed during the delay on TV, and
says he's gonna try to take Lee to the opposite
field. The game resumes, and in the ninth,
Spaceman throws Bench an outside pitch, which
Johnny smacks to the opposite field, starting the
Reds' game-winning rally. Lee: "40 million people
heard Bench saying what he was gonna do against
me, and nobody tells me??"

AJM said: Lee had a better ERA, and gave up less hits
per inning to the Big Red Machine in that World
Series than El Tiante (speaking of Cubans). A couple
pitches go a different way, or if the offense had
helped him out (remember, Jim Rice was injured and
missed that series), and Bill Lee is known more as a
World Series hero than just that wacky Spaceman.
See, these are the things that used to keep me up at
night. All that woulda, coulda, shoulda. Now I can
just pop in the 2004 World Series DVD. . . .

Macho in Florida said: Commie bastard. This is the
last time I go to your blog, commie-lover.

KGNumber5 said: Now there's somebody who hasn't
seen "Sicko."

CHAPTER

12

Jack Lagunas shot himself through his ears. The bullet entered his right ear and lobotomized him before it exited his left. The officers at the old crime scene, which was now a new crime scene, couldn't find the bullet. But it might have traveled a good fifty yards into the fens. Because Lagunas's handgun of choice—lying ten inches from his right hand—was an FN Five-Seven which fired bullets at such a high velocity they could punch through a cop's vest. It is illegal to sell or possess such a gun in the Commonwealth of Massachusetts, the only state the gun lobby has been unable to hold hostage—cops had to dodge those bullets everywhere else, though. Boston PD would find out where he'd bought that gun.

It was a hot summer day. The perspiring medical examiner said to Rocky, "I hope your guys have a couple of metal detectors with them."

"*Spotshooter?*"

"Nearest sensor is half a mile away."

"It seems they're always a half-mile away."

"What good is it to come up with a system that detects gunfire, pinpoints the discharge and beeps 911 in two seconds when there's not enough of them?"

Rocky said nothing because there was nothing to say. He looked down at Jack Lagunas. Not a tall man, but he was slim and toned. Rocky couldn't get over that the man he'd questioned at D-4 was his own height, 5' 8", not six feet. Only now Rocky noted that the dead sports agent was wearing LA-style cowboy boots, and had high hair.

The gun was lying seven inches from his right hand.

Rocky walked the area with one of the officers who pointed out that the ground was heavily trampled.

"We hoped to find his boot prints, but it's prints, on prints, on prints."

Another officer told him, "One interesting thing in here—outside of the corpse—is that the cross is gone."

"The cross?"

"Yeah. Little wooden cross. The Victory Gardeners it put up for Cinthia. It'd been right there."

He pointed to an area a few feet from the body.

"And the flowers are gone, too. Last time I was here, there were like, a thousand flowers. Well, there's still a few," and he gestured at the few strewn petals and some withered leaves. "We figure the family must have come and gotten the cross. A couple of the gardeners were surprised at that though."

So was Rocky.

When he was about to leave the double crime scene, a patrolman came running out of the reeds, breathless. It was Ryan, everybody's favorite rookie. He called out, "Hey! Have a look at this, Detective. I mean, like, holy shit!"

The examiner went back to his own work and the excited officer led Rocky and two other cops into the reeds, up a small rise, and around an oak tree that had sprouted from an acorn around the time of the Civil War.

In the small clearing, behind the tree, stood a three-foot high marble niche with a ledge at the base meant to hold candles. The niche was paved with a mosaic replica of a Byzantine icon; a luminous, baroque image of the Madonna and Child. Their halos were sunbursts spreading out from behind their heads, and the brilliant rays were made up of hundreds of tiny gold tiles.

Ryan said, "Will ya look at that. I feel like I should bless myself or something."

The flowers that had surrounded the cross, the ones taken from the spot where Cinthia died, were there, but had not been arranged. Rocky felt someone meant to arrange them again at this new shrine, but hadn't gotten around to doing that. Had maybe been interrupted.

The day was overcast. The grounds crew was about to arrive at Fenway Park. Just at that moment, while Rocky and the officer stood looking at the shrine, thousands of watts of electricity flowed up the park's light stanchions. The mosaic shrine faced the tower in left field, above the green monster. Seemingly, one by one, the gold tiles of the halos lit up. They came ablaze—radiant, dazzling, almost blinding in splendor and glory.

Rocky actually felt his breath taken away. And Officer Ryan, who had thought he should bless himself, did.

While Rocky returned to headquarters to see if there was word from Marty, and before he would return to Edgerly Road, a Victory Gardener called the hot line. The woman identified herself as Anne Winthrop, and insisted on speaking to the "person in charge of the case." She did not mention that she was a descendant of the most prominent founder of the Massachusetts Bay Colony.

The officer recognized her name from the fund-raisers she conducted and said as politely as he could, "Detective Patel is out conducting our investigation, Miss Winthrop."

"*Ms.* Winthrop."

"Uh. . .excuse me. I will be sure to pass along whatever it is you'd like to tell Detective Patel."

But she persisted, wanting to speak directly to the detective.

That was when Rocky walked in.

The cop pressed his hand over the mouthpiece. "A Victory Garden lady wants to talk to you. She's. . .uh. . .pushy. That's because her name isn't Mollie Malone, it's Anne Winthrop. Of the *Mayflower* Winthrops. Ms. Winthrop, unless you want her to bite your head off."

Rocky took the phone, identified himself, and listened as the elderly woman told him succinctly what she'd seen the night before.

"Detective, I've just heard about the body of a man found in the fens. I felt compelled to contact you. To tell you what I, by chance, happened to see last night on the Agassiz road."

Rocky was polite too, but then he was always polite. "I appreciate your willingness to help us, Ms. Winthrop. Thank you."

"You are quite welcome. Here is what I have determined I must tell you: Last night, I dashed over to my plot at seven o'clock because severe thunderstorms were forecast, and I wanted to make sure my new pair of lilies were protected as they are just about to come into bloom. *White Merostar.* My only August-flowering lily. By the time I left, it was dark. We need a few more street lamps in that section of Gardens near the reeds. But never mind.

"I drove from Boylston into the Agassiz road, and I saw Cinthia's husband. He was with another man, and also a woman. I would say the woman was not a Latina."

"Where exactly did you see them?"

"They were walking across the strip of grass—the ground there—into the reeds. They were carrying something. The two men were. It was a small crate of some kind. They went into the reeds toward. . .to. . .where Cinthia was found. So horrific, Detective. The poor dear girl, full of life. Now that life has been cut short and a motherless child left behind. It's too terrible."

Rocky sympathized with her at how terrible it was and then he asked, "Is there anything else, Ms. Winthrop?"

"Well, of course there is or I would have been willing to speak to the officer who answered my call. You see, I'm afraid Cinthia's family is in yet more danger. I drove by later that night with two friends. We'd been to dinner at the home of another mutual friend, who'd arranged to have a private piano recital with Jean-Yves Thibaudet. Have you heard him play, Detective?"

"Yes. With the symphony."

"Brilliant, wouldn't you say?"

"Yes."

"If ever he consents to another recital, I will see to an invitation for you."

"Thank you."

"At any rate, we drove home along the Fenway, and when we passed the other end of the Agassiz Road. . ."

"The other end?"

"That would be the east end, driving along Fenway toward Commonwealth. I saw a large car—one of those SUV horrors—parked on the Agassiz Road with its engine running. The lights were off. My friend who was in the back seat swore she saw someone in the driver's seat just sitting there. She had turned and was looking out the back window."

"And what time was that?"

"I would say very near to ten-thirty. We'd left the recital

just ten minutes earlier at ten-twenty. My friend happened to mention the time when we were getting our wraps."

Rocky considered that she might have seen a man in a car looking to hook up. But he didn't go there.

Instead: "Ma'am, did your friend remark on the make of the SUV?"

"My dear man, how does one even hazard a guess as to the make of such a hideous vehicle? I will say it was the larger variety. Larg-est, in fact. But the thing is—and here is my main reason for insisting I speak to you—I craned my neck to see what might be going on, only to spot another man running out of the reeds toward the car."

The timing provoked Rocky's interest.

"And Detective?"

"Yes, Ma'am?"

"It wasn't a hook-up, if that's what you might be thinking. Since the murder, the men have found other places to meet. The young boys. . . They're all but gone too. This fellow running out of the reeds was determined. He ran directly to the car. The car was waiting for him. He got in. That was all I saw."

"Let me ask you this, Ms. Winthrop. As you drove along Fenway, before you reached Agassiz, did you hear a sound like a car's backfire? Did you hear anything that could have been gunfire?"

The silence that followed Rocky's question was thick with the woman's thinking. Then, "My God, Detective. The Sanchezes. . . Are they all right?"

"As far as I know, yes. They are."

"Well, I heard no such sound. But I will ask my friends."

Rocky thanked her profusely. He also said to her, "I'm glad the thunderstorms predicted didn't materialize. I presume your lily is doing well."

First, a pause. Then: "Detective?"

"Yes, Ma'am?"

"Where have you been all my life?"

Then she laughed heartily and hung up.

⚾

A short time later, Rocky was sitting at the kitchen table of Alicia Sanchez, on Edgerly Road. Rocky wondered if Anne Winthrop referred to the street as *the* Edgerly road, as she did with Agassiz.

Also at the table was George Sanchez, Cinthia's brother Carlos, and Carlos's wife, who Rocky hadn't met before. Her name was Emily. It was explained to Rocky that Cinthia's sister-in-law had come up from New York—was there to help with the baby. She had a long blond ponytail which she wound around her fingers.

Rocky and Emily shook hands.

Rocky asked them about the new shrine, when they had placed it there.

At first, they exchanged glances, and then Emily proved to be as talkative as the others were reticent.

"We wanted to replace the cross that the Victory Garden people brought there. It was very nice of them. But we'd decided to have something more special for Cinthia. Something more permanent. A *shrine*." She'd gone back to winding her ponytail round and round. Her eyes had filled.

George reached over and patted Emily's hand. He said to Rocky, "Emily made the mosaic. Cinthia was always so proud of what Emily could do, of her great talent. And now Emily has done her friend proud."

Emily twisted her ponytail and reached out to pull a Kleenex from the box on the table. She said "I had the idea of placing it so that it faced a Fenway Park light tower. When all the lights of the tower are on, the mosaic becomes. . .it. . ."

Her husband said, "It becomes radiant. There is now a beacon in the darkness there."

Rocky nodded, "We have seen it. It is a most moving tribute to Cinthia."

Rocky could not forget how mesmerized he'd been by the sight, the dazzling halo drawing his eyes right into the center, into the Madonna's eyes, so full of pain despite the smiling, chubby baby in her arms.

The matriarch of the Sanchez family said, "We took the niche from my husband's grave. A place to put candles. You see, Arturo called to me. Called to me to somehow allow him to share our grief."

Rocky said, "But it is not where the cross stood."

George looked up. "No. We did not want it there. . .in the place where some monster left her to die." He swallowed. "We saw the beautiful tree nearby. We found a space just behind the tree that can't be seen from the road. We thought this would allow for more comfort to us, and to other people who want to visit. . .her shrine."

Emily said, very quietly, "And it was drier there, too."

With that, the young woman leaned into her husband and began to sob. Carlos put his arm around her. He said to Rocky, "My wife and sister were best friends. Neighbors since they were little girls. They went to school together. To Archbishop Malloy High School. In Brooklyn. Then to NYU."

George knew why Rocky was there. He didn't wait to be asked. He said, "We were almost finished with our work when we heard a noise. Someone was coming. We thought it was the police. We put out the light we'd taken in there with us. But it was a guy. We couldn't believe it. He was coming through the reeds."

Carlos said, "It was dark. We heard a shot. It happened very fast."

He stopped speaking. Rocky waited.

"There was nothing we could do."

"He wasn't anyone you'd seen before?"

"No."

"And then?"

Emily said, "It was so horrible. We ran."

"Where did you run to?"

"To our car."

"Was your car on Agassiz Road?"

George said, "No. It's illegal to park there. We were over on Fenway."

"Did you see a car parked on Agassiz Road?"

Their heads lifted. All four stared at Rocky. Carlos finally said, "There were cars going by, crossing over from Boylston to Fenway. I didn't see a car parked on Agassiz."

Rocky looked at the others. "George? Emily? Did either of you see a car there?"

They both shook their heads, no.

"And when you returned home, you did not call the police?"

"No."

"Why not?"

Emily said, "We were so upset. We didn't know what to do."

George had a better excuse. "There were people around there. The police patrolled often. We knew he'd be found."

And Carlos: "We couldn't deal, man. I mean, some crazy guy goes and. . ."

Alicia spoke. She said, "My family is too distraught to act in a rational way, Detective. We are in a terrible condition. The man was dead. To think. . . Cinthia's life was taken away, and then someone comes and. . ."

George took his mother's hand. "It's all right, *Mami*."

Rocky could barely stand the grief in Alicia's face. She said, "I need to know this. Will you take it down? The shrine?"

Rocky said, "No. But I'm sorry to say that, eventually, it will have to be moved. Perhaps, soon."

George sighed. "I spoke to our priest at St. Clement's. He said they had a policy. There is no place for it there."

They were all silent. Then Rocky said, "I belong to Father Connealy's Church. Do you know of him?"

Alicia nodded. So did George.

The priest was a local celebrity. He had turned a down-trodden neighborhood church into a showpiece, filled it with people from across the city. He had no policies. The church was down the street from the motel the Patel family ran when Rocky was a boy. "Father Connealy will find a place for your shrine, I promise you."

Alicia Sanchez said, "We decided we would wait for the time when it had to be moved, and we would go and get it. We planned to think of a place for it. Some place, we hoped, where it would be revered. Now. . . I appreciate your concern for us. . .your willingness. A willingness that goes beyond your intention to seek justice for Cinthia, who I loved as if she were my own daughter. A girl who was becoming the daughter I'd always longed for."

And at that moment, a lusty cry came from another part of the house. Emily dashed out. She returned with baby Arturo, and was followed by three Sanchez grandchildren, visiting Alicia for the weekend.

Emily said, "Before I change him, Detective, I thought you might like to say hello."

Rocky admired the infant, and paid compliments as to his charm. And of course he thought of his own baby, who he

would be sitting with late that night when he cried out from
his crib at 2 AM.

Arturo's grandmother took Arturo from Emily, and told
her she would see to him. That the detective might still need
to ask more questions.

As soon as she'd left, Emily was the one to ask Rocky a
question, "Did the man who killed himself have anything to
do with Cinthia?"

Rocky answered, "I don't know that yet. But now it is with
great trepidation that I must ask you the same question."

Their eyes grew wide. They seemed unable to take in such
a question. All of them. And when the question did sink in,
they because more agitated than ever.

Carlos said, "Listen to me, Detective. Cinthia was twenty
years old. A girl. She went to college for a year. NYU. . .with
Emily. She met George. She fell in love with him. He was
serious, she told me. A serious person instead of a silly one.
She left school, she married George. It seemed she married
his *family*, not just him. That's the kind of person she was. A
girl who found someone she could trust, a secure place. She
wanted a husband, a home, a baby." His face was lined with
worry and sadness and regret. "I was angry with her. She was
a smart girl. I told her Emily was staying in school. But she
said to me. . . She said the kind of thing she'd always say. I can
hear her: 'Carlos, NYU isn't going anywhere. And there's a
million schools in Boston.'"

He broke down.

Rocky was finished.

Rocky chose to end his questioning the way he always did;
he told the family that if they thought of anything else to call
him. Then he thanked them, and promised yet again that he
would find whoever it was who had murdered their loved one.

When he left, he looked over his shoulder in the doorway

and gave a little wave. He did that to see if there were telling glances from one to another of them. There weren't. He could see only the faces of people who had recently been left devastated—that heart-breaking combination of wretchedness and impotence.

In his car, Rocky mused as to whether they'd lied. If they'd seen more than they'd let on. He knew one thing though; throughout, George and his brother-in-law disciplined themselves to avoid any outbursts of the variety that had put them in a jail a few days earlier.

Then he asked the Virgin Mary to intercede with Jesus and ask that they be protected. And finally, he acknowledged Shiva because he could feel him racing through his blood, warning him to never let down his guard.

Tomorrow was Sunday. It was unacceptable to Rocky that it would take more than a week to find Cinthia's killer.

In his car, he called to find out if Anne Winthrop had found a chance to speak to her friends. She had, and saw to leaving her number for Rocky.

The dispatcher said, "Couldn't get her to talk to me, Rock. You're her main man."

"Just give me the number."

Anne Winthrop said to Rocky, "We were sure we hadn't heard anything, Detective, but. . . Can a gunshot sound like a crack rather than a bang?"

"Yes."

"You see, the three of us recalled running over a branch. At least we thought we had. Perhaps a minute or two before we reached the Agassiz Road. There was this. . .*snap*."

Jack Lagunas was not shot somewhere else and then left in the fens.

◍

After Rocky hung up, he called Jay, the blogger.

"You've heard about Jack Lagunas?"

"Yeah, I heard."

"I need to see you and your. . .uncle."

"When?"

"Now."

And the blogger could tell the detective meant business. He got back to Rocky a few minutes later.

Jay said, "The game starts in less than two hours."

"Meaning?"

"My uncle will have to meet us at the park. Is that okay?"

"Yes."

"He'll be waiting at Gate D in half an hour."

Rocky recognized Victor Hauck. Whenever he was home in the evening—from early spring and into the fall—he would join his wife on the sofa and watch the Red Sox game. He had come to note the regulars, whose faces were visible at every pitch, sitting behind home plate, front row. Victor Hauck stood out—big guy, well-dressed, designer haircut. Sometimes, he was late to the game, but he always came. Often, he would be speaking on his cell phone, though he never took his eyes off the game. The man had a face Rocky liked—open, calm, contented. He had accomplished in his life what he had set out to accomplish.

When he shook Rocky's hand, he said, "Always an honor to meet a peace officer."

Rocky responded, "The pleasure is mine."

After Jay made the introductions, Victor led them to his office. Along the way, he greeted and shook hands with every Fenway Park employee whose path he crossed. He knew all their names. He was received with huge smiles and he returned them. He gave a big hug to a security guard named Craig, and Craig acted as though someone had just handed him a million dollars. Victor seemed a man at a party.

When he wasn't greeting people, he was taking calls on his cell. His response was always the same: "Listen, I've got someone here. Call you back."

When they reached his office deep within the bowels of the ballpark, Victor took another call while he waved Rocky and Jay toward a sofa and two comfortable, cushy armchairs. When he hung up, Rocky said, "I would ask you to turn off your cell. Please tell your secretary to see that you are not disturbed."

Victor remained merry. "How about I set it to vibrate? Just so I know. . ."

"Indulge me, sir. I do not want your train of thought interrupted.

Victor knew the alternative to his office was Rocky's. Buzzing his secretary was not a problem, but then he looked down at his cell phone.

"Hey, I've never turned this thing off before."

Jay shook his head. He said, "Give it to me, Uncle Vic."

The phone was passed to Jay who turned it off.

A look of concern crossed Victor's face. Jay smiled. "Don't worry. I'll turn it back on for you." And to Rocky, "He's always afraid he'll press the wrong button and the phone will blow up."

Rocky said, "I sympathize. A generational difference. Yours, Jay, will press every button in sight. Ours. . . Well, we tend to be cautious."

Then Victor said to Rocky, "I can't get my mouse to work lately. I tried spitting on it, ya know? I tell people, Don't email me. Call." He looked longingly at his dead cell phone in Jay's hand.

His nephew rolled his eyes.

Rocky did not allow himself to be disarmed by this man's rather eccentric charm. "Mr. Hauck, is it within your capacity as an employee of the Red Sox that you have a connection with Jack Lagunas?"

"No. I'm the resident trouble-shooter."

"And your regular seat at the park, I would guess, allows you to determine where you should be shooting.

Victor laughed. Then he said, "Detective, here's the connection. I was once. . ."

"I know what you were. You were such a superb, committed and innovative agent that you created the free agent system as it is known today. I know that at one time, you yourself represented Cuban ballplayers. But Mr. Hauck, the reason I am speaking to you now is simple—to ask you if you know the names of the men who worked for Jack Lagunas. The men who smuggle Cuban ballplayers into this country via the Pestano Pipeline?"

Victor was as forthright as Rocky. "I know the names of the players who have been smuggled here. We all do. But the criminals who actually accomplish the deed. . .? No. Lagunas paid them to infiltrate Cuba; to make promises to the players; to traffic them out of Cuba and into Florida. He paid these men to accomplish this activity, and he paid them to keep a low profile. He paid them not to get caught.

"And I know this too. Lagunas has enforced his monopoly through threats and violence, a monopoly on the phenomenal talent in Cuba that is worth millions and millions of dollars."

"The reason you had an appointment to meet with him?"

Victor looked to his "nephew."

"I told him Uncle Vic. Told him you like to keep up on things."

Victor nodded. Jay had done no wrong. "I check in with everyone. I knew there was trouble when I heard about Luis

Sanseverra. I'd hoped to talk Jack into coming clean about his operation. . .to save himself before. . . Well, I was going to say, before it was too late."

Rocky's voice grew a little deeper. "Yes, you were too late. But aside from Mr. Lagunas taking his own life, it was too late for him to come clean. Some of the people who have worked with Jack Lagunas—the criminals you just spoke of—have been caught."

"But not arrested."

"Now they have been arrested. And Mr. Lagunas had been named in the federal indictment against them."

Victor leaned back. "Then that is what accounted for his suicide."

"Maybe. But while you were outing Jack Lagunas, someone else was blackmailing him. I believe the combination of these two elements has virtually ended the monopoly you speak of. But so much money is at stake. . . Somebody will undoubtedly step in. . ."

Victor Hauck interrupted. "No one else will step in if the government and Major League Baseball take a stand. I could have taken a stand many years ago. I saw this coming. I wanted no part of it, though I knew someone would create what came to be called the Pestano Pipeline. I washed my hands when what I should have done was prevent it. It is the only thing in all my years in baseball that I am ashamed of."

Rocky took out a card and held it out to Victor Hauck. He voice became stern. "I am the government, Mr. Hauck, and I am taking a stand. You are Major League Baseball. Take a stand. Someone must be the first to rise. Now is your chance to remove the stain you see on your career."

Victor took the card and Rocky stood up. "Jack Lagunas shot himself in the very spot where Cinthia Sanchez's body was found. Perhaps this criminal activity has begun to take its toll on the innocent. That is the basis for my stand. Your own stand would be based on your reputation to do what is morally correct, Mr. Hauck."

The detective left the young man and the older one to stare at his back.

◍

Rocky and Marty read Jay's blog together.

"Jay is passionate, isn't he?"

"Yeah. That's what it takes to be a blogger. Passion." The sergeant noted a second trait. "And a shitload of arrogance. So who was the uncle?"

"Victor Hauck."

For once, Marty was rendered speechless. Aside from, "*Holy Mary, mother of God!*"

THE NUMBER ONE PLACE
Saturday, 5:00 PM

Jack Lagunas has committed suicide. The Pestano Pipeline has been flooded out. Somewhere else, this travesty will be rebuilt. I want Americans to know—particularly baseball fans—that the Cuban embargo prevents some of the most talented players in the world from becoming part of the game. And that there are criminals who get around the embargo, make a fortune, and put players' lives at risk. And perhaps caused the death of Cinthia Sanchez, who was pushing her baby in a stroller in the wrong place at the wrong time. In the shadow of Fenway Park which should never be the wrong place.

I'm at the park right now. Trying to get back to the reason all of you are reading my blog and feeling free to give me your opinions and join in on discussions. So here is a little live update. Kevin Millar just homered into the Monster Seats, and was giving big smiles and waves to the Fenway Faithful who still love the guy. I always try to snag Orioles tickets just to watch him goof around with his old teammates in batting practice. Right now, even with the Millar dong, the Sox lead 7-3 in the sixth.

COMMENTS:

KGNumber5 said: A friend just e-mailed me and said "Scott Boras killed himself." See, people are still so unfamiliar with this situation that they don't know who's who. So, was Lagunas back in LA when this happened?

Jay said: No, he was right here in Boston.

RebGirl said: And we still don't know where that Sea Dogs pitcher is. This is crazy. Lagunas must've had serious problems.

Leg It Out said: This is a Fox game, so technically you *could* go up to the broadcast booth and give that favorite announcer of mine a smack for me. Technically.

Jay said: Leg It, if I was allowed up there, I'd probably skip the Fox booth and just go straight to Joe Castiglione to shake his hand. I've been listening to him call Sox games on the radio since he was the "new guy" with the late great Ken Coleman.

Amy said: Jay, here's another diversion for you. Have you noticed Stephen King in the crowd? The in-crowd Fox reporter interviewed him and brought up how King's reading a book between innings. Stephen said, "There's plenty of time, it's a Fox game."

Jay said: Amy, I love it. Knocking Fox right on Fox itself. It's true, you notice just how long the between-inning breaks are when you're here at the park for a Fox game. I shoulda brought a book myself. Funny you should mention Stephen King, as I've been thinking: Watching Mirabelli today, he just hasn't been the same in this, his second tour of duty with the Red Sox. It's almost like Theo buried him in a Pet Sematary and then dug him up again. Sometimes you just have to let a person go. . .

MattySox said: Hey ho, let's go. Ayuh.

CHAPTER
13

Before Sargeant Flanagan had left LA the previous day, several things happened. First, he called Gloria who turned down the request for a second date. She'd said, "Can't. Too busy. I'm looking for another *job*. And by the way, just so's you know. The picture wasn't colorized."

She hung up. This confirmed to Marty she was not in on any of it. She hadn't said, "You know I didn't have any part of all that stuff, right Marty?" He liked a girl with integrity. Also one with no time, but who made time to find out if a picture of Ted Williams had been colorized. If he ever was in LA again, he'd have another go.

Then the sargeant tried to see Byington again, but the closest he could get was Byington's lawyer, which didn't surprise Marty now that Byington's partner had offed himself leaving Byington holding the bag.

The lawyer invited Marty to his club. This invitation told Marty that the fellow was treating his client's difficulties as a little behavioral glitch, rather than criminal behavior. It also told him that the lawyer wanted him to see how the other half lived. As soon as he laid eyes on the guy, Marty thought, *Fuck him*. He was damned sure that the man had never experienced the likes of Gloria of the whitest teeth and scarlet lips.

The lawyer was an elderly gent who had represented the

Byingtons for fifty years, as had his father before him. After Marty was led to his table, the lawyer ordered two brandies from someone who looked like a librarian rather than a waiter. The librarian gave Marty no chance to put in the order he'd planned, as in: "Gimme a Bud, Jack."

The lawyer told Marty that his client was presently under a physician's care and therefore wouldn't see him. Marty had figured that word of Lagunas's demise would pretty much freak Byington out, and he couldn't wait to tell Rocky how, in California, you are not subject to interrogation by local police if you are in a psycho ward, which is where the lawyer had managed to stash Byington for the time being.

The brandy arrived. The snifters were the size of bowling balls. While the lawyer swirled the brandy around the glass, noting its fine color and the perfect film left behind, Marty knocked his down and told the librarian to fire another one on him. The lawyer reminded Marty a lot of the guy on the Kentucky Fried Chicken box. Colonel What's-His-Name. He tried to think of the name while the lawyer got over Marty's attack on the brandy, but then went on to talk about what a wonderful boy Byington was.

Oh yeah. Colonel Sanders.

Colonel Sanders said to Marty, as helpfully as could be, "Sargeant, you'll be glad to know that I have succeeded in showing Chipper. . ."

"Scuse me. Who?"

"Chipper Byington."

"Oh."

"I believe. . ."

"What's his real name?"

"Whose?"

"Chipper's."

"Oh. Same as his father's and his father's before him. Horace."

That explained a lot.

"I've known the boy quite literally since he was in swaddling clothes." Colonel Sanders leaned in and lowered his voice. "Harmless little pea." He leaned back again. "As I was saying. . . I am sure I was able to make Chipper understand that having knowledge of an operation that may or may not be illegal is not the end of the world. Yes, the whole thing is certainly unpleasant, his late partner's dealings perhaps even *shady*. But he certainly can't blame himself that this Lagunas chap was unstable. Absolutely none of it has anything to do with him. His duties at WorldWide Baseball were simply to legitimize it. Obviously, Chipper was being used, but at this juncture, we here at the firm have no evidence to show his ever having taken any actual part in Mr. Lagunas's possibly clandestine activities."

We here at the firm. Marty thought, *Asshole.*

Now the lawyer looked from side to side out of the corners of his eyes as if he were about to give Marty an insider stock tip and said, "I think my client is having a nervous breakdown. I'm not exaggerating either."

Marty finished his second brandy. Not bad if you like your pancake syrup at ninety proof. He said, "As much as I'd like the opportunity to speak to your client, I will make do with the transcript of the conversation he will be having any minute now with the FBI. I do believe they're probably at Chipper's bedside. Probably issued a warrant to his shrink. The FBI—not that it would be news to you—doesn't have to abide by the hobbles the cops around here put up with."

The lawyer dropped his brandy snifter. Fortunately, the vintage Persian carpet was especially thick. The snifter bounced. Marty thought it was too bad the carpet was such a nice cream color.

The sargeant took a couple of cigars from the humidor on the table and put them in his pocket. He had a friend or two who partook. Would they ever be indebted. He said to Colonel Sanders, "Cubans, I'm sure."

⊕

On Saturday morning, while Marty waited at Logan, preparing for his next flight—the one to Memphis with an agent waiting at the airport to take him to the Arkansas pen—he opened his laptop and read reports now forwarded to him from Rocky's office. Of the named suspects in the completed indictment, one had an asterisk next to his name. It was noted at the end of the document that Juan "Jack" Lagunas was deceased.

The rest of the named co-conspirators had been detained, and weren't going anywhere because none were granted bail. The judge in the case determined they were flight risks. The men had been given various assignments by Jack Lagunas, and all these assignments were in violation of the laws of the United States. They were felonies. The formal charges against them were: *Conspiracy to Commit Alien Smuggling* (maximum penalty five years imprisonment); *Transporting Aliens* (maximum penalty ten years imprisonment); *Harboring Aliens* (maximum penalty ten years imprisonment). It seems these were the men who waited in vans for the smuggled Cubans, drove them across the country to California, and then saw to their being housed and fed, while they were kept in shape till they could be sold to various major league franchises.

The two men unnamed—meaning not accounted for— were charged with the same violations as the others, plus a couple of additional counts: *Attempt to Commit Alien*

Smuggling (maximum penalty ten years imprisonment); and *Assault on a Federal Officer* (maximum penalty twenty years imprisonment), and *Threat to a Federal Officer with Deadly and Dangerous Weapons* (maximum penalty life in prison).

The laptop made a chirping noise. An email from Ryan read: *Call Rocky like the minute after you speak to the prisoner.*

⦾

Sargeant Flanagan really hated leaving his Glock with the Feds, though he did appreciate they're allowing him to meet with the prisoner in the visitors' yard rather than the cage. Marty didn't like the smell of criminals. He had a girlfriend, who once said to him, "They smell?" And he'd told her, yeah, they did. So she asked, "What does a criminal smell like?" And he explained it wasn't just one criminal that smelled, but when there were a lot of them together—Whew! She was a persistent sort, which was probably why the relationship didn't last, and so went on to ask what the collective group smelled like. Marty just chucked her under the chin and said, "The opposite of you, sweetie."

Though the prisoner had a name, he told Marty he was known as *El Jefe.* Marty loved nicknames and, in fact, drove Rocky crazy when he'd refer to people as, say, *Colonel Sanders*, instead of their real names. The prisoner explained to Marty how, as a toddler, he used to bully kids around in Havana and ended up with his nickname—*The Chief.* And when he was five years old in Miami, he got thrown out of kindergarten for shoving a fellow student down the stairs.

Like Marty, the prisoner was glad to be outside despite the depressing sight of the guard towers, the cyclone wire and the four corrections officers posted at the door in the wall. It was hot outside, but Jefe wished it were even hotter. He missed Miami.

He told Marty, "I was the coordinator. Like, one thing I

was in charge of was making sure the satellite phones were all in working order. They tended to get wet."

"What else did you coordinate when you weren't blow-drying the phones?"

Jefe laughed. "I saw that everything was what and where it should be: the boats ready; the middle-men at their stations in Cuba; the food in place when the players got to Florida; the clothes; the vans set and gassed up to take them and their. . . uh. . .guests to California; the welcome committee ready in LA. Everything."

"And the reason you absorbed the fall?"

The prisoner shifted himself on the bench. "See, the operation took a turn I didn't approve of. I wanted out. I'm the first guy to risk a prison sentence—high risk, high gain and all that. But I wasn't about to do the time that. . ."

"So what turn was that?"

The prisoner smiled at Marty. "What did you say you're going to do for me again?"

"I'm going to get you a reduction, Hiffy."

"*Jefe.*"

"Yeah. Heffy. Sorry."

El Jefe's eyes narrowed. "You going to tell me how much of a reduction?"

"Can't say. Depends on Justice. I'll do my best. I'll get you as much as is possible."

"I have no choice but to believe you, do I?"

"That's right."

The prisoner looked up at the guard towers then back at Marty. "I wouldn't have even considered seeing you if I hadn't heard about Jack. Won't need to be in a federal protection plan with him out of the way."

Marty listened. No reaction was a good way to keep someone talking.

And Jefe kept talking. "The two guys you're interested in? They're the two who had the boat operation. See, they had a lot of shit goin' on, and Lagunas's operation got busier than they could handle. They whined to Jack. He told them they couldn't involve anyone else—too many cooks spoil the broth. And any cooks these guys rounded up wouldn't be cooks— they'd be low-level drug-runners. Unreliable. Lagunas didn't want to hear about it, so he promised them extra money. But just to cover all possibilities, they saw to finding room on board for a few extra people in addition to the ballplayers— wives, girlfriends, kids. Guys."

Jefe changed the subject. "Wish I had a smoke."

Marty said, "Don't look at me. If cigarettes and matches weren't considered contraband, I'd light you up."

"Just dreamin' out loud."

"Can ya get back to reality? We haven't got a lot of time. About the guys who weren't ballplayers. Were you trying to tell me something?"

"Other guys. They were nobody. Teenagers. Prido promised them. . ."

"Who?"

"I'm gettin' to *who*. The guys were promised things like— *Come to America and I'll get you in a band. Yeah, sure, bring your fuckin' guitar.* Shit like that. But these kids didn't end up pounding a drum in some band. They were forced to work the boats."

"Work the boats?"

"That's what I said. Lagunas's guys. . ."

"I believe you said *Prido*."

"Yeah. Prido. Once these boys were on the boat, he told them they'd work for a year, then they can go join a band. Do whatever the hell they want. They'd be in *America*. But if they didn't work for a year, they get thrown in the water. And Prido would've done it too. So he was gonna get his extra money *and* have the help he needed."

"Jesus."

"Yeah."

"Indentured servants."

"That would be one way to put it."

Marty thought for a minute. Then, before he got to his main thrust, he decided to satisfy his curiosity. "So Heffy, were you surprised that Lagunas killed himself?"

This prisoner knew it would be useless to try and correct Marty's pronunciation of his name. "Well, I knew he might be a dead man—sooner than later. But I didn't figure he'd do himself."

"Why'd you know he might be a dead man?"

"Because nobody deserves to get a gun shoved into his ear more than Jack Lagunas. He liked to stiff us. Enjoyed it. Had more money than God, and cheating us out of what he owed us was a fucking riot. Made him feel like. . . Oh, who gives a flying fuck? He don't feel too good right now, does he? He was a son of a bitch. You're sure Jack offed himself, right? Because those two guys. . .the ones you want to hear about? One of them is nuts and the other one shoots more shit into his veins and up his nose than he'll ever be able to pay for in a million years. Another one of the those indentured servants, matter of fact."

And Marty said, "So now it's time to tell me Prido's first name and who the junkie is."

"Alberto Prido. A psycho. The other guy is named Machado. Don't know his first name. He's got a nickname, goes by Cha-Cha, naturally. Put these two guys together? You got yourself Charlie Manson."

"Where do they live?"

"They're both in Miami. Prido somewhere in Little

Havana. Cha-Cha, he mostly lives on the boats. Or else with the roosters in Prido's back yard."

"If you don't know where Prido lives, Heffy, how come you know he has roosters in his back yard?"

"We all got roosters in our back yards. We're Cubans, remember?"

Marty called Rocky from the car. The notes they compared meshed.

THE NUMBER ONE PLACE
SUNDAY, 1:00 AM

Two months ago, when I bought tickets to tonight's show at the Middle East in Cambridge, the last thing I would've thought people there would be talking about is baseball. But everybody's talking about the pipeline because it goes so far beyond baseball. So, after Disaster Strikes played their set, while waiting for The Pist to hit the stage for the first time in years, as this was their big reunion show, I chatted with a bunch of punk rockers about Cuban shortstops.

How come when I'm at a rock concert in Massachusetts, I always see Red Sox hats? Whereas I don't necessarily see Yankee hats at concerts in New York. Maybe it's because if you're from New England, the Sox are such a part of your family, that even if you don't have as much interest in baseball as you used to, you've still got a ratty old Sox hat you can put on. But in New York, well, as far as the younger crowd goes, nobody's really *from* New York. They all came from somewhere else, so they have their hometown team. My conclusion: If a musician is wearing a Sox hat, he's probably a Sox fan. If a musician has a Yankee hat on, he's just shielding his eyes from the lights.

COMMENTS:

ConnecticutSoxFan said: Jay, you said, *Nobody's really* from *New York*. Yeah, all the New Yorkers moved up here to Connecticut! So we're stuck with all the Yankee fans.

AJM said: Speaking of Connecticut, isn't that where The Pist were from?

Ridiculum said: Yup, CT representin'. You know, Jay, I was just at a dinner, and all anyone could talk about was the Cuba situation. I think it's good that this is finally out in the open. . . .

CHAPTER
14

A break is not the lucky stuff of a batted ball taking a for-tuitous bounce, allowing the batter to get on base, as in, "Hey, I caught a break that time." It's more like breaking the back of winter: You're out in the cold, you can't stand it, and all of a sudden, a robin hops across the snow. Yes, it could prove helpful now to have the names of Alberto Prido and Cha-Cha Machado, considering they were presently facing a life sentence in a federal penitentiary. But helpful is not a break.

A break is when a conscientious rookie cop, inspired by a glittering mosaic of the Madonna and Child, returns to the scene of a crime during his off hours, lies down flat on his stomach and gazes across a muddy moonscape of shoeprints where none of the pits and depressions look anything like the sole and heel of a shoe. He isn't even sure what it is he might see. He simply so desires an epiphany—one that will give him insight into who killed Cinthia Sanchez, a girl who was his own age, when she was left to die in a swamp.

The sun is setting. The pock-marked ground is in shad-ows. The rookie thinks he sees a broken line—a groove; it cuts a faint four-foot-long path across the ground. His eyes follow the groove. He can make out more bits of that groove running toward Agassiz Road. Then he follows the groove in the other direction and not only makes out yet more bits and pieces heading into the reeds, he sees a second groove parallel to the first. He blinks. He leaps to his feet shouting to the two officers on patrol who have humored his hunt for "a clue." They have actually seen far more bizarre behavior in unjaded rookies than what this guy was doing.

They walk toward him, but he screams, "Stop, stop!"

They do. There is a clear indication that this rookie fell between the cracks during psychological testing sessions.

He shouts to them what he has discovered, shouts out, "Don't walk on my drag lines!"

They both pull out their phones.

Detective Patel and Sargeant Flanagan often disagreed. This allowed for extensive discussion which, in turn, brought them to eventual agreements or compromises they both felt comfortable with.

Not today.

Rocky was furious. "We will bring them in. They are victims, yes, but now they are also persons of interest."

"Rock, it's not like we'll be surprising them. They know we're not idiots. Neither are they. They knew we'd find out one way or another. So they've already concocted a story. We let that get away from us. But let's hear it from the three of them together. They trusted us once. Now they don't. Not because of anything we did. Something else. If we sequester them, they won't go back to trusting us and we need them to do that. Or they'll continue to lie. They're on a sinking ship, Rock, they're. . ."

"I know where they are. They lied."

"A lie that comes under the category: bad decision. They want what we want."

"I made the mistake of trusting them, Marty."

"Oh Rock, for Chrissakes. Who wouldn't? What they've suffered. . . What was not to believe? People who have never been in trouble before. So something really bad happens. They don't know what to do about it. They lie. Way I see it, it's our job to figure out why they chose to lie. Why they concocted the lie. Let's go find out."

Rocky's palms came together. He closed his eyes.

Marty shouted at him, "Jesus, Rocky. You're thinking *too* hard! Let's just go over there and talk to them again. We can't bring them in. Guess what happens if that's in tomorrow's headlines?" Rocky did not respond. "Ya know what, Rock? You're embarrassed because they pulled the wool over your eyes. Happens. So get over it."

Rocky blinked. He took in the large bulk of his partner who was pacing the office floor. Marty's loyalty meant everything to Rocky. The sargeant was right. Perhaps Marty was witnessing his own impulsiveness coming out in Rocky and he didn't like what he saw.

Rocky stood. "You have clarified the influence of my ego upon my judgment, Marty. We will rely on your gut feeling rather than my ego. But I am afraid compassion has precluded your own judgment."

"Compassion? Me?"

"Yes."

"I'm getting soft? I'm not tough enough for this?" Marty, still standing, leaned over Rocky's desk and into his face. "Is that what you're tellin' me?"

Rocky stood up. "My wife tells me I have no understanding of the quintessential American form of expressing anger. Bickering. It's true. I don't. Let's go."

As they walked out to their car, Marty had to force himself not to continue bickering. It wasn't easy.

〇

Detective Patel and Sargeant Flanagan sit—yet again—at the table in Alicia Sanchez's kitchen. It is Sunday, a week since Cinthia died.

Rocky was frustrated. A week had gone by since the crime was committed. Maybe that was his problem.

The two men refuse the coffee graciously proffered. George, Carlos and Emily seem awash in anxiety. Marty is thinking: *Here's what happens, folks, when you make the wrong decision.*

Rocky said to them, "You lied."

They did not respond. Marty worried that they were not sure which lie the detective was referring to. Rocky told them. "You didn't see Jack Lagunas shoot himself. He'd been shot earlier and dragged into the fens and left there. We have found the drag marks that the heels of his boots made. Tell me again what you saw, only this time, tell me the truth."

Carlos narrowed his eyes. He was angry too. He said, "It was the same god damn way Cinthia was dragged into the fens and left there. Except she wasn't dead. She could have been saved!"

Alicia reached across the table and closed her fingers around Rocky's wrist. Her eyes were wrenching. "Detective, these children witnessed something terrible. They are afraid, Detective."

Marty looked to Rocky. Their thoughts matched: *Children.* That's what they are to her.

Carlos put up his hand, "No. We are not afraid, Detective. We are cautious. We have no choice if we want to be safe."

Emily looked over to Carlos, then back to Rocky. "We didn't think you'd believe what we saw. Because *we* couldn't believe it. That was part of it. We have been shocked. Our good intentions that night. . ."

Rocky interrupted her. "Just tell me, Emily... Tell me everything you saw. Don't leave anything out." And then he looked at Carlos and repeated a refrain he so often found necessary. "I understand your caution. But I am not from immigration enforcement. Talk to me."

In the end, it was Emily who was the one to describe exactly what the three of them had witnessed, though she would still introduce what she had to say with a prelude. "Detective Patel, we are like wreckage. That's what it feels like to me. We are grieving with a pain we never knew was possible. We were trying to do something for Cinthia. We needed to comfort ourselves. That's all. It was our first step out of what we are going through.

"That night, we had almost finished with what we'd set out to do: build something very special for my friend—for my sister-in-law—in the Latino tradition."

George said, "Something more than the *crucecita*, though it was a gesture we will never forget."

"We heard someone coming into the reeds. We were scared." She turned to her husband. "Yes, Carlos, we were."

Rocky steered her back. "Go on. Please."

But George would finish. "We put out our light. We stayed behind the tree. I saw him. It was a man and he was pulling something behind him. A body. He didn't see us. The tree was in the way and. . . He was struggling with the body. He was dragging it as if it were a load of garbage. Then he let the body drop, just let it go. He stood there and then looked up. We ducked back behind the tree. I didn't see what happened, but then a gun fired. We heard him run. Then we heard a car take off."

Rocky said, "A body was left there. A gun was fired. The man ran off."

"Yes."

How Rocky hated to say what he had to say. "The man was not simply unconscious?"

Alicia gasped again.

George choked out the words: "We have discussed this. We saw his eyes. His eyes were staring."

Emily looked back and forth from one to another. They were all shaken. She took a breath and it was her turn again. "After the shot, I saw the man standing over the body. He put a gun down on the ground. Then he ran."

Carlos said, "But George and I, we didn't see that. Emily told us later what she just told. That she saw the man put a gun down. I never even saw a gun. I am trying to tell you what I saw even if it's different from what Emily saw."

Emily's face was in her hands now. Rocky said, "Emily?"

She took her hands away. "I realized they didn't see the man put a gun by the body before he ran. I didn't think George and Carlos could handle what I saw. The man with the gun wanted it to seem as though the dead man committed suicide. I didn't want to scramble their brains any more. I thought maybe I was imagining what I saw, dreaming it. But I didn't imagine it. All the horrible movie scenes in my head have been *real*." She let out the deepest sigh, and looked into Rocky's eyes, and then into Marty's. "I want my friend Cinthia back. I want her *back*."

With that, she began to cry. To cry with terrible sobs.

Carlos put his arm around her shoulder "Maybe you *did* dream it, Em. Maybe we dreamed the whole thing. How I wish that could be true."

Alicia poured a shot of scotch into a glass. Carlos got Emily to drink it. Rocky did not let up.

"You heard a car after the man ran off." All their faces raised to Rocky's. he didn't wait for an answer. He knew the answer. "But *before* you heard someone coming into the reeds, did you hear a car then? Before? Did you hear a car stop?"

George said, "I don't remember if I heard a car stop before. There were cars going by the whole time."

"I ask you because I am wondering if you chased after the man who ran. The man who Emily saw leave the gun by the dead man."

They were silent. Then George answered. "We did. First we looked to the man on the ground. We wanted to be sure he was dead. Because when Cinthia was left there, she was still alive, as you have brought up."

Marty asked, "You saw no gun?"

"Only Emily saw the gun." George banged the table with his fist. "But I don't care about that. I want to know who would leave my wife to die in that muck!" His late wife's best friend put her arm around him. His mother came back to the table and stroked his hair.

Carlos, his voice shaking with emotion, said, "The man was beyond our help. So yes. Maybe we did hear a car earlier. A car that stopped. If we did, we paid no attention. But after the gunshot, what we did hear was the man running. And yes, I heard his car take off because I ran after him and I saw it. I reached the edge of the fens in time to see him get in the car and speed away."

Rocky leaned forward. "Please describe the man you saw."

"It was night. Dark. He was just average size. Not too big, not small. It was dark"

"And the car? Can you describe the car?"

"It was an SUV."

"The make?"

Carlos shrugged. "I don't know."

"The license?"

"Listen to me, Detective, I tried. I wasn't fast enough."

"There are street lamps."

"The car wasn't under a street lamp."

"The more costly SUVs have light bulbs over their license plates. At a short distance, you can make out the plate."

"There was no light. I couldn't see the plate. Maybe the guy got rid of the light. Broke it. I only saw the car speeding away."

"Did the man you saw running. . . Did he drive the car away?"

"No. He got into the passenger side. The car sped away before he closed the door."

"And then?"

Emily, wiping at her eyes, answered. "George and I ran, too. But when we reached Carlos, the car was gone. We went back and got our stuff. We had to leave the flowers. We weren't able to put the flowers around the niche. We hurried to get home."

Emily's eyes were red, her face ragged. She said, "I have to tell you what George and Carlos are too ashamed to say. Since then, we have spent all morning looking for the car. An SUV with a broken light over the license plate. We went up and down the streets. But we couldn't find it!"

She ran out of the room.

Rocky knew that, at the moment, he could push no further. Marty felt exactly that way too, and he was the one to say, "Please. If you think of something else, call us."

Alicia stood. "Yes. We will."

In the car, Detective Patel and Sergeant Flanagan were now in agreement. The three had taken the law into their own hands and had come to see the futility of it. Happened every day.

As word of Jack Lagunas's suicide came out of news web-sites, Rocky found that his office had received several reports from motorists and area residents of the Back Bay claiming they might have heard gunfire the night before.

The bullet was found deep in the muddy soil of the fens. It had been examined. The brain tissues between a person's ears do not leave much of a mark on a bullet. And any brain tissue residue on that bullet had been washed away in the tidal mud.

Rocky read the report while he drank a cup of tea. In the space of time Rocky took to sip half of it, Marty had slugged down three cups of black coffee. While Rocky thought, Marty waited for him to finish his thinking. Marty knew the level of tea would have to drop to three-quarters before Rocky would come back from whatever mother ship he was visiting. Fortunately, Rocky's favorite cup was a glass mug celebrating the 1980 Moscow Summer Olympics. Marty had figured it out—Rocky must have been on Team USA, a boxer. But Team USA couldn't go. Someone got him the mug. Embargoes, Marty thought, sucked.

The tea reached the three-quarters empty level and Rocky looked up.

He said to his partner, "We have to surmise that Lagunas didn't give in to the demands of whoever killed him. But there was further purpose to his murder, which is why his body was-n't dumped into the harbor. His death was a threat aimed at Lagunas's partner. And Byington knows who these people are. You know, Marty, I never cease to be amazed at the reck-lessness inherent in vengeance, when the vengeance is rooted in. . ."

". . .getting shafted."

"Yes."

"But maybe, Rock, the perps figured an eruption of scandal—a sports scandal, and it sure as hell doesn't get bigger than that—would divert LA. The cops in LA are dealing with a really public situation, and because of Byington being who he is, and Major League Baseball being what it is, political shit is oozing out of every seam. Man, how those seams are opening up. Our perps figure nobody's in a big hurry to arrest Byington. His family is crying about his being persecuted, when all he'd done was try to help. Like, he's just an innocent bystander, blah-blah-fucking-blah."

"And all this gives Byington the time he needs. . ."

". . .to wire the perps the money they want—the money they *earned*—so that he doesn't experience a bullet through his own ears. And it's not like us and LA can just throw out a dragnet around them, and Boston, and Florida to boot."

"But Marty, there is an ever-expanding dragnet, a Federal dragnet." His cup was empty. "It is time to check in, isn't it?"

Marty loved it. *Check in.* He was partnered with a cop who could just *check in* to the FBI whenever he wanted. Rocky picked up his phone and Marty said, "It's Sunday morning, Rock."

"There are no Sundays in law enforcement."

"Oh, yeah. I forgot."

But Rocky wasn't aware of Marty's sarcasm. He was concentrating on checking in with the agent Poppy Rice referred him to. Marty watched in utter admiration as Rocky asked for the favor he needed without so much as a hello-how-are-ya. And marveled while Rocky explained the need for the favor without any bullshit.

"I cannot risk asking Miami PD to do this even though, obviously, that might seem more appropriate." Pause. Rocky listened. Then: "The difficulty is my needing to avoid dealing with Cuban-American police officers over the age of fifty.

Such persons might have a bias which would require I placate them before they agree to the action." Pause. "I haven't got the time to be placating anyone. *Anyone.*" Meaning the agent, too.

The agent Rocky was speaking to agreed to the request, but then asked him how he found out the perps' names.

Rocky answered, "I will get to that. When there is time. For now, I need you to question anyone who might know of the whereabouts of Prido and Machado. These men are likely in Boston though they might, at any moment, be recipients of enough funds to have fled the country."

The agent all but shouted at Rocky, "*They're in Boston?* How do you know that?"

"They are the prime suspects in our murder investigation of Cinthia Sanchez, the young mother of the baby found at Fenway Park a week ago. There might be some involvement with her, or her family, that we are unable to detect. I believe the two men murdered Jack Lagunas, as well."

"*Murdered* Jack Lagunas? Last I heard, Lagunas killed himself."

"I'm sorry the accurate information hasn't been passed along to you yet. Again, the overriding issue here is time. These men, in fact, met with Jack Lagunas here before he was killed."

"When did they meet with him, and how long have you known about that, Detective?"

Shiva began to rise. Marty, listening and watching, felt, in his bones, the deepening of Rocky's voice. His partner, the former boxer, once came to Marty's rescue when Marty was about to have his neck broken by a man who'd decided Marty had to die. Marty was bound with phone cable, tied to a chair, as was Rocky. Rocky broke free, punched his fist into exactly the right spot, and ruptured the man's left kidney.

Rocky said to the agent, "They met with him four days

ago. Thursday. I didn't know about the indictment until the next day. Prido and Machado have been fingered by the prisoner known as *El Jefe*."

"Jefe talked?"

"Yes."

"To who?"

Now Marty could swear he saw smoke rising out of Rocky's head. He grabbed the phone right out of Rocky's hand. "This is Sargeant Martin Flanagan. I'm Rocky Patel's partner. I'm the one who talked to Jefe." Marty pronounced the nickname perfectly. "Under Detective Patel's direction, I promised him a deal."

"You can't do that."

"Yeah, I can."

"Where the hell is Detective Patel?"

"He's had to take another call. . . Uh. . .from Washington. From Agent Rice." Marty could see Rocky's color was returning. "Wait a minute. He's just hung up. You want to talk to him again?"

Rocky took the phone from Marty. And Jesus whispered the sentiment of David Ortiz into Rocky's ear, what Big Papi had expressed at D-4. Rocky repeated it. "You are doing your job, Agent. I'm sorry I hadn't had the time necessary to procure the cooperation I needed from Justice. But this is a matter of life and death. Lagunas's partner is under a serious threat. The man is a member of a well-known and well-connected California family. I have, in the past, found myself up against the constraints that such a complexity creates. There is really but no choice for you to get done what has to be done."

The agent sighed fairly audibly. It was a damn good thing Poppy Rice had taken this Patel guy under her wing. But he had to ask: "What exactly did your partner promise him?"

"To do the best he could to see to a reduction of his sentence."

The agent said, "Okay. If Prido and Machado are caught, tried and get sent up, Jefe's sentence will be reconsidered."

While the Feds were invading the home of Alberto Prido, Rocky was receiving ongoing information from his newly cooperative agent contact: Prido owned a radar-equipped 40-foot Sea Ray which was confiscated as evidentiary material. Stowed aboard the vessel were night-vision scopes which enhanced sight as much as if there were full sunlight. There were weapons—a lot of weapons—all loaded with spare mags in a crate. There were also medical kits that were more advanced than what is found in many hospital emergency rooms. The boat had been reconfigured to seat thirty people uncomfortably. There was scuba equipment and wet suits, but only for two.

Prido also rented a couple of other boats for back-up.

Both Prido and Machado had several priors on drug smuggling charges, no convictions. Prido drove an SUV. But no motor vehicle was registered to him.

He also had a FedEx account. Rocky received a fax with a copy of the account's activities attached. Prido had FedExed a letter to ESPN corporate headquarters in Bristol, CT, the previous week, addressed specifically to news anchor, Michael Kim. The letter had been sent from the FedEx box on Mass Ave near the Christian Science headquarters.

Rocky said to Sargeant Flanagan, "That's a few blocks from Edgerly."

"Shit. It is."

Rocky was reading on, concentrating on something the

agent had written and tacked on to the reports. He chose to
read it again, aloud, so that he and Marty could think together as to its consequences:

*"The citizens of Little Havana don't abide by zoning rules.
There are McMansions next door to shacks. Behind the
McMansions are chicken coops—the people like their eggs real
fresh. Behind others there are training rings and roosters in cages.
Prido had reached a level of success where he could live in such a
MacMansion, but he wisely chose not to—didn't want to be
noticed. Rest assured, however, that his family no longer lives in a
shack with the chicken coops and caged roosters.*

*Both men graduated from the Mariel boatlift, and continued
working the same crimes they did in Cuba—pimping, illegal gam-
bling, etc.—before moving on to the drug industry. So now Prido's
family is ensconced in a middle class home in a nice section of Little
Havana. Machado lives on the boat—guards it.*

*Our agents found Prido's front door open, his two teenage sons
tied up in a bedroom, and his wife tied to a chair at the kitchen
table where there were cups of coffee, a bowl of sugar, and a pitcher of steamed milk gone cold. They untied the dishtowel wrapped
around Mrs. Prido's mouth. She took that opportunity to spit out
a string of obscenities so the agents chose not to ask for her help.
Instead, they replaced the dishtowel. They left her tied up while
they scanned her kitchen. An agent spotted a laptop at one end of
the kitchen counter. It's been confiscated.*

*The sons told us their father was in some little hotel in Boston,
a Bed and Breakfast. They didn't know which one. His father
called, apparently very upset, because he wasn't pleased with the
accommodations.*

*The sons said the people who got there ahead of us wanted to
know the same thing we did: Where their father was. The sons
didn't recognize them, only stated that they were Hispanic.*

Since our agents were in less of a rush than the previous visi-

*tors, they locked the doors behind them. They passed the Miami
police cruisers as they drove up 7th Avenue. The Prido neighbors,
having called the police, did not necessitate our calling them, but
we did anyway for the sake of relations.*

*Prido and Machado used a credit card to pay the bill at the Bed
and Breakfast when they checked in. The card belonged to
Machado's wife. They checked in a week ago Friday and they left
Wednesday. The manager there is expecting you. It's the John
Adams B & B at 11 Edgerly Road."*

Detective Patel and Sargeant Flanagan once more found
themselves on Edgerly Road, but this time three doors down
from the home of Alicia Sanchez.

The manager of the B & B was helpful but visibly anxious.
He said to Rocky, "Our little neighborhood here is still
mourning the loss of that sweet woman. And now the FBI
calls and tells me you people are on your way. I can't believe
there's some connection between Cinthia Sanchez and the
two guests staying here when she was killed. It can't be true.
It's not true."

"You feel strongly."

"I most certainly do."

"Why?"

"Because the two men were sent here by the tourist office
on the Common. They hadn't planned to be here. They called
me to see if we had a cancellation. It was a busy weekend.
That big crafts convention was on. They get, like, a zillion
people. The Red Sox are home. And it's *summer* besides.
We're full of tourists. We're booked through Labor Day. And
forget about a hotel in October. The Red Sox are always con-
tenders now, aren't they? These optimistic fans. . . They plan
their weddings around possible playoff dates."

Rocky said, "Please continue as to these particular guests."

"They walked in, they looked totally stressed. One of them was basically stoned, and the other had a very short fuse. They weren't the least bit grateful that I managed to get them a room, none too happy that they would have to share a bathroom, even though I explained to them that they would be sharing it with the Stella Marie Soap lady, not some drunk. She left me a whole box of soap for my bathrooms—*Big Poppy* soap—mango-scented. With poppy seeds to. . . oh, never mind. I told them it was the best I could do, that we weren't the Omni which, by the way, was *over-booked*."

Rocky said, "Did they have a vehicle?"

"Unfortunately, yes. I have three spots behind us in Public Alley 903. Their car took up two. The SUV that Cadillac makes. An Escalade. I had to ask them to hug the stoop back there because that car stuck out so far no one would get through. God, they were a pain."

"What color was the car?"

"Black. Most of them are."

Sargeant Flanagan asked. "Then you took their license plate number?"

"Well I *asked* for it when they checked in. The number they gave me didn't match the plate. By the time I happened to be back there to take notice, I didn't care about the phony number. Those guys were too scary."

"A Massachusetts plate? Do you remember that?"

"Out of state. Don't remember which state."

"And they left no forwarding address?"

"*Please*, Detective. They never even checked out. Just disappeared. They even left some of their stuff."

The man looked at the housekeeper's notes. A pillowcase was missing. He told Rocky about it. "Probably scooped excess stuff into the pillowcase because they were too lazy to pack in an orderly fashion."

Rocky waited.

"We keep things guests leave in their rooms for thirty days. If we get no requests for the items, we pitch them. Usually undershirts that somehow—and for the life of me I can't figure this out—get kicked under the beds. Toiletries mostly."

"I would like to see what they left."

"You can have it."

After asking, yet again, to be called if any more information came up, Rocky and his partner were back outside the B & B carrying the small cardboard box that contained dirty underwear and socks. Prido and Machado would buy new underwear rather than bother with washing things in a sink.

The detective and his partner quickly departed the neighborhood so that Cinthia's family would not see them and wonder what they were doing down the street. They drove out of Edgerly, to Haviland, onto Hemenway, crossed Boylston and parked in the little lot at St. Clement's Church, on the corner of Ipswich.

Sergeant Flanagan said to Rocky, "How the hell are we supposed to believe that these two guys came here to kidnap a baby and put him in Fenway Park? To scare their boss into giving them the money he owed them? I don't think so."

"They never planned any such thing. What they wanted was to create some public event that would throw Lagunas into the limelight. They'd gotten a picture of Luis Sanseverra's girlfriend. Who knows how? Probably the smuggled Cubans had to turn over their possessions. Prido needed to entice Lagunas to Boston. They couldn't go to Newport Beach. That's his domain, not theirs."

"Well they got his attention, all right."

"Yes. The man was on a plane to Boston within hours. I think, at first, they'd decided to leave the photo of the girl at Fenway Park, maybe with a message. They got a press pass. If you have enough money, you can get one on the street. Apparently fans do that quite often. Of course, they generally get caught. But I think Prido and Machado hatched something else impulsively when they happened to see the Sanchez baby with members of his family."

"Something that would really freak out Lagunas."

"Yes. They are criminals and they are facing a conviction with a life sentence attached. Combine that with the fact that they are experienced smugglers. They smuggle people. They *steal* people. That is the word David Ortiz used when he was coming to the aid of the young ballplayer. They have a lot of practice eluding both the Coast Guard and Federal investigators. Now they only had to steal one more human being. A baby. The baby they would lead people to believe was the child of a talented young ballplayer from Cuba. One who was posing as a Dominican—something Jack Lagunas couldn't be let known."

"Fuck."

"Yes. Fuck. We have discussed the ramifications of vengeance and greed, Marty. So they'd seen Cinthia—probably walking the baby up and down the street. They saw her take him to that little park almost next door so she could be with the other mothers. They watched her. And then on Sunday morning, when things are quiet, Cinthia comes outside with the baby, puts him in his new stroller and they follow her and George. George leaves her to go to work. A stroke of luck. When all is said and done, Lagunas will know they mean business, and Cinthia will get the baby back. But Cinthia is typical of any new parent. When they try to grab the baby, she fights them. Maybe she hung onto the car. Maybe she stepped in front of it after they got the baby inside. But the thing is, they knew they had to grab her too.

"They didn't want to kill her but they had to hit her. They didn't want to kill the baby either, obviously, though they could have certainly killed him with the barbituate they gave him. And when they had to get rid of Cinthia, they dragged her into the fens where they didn't know she'd end up face down in water."

"But she did."

"Yes. And the baby, Marty. . . the baby was fortunately saved by the Boston Red Sox."

Marty struck his right fist into the palm of his left hand. He said, "Shit. Let's get the bastards, Rock. Let's fucking get them."

Rocky's cell rang.

THE NUMBER ONE PLACE
SUNDAY, 11:00 AM

The Feds dropped in on a couple of people in Miami today in a house that belongs to a guy who worked for Jack Lagunas. They utilized the same number of agents and the same number of vehicles as they did when they grabbed that kid, Elian Gonzalez, before getting him back to his family in Cuba.

And it has come out that Jack Lagunas did not kill himself. He was murdered.

I don't think I'm in the mood to talk baseball.

COMMENTS:

KGNumber5 said: This keeps getting weirder. I don't blame you, Jay.

RebGirl said: Usually we have the Red Sox to cheer us up when things go bad in our personal lives. Now even the team itself probably feels the same way we do. Very sad.

HaroldTheGuard said: We will get back to baseball, Jay. The sun never sets on Red Sox Nation, right?

MikesFriendJen said: Don't worry, we didn't come here for the baseball scores today, Jay.

RedSoxAnnie said: Jay, barbecue at my place today—if you wanna hang out during the game, feel free, neighbor.

CHAPTER
15

In the movies, cops get tips: they receive anonymous phone calls; they hear from a con who wants to trade information for a deal; they follow provocative "leads" that seem to come out of the blue; they rely on homeless informants who reside happily in gutters where they witness important phenomena; or thousand-watt light bulbs miraculously go on in their heads.

But real cops think. The greatest part of a cop's work is thinking. Tenaciously, they go over and over and over the same envisioned ground, searching for what they might have missed the first, second or 100th time around. Going along with the thinking is the hounding of subjects they feel have something more to give than they've already given. This often annoys the subjects mightily, straining a cop's patience. But patience is prime.

So it was an annoyed proprietor of the John Adams B & B on Edgerly Road who became fairly testy.

He said to Rocky and Marty who appeared at his desk after they'd just been there, "Listen, I really *really* want to help. But I'm *spectacularly* busy. My housekeeper just dropped the coffee maker carafe. The replacement that came with the coffee maker does not exist because she broke the original two weeks ago, neglecting tell me. That's about as bad as if my computer crashed. I have sent her off to buy another coffee maker because the owner. . ." he rolled his eyes ". . .insisted on a coffee maker from Belgium. Just *try* to find a carafe that fits that monstrosity. So I've got my handyman—who fortunate-ly wasn't in hiding for once—picking up the pieces of glass strewn all over our parlor. It is now. . ." He glanced down at his watch giving Rocky the opportunity to interrupt him.

"Do you meditate sir?" Rocky asked.

The man looked up. "Excuse me?"

"Do you meditate?"

While Rocky asked the question the second time, Marty was trying to control his urge to take out his gun and shoot out the guy's computer so that he could actually contrast a real inconvenience with an imagined one.

The manager, having profiled Rocky's race, said, "Actually, I have tried to meditate. But I get interrupted by. . .by all of this." He waved his hands across his little office.

Rocky said, "I would please ask you to meditate right now, now that there are no more carafes to be smashed, and close your eyes and imagine the Cadillac Escalade driven by the two guests we have discussed previously. The Escalade parked behind this establishment in Public Alley 903. It was late at night. . ."

The B & B manager chose not to humor the detective. Instead: "Exactly. It was late at night. . .dark as hell back there. Too bad the guest wasn't *in* the car starting it up. Then I could help you. Because the lights over the license plates of those cars are so bright you can read them from a hundred yards. Maybe I might have. . ."

The small lurch Rocky felt in his stomach was matched by the one in Marty's. The man could only shake his head at the speed in which the officers thanked him and made their exit.

Out on the sidewalk, Marty spoke first. "Emily was the one. Oh, right, the light must have been broken. *We believed her!*"

And now, Rocky was the one to remain calm and reasonable. "We must recreate the deposit of Lagunas's body and make use of our watches and tape measure."

Marty was always amazed by Rocky's ability to leap into action before griping first the way normal people did.

As the crow flies, it was about two minutes from Edgerly Road to Agassiz. But in Boston, the Back Bay streets were designed for horseless carriages: Every street was one-way, and it was often difficult to squeeze even one car down a road. As for the numbered Public Alleys, garbage trucks had been known to become wedged. The detective and his partner made their way through the winding passages until they came out at Boylston. They next had to proceed along a circuitous route all the way to Fenway Park, and then turn back, winding their way to Boylston with only one illegal U-turn. They skirted the fens and turned left on Agassiz. They pulled onto the sidewalk so no one would sideswipe the car, and got out. Rocky took the tape measure out of his trunk. It was of the variety that surveyors used.

They measured the length of ground from the place where George, Carlos, Emily, and Miss Winthrop and her friend, saw the car with its engine running. They stepped across the strip of grass and then through the reeds, past the place where Cinthia's body had lain, as well as Jack Lagunas's, and up the little rise to the tree. The path they took was worn, the shrine having fast become a place to visit—everyone wanting to pay their respects to the young mother who was murdered, whose baby was rescued by the Boston Red Sox.

The distance between the shrine and the road was 218 feet.

At the shrine, Rocky said to Marty, "I'll give you a fifteen-second lead time. It probably didn't take any longer than that for George and Carlos to determine Jack Lagunas was dead, and to start their run."

Rocky took out his watch. Marty got ready. "Ready. . .get set. . .go!" And Marty sprinted back toward their car with Rocky in hot pursuit. When Marty reached the road, Rocky gave him five seconds to get into an imaginary car with its engine running and for the car to speed away. Rocky was seven feet out of the reeds and six feet from the road.

The two men sat in their vehicle while Rocky spoke to a technician: "This is high priority. . ."

"To do with Cinthia Sanchez?"

"Yes."

"Shoot, Rocky."

"On a dark night. . ." and he gave the technician the date, time and place so he could go back and check the level of brightness thrown by the moon, street lamps, whatever ". . . how many feet must someone be from a Cadillac Escalade and still be able to read a Florida license plate?"

"Agassiz Road?"

"Yes. Probably just a few feet east of the bridge."

"Twenty-twenty vision?"

George, Carlos and Emily did not wear glasses. "Yes."

"I'm on it."

The detective and the lieutenant walked back over to Boylston to the gas station and got a cup of coffee, a cup of hot water and a tea bag. Forget driving. Then they returned to the car, and got themselves back to Edgerly Road. They were able to park discreetly on a short, dead end road off Edgerly which allowed them to contemplate the Sanchez home and the John Adams B & B while they drank the tea and coffee.

The call they were waiting for came twenty minutes later.

"Based on what you gave me, Rocky, eight feet."

"You're a magician," Rocky told him.

"I know."

Rocky thanked him and said to Marty, "Let's go. Before I arrest them I'm going to give them rope."

"I'm sorry, Rocky."

"You weren't there when I was alone with them. Your instinct varied from mine."

"I *am* fucking going soft."

"Enough! Let's go."

They got out of their car and walked out onto Edgerly until they came to #5.

Inside, Emily was sitting at the dining room table, the formal room used for Sunday dinners and holidays. She could see the two police officers through the sheer summer curtains. The bell rang. She went to the front door and opened it.

She looked pale. He said, "We have more questions, Emily."

She stammered just a little bit before she managed, "George is at work and Carlos has gone out. Your office called this morning. We can have Cinthia. We can bury her. Alicia and I are planning to go to the funeral home in a little bit. When she finishes bathing Arturo. We're in here." She gestured to somewhere over her shoulder.

Rocky first turned to Marty and made eye contact. Marty nodded. In the foyer, Rocky asked Emily to leave the door ajar. "Marty has to go to the car—he'll be right back."

"All right."

She led Rocky to the kitchen. Rocky could smell something sweet baking. Alicia stood at the sink, a shallow, blue, baby tub set in place. She looked over to Rocky, and then went back to the baby. Arturo was gazing up at her while she held him firmly and ran a washcloth over his glistening hair.

Rocky thought the baby should be gurgling with pleasure. He was enjoying his bath. But he wasn't gurgling. Rocky was sure Arturo was remembering his mother.

Rocky spoke softly to Alicia, taking care not to startle the baby. "Where exactly is Carlos?"

He watched as she slid the wet washcloth again over the baby's head. She didn't answer the question; neither did Emily. And then Marty appeared in the kitchen doorway. He said, "George isn't at work."

Emily stared at Alicia's stooped back, and then back into Rocky's eyes. "I'm sorry. . ."

"You're sorry about what?"

"We *were* able to read the license that night in the fens. We wanted to find them."

Alicia finally had something to say. She turned to Rocky. "I tried to stop them. It was all I could do to stop Emily."

"What did you do, Emily?"

"It was a Florida plate. So we called the State Police headquarters in Tallahassee. To see how we could find out who the car was registered to. They. . ."

Marty couldn't help himself. "You called the Florida State Police?"

"Yes." Her blue eyes were clear, her face that of a law-abiding citizen who depends on the police. "They gave me the number of the DMV. But then it turned out there were forms we'd have to fill out. If we filled them out on-line, it would take five business days to respond. That's what they told me. So Carlos and Cinthia—they have a cousin in Florida. Ocala. He works at a farm that breeds horses. Race horses. Famous race horses, Carlos told me. So Carlos called him. His cousin called some other guys and he found out who the car belonged to."

Rocky asked her, "And then what happened?"

"I don't know."

"Who invaded the house in Miami?"

"Invaded a house?"

Rocky breathed deeply and continued. "That is police talk. Who went to the home of the woman who owned the car?"

"Some friends of Carlos's cousin. They all know about Cinthia. They wanted to help. They found out the woman's husband had the car. That he was in Boston."

"Did she say where in Boston?"

Emily pressed her lips together. Alicia went back to the baby. Emily did not know how to take the woman's silence. Then Arturo made a little baby noise, a kind of, "Ooooh..." When he did, Emily's gaze had shifted from Alicia to the blue summer sky beyond the window. She decided the small sound from the baby was a sign that Cinthia wanted her to answer the policeman. Her gaze travelled to Rocky.

"Carlos and George told me the woman didn't know where he was. I told my husband I knew he was lying. I told him I would leave him if he didn't tell me. George said I shouldn't worry—they planned to go to you with what they knew. He said they had to find you. They didn't want to speak to just anyone. It wouldn't be easy. There was no time to explain things to me. They left. George was lying too. I got so mad. "

"When did all this happen?"

"An few hours ago."

"Who is this cousin? How can I reach him?"

Alicia still hadn't turned. Rocky saw his own mother's back in hers. She was abdicating responsibility. Emily had to decide whether or not to take on whatever might become of betraying her husband.

She said, "Wait a minute."

She left the room and came back with her purse. She rummaged in it and took out her cell phone.

She said, "Carlos forgot to charge his phone. He used

mine." She held it out. "They wouldn't take me with them. I begged them."

Now Rocky thought, she and her husband are even. He took the phone from her. Marty took out his pad and wrote down all the phone numbers with Florida area codes. There were over a dozen. One of them turned out to be the Florida State Police. Another, the DMV in Tallahassee.

Alicia lifted the dripping baby from his tub. Emily reached for the towel folded neatly, and placed on the surface of the oven to make it warm. The two women wrapped him up. Emily took him into her arms.

Alicia said to the police officers, "Please. You must hurry. I'm so frightened. I do not want to bury my son too."

Marty looked to Rocky. They both knew there would be nothing productive to come from arresting Emily.

They left. Rocky called a judge. He got a warrant. During the wait for Verizon to send him a transcript of the calls, Rocky and Marty exchanged *mea culpas*. Mostly Rocky tried to comfort Marty who was agonizing again. Marty had a new term for what he perceived as his weakness. "I'm burned out, Rocky. I'm fuckin' *burned out*."

Rocky said to him, "If we'd tortured them, they wouldn't have told us. They are in the throes of agony and they wished to inflict the same agony upon whoever killed Cinthia. To feel revenge is to experience a passion that has no logic. Neither of us is at fault. And what is burn-out, after all? It is. . ."

Marty listened to Rocky's Hindu philosophizing and realized how much it comforted him. It certainly comforted Rocky, who felt equally helpless, waiting and talking until the call finally came.

Carlos had found out from his cousin in Florida that Prido and Machado had moved from the John Adams B & B to the La Quinta Inn, in Somerville.

Rocky went to the chief. The man listened; he approved the plan. High risk, high gain. It took Rocky just under an hour to assemble a SWAT team. There were forty police officers who were members of the Boston PD SWAT team, and it had been determined that Rocky required twenty. They gathered with Rocky's own men at police headquarters in a room similar to a college classroom with two tiers of seats.

Behind Rocky, on a large board, there was a diagram—the inn, a restaurant, the small parking lot between the two, and the vast shopping mall on the other side of the access road that ran behind the La Quinta. Rocky told them, "We cannot evacuate the hotel without causing a great deal of commotion and noise. We are talking about a hotel filled to capacity. . . *Filled to capacity*. Our goal is to surprise the men in the room, to confuse and intimidate them, and to arrest them. If we meet that goal, we will avoid gunfire. If that isn't possible, if a weapon of theirs is pointed at you, your training and instinct to survive will take their course. "

The SWAT officers had placed their Kevlar helmets and panels against the wall. Since their personal weapons were of the variety that each officer felt most comfortable with, Rocky's reproach to the men was almost surreal in that the officers carried an arsenal—Glocks, Berettas, H & Gs, Colts, a Walther P99 and one Sig Sauer P220. And they had semi-automatic weapons plus several 12 gauge shotguns that could hit a close target without requiring a lot of time to take aim. Shotguns tended to just blow people away. Then there were the stun grenades, and pepper spray, and mace, and tear gas. . .

Rocky pointed to a delivery area behind the mall, up against the access road. "And right now their vehicle is here near a row of dumpsters, parked in the middle of the cars driven by the mall's night crew. If by any chance Prido or Machado, or both, go to their vehicle, our task becomes simpler; we surround the vehicle, arrest them, take them in. We can only hope.

"We have scoured the area for any sign of George Sanchez and Carlos Vega. Security video tapes at the mall were checked out. They haven't turned up and we are watching for them too."

He touched his finger to the restaurant on the diagram. "Prido and Machado went in here at six-forty for dinner, and returned to their hotel room at seven-thirty-five. Their room faces the restaurant. They each had two beers with dinner. It's too bad the restaurant isn't facing the mall. We could have started our work earlier. It is now. . ." he glanced at his watch ". . .eleven-ten. The restaurant closes at midnight, and the manager leaves at one. We will have lights set up on the restaurant's roof within fifteen minutes. Our Special Unit—snipers—will move into their positions.

"We will not go into the hotel until two-thirty. At that hour, most—if not all—of the hotel guests will likely be asleep. There are two desk clerks, but only one is on duty after midnight. At two-thirty, we will remove the desk clerk. We will have someone at the phone for any calls from guests, or from the outside.

"We will need two point men, one leading my team, and the other leading your snake of eleven. We'll go to the third floor, where the eleven SWAT members will take over the corridor. Any guest who might come out of a room, will be put back in the room.

"At a signal from me, when we enter the room at two-thirty, the lights on the restaurant roof will come on, and the interior of the room will be illuminated. In addition, the point man you've assigned will throw in the stun grenade so that, in addition to the noise and the flash, we'll still have the outside lights. The blinds at the room's windows are slightly open. That's all we need. The element of surprise is of the utmost importance. We will arrest Prido and Machado in their beds. If it is clear that we will take gunfire, the snake will attack the room."

With that, the SWAT members huddled with a map of the hotel floor so that they could determine and memorize each position. The two point men identified themselves to Rocky. The one who would lead Rocky and Marty into the room was Jan O'Keefe, Boston's first and only female SWAT officer. Because of Cinthia, she would be the one. She shook Rocky's hand. She was five feet two, and she weighed ninety-seven pounds. The strength in her handshake could have broken Rocky's fingers if she chose to do so.

Rocky told them all, "Again, we will only initiate fire if we enter the room and find the men awake and pointing weapons at us. If we hear gunfire, we will return it."

Only Rocky had noticed the chief enter the room; he'd been standing in back since Rocky began speaking. Now he came forward. The men and Jan O'Keefe tracked him with their joint gaze, and then he stood in front of them.

He didn't have much to say—Rocky had said it all. But he did have something he needed to add. He told them, "I don't want to lose any of you. I don't want any of you to suffer injury. I don't want loss of civilian life. This is a challenge I know all of you will all face with courage. You have the training. You're professionals. But at the same time, if you are in mortal danger, you must still rely on your instincts. You can do the job. Good luck."

THE NUMBER ONE PLACE
Monday, 11:15 AM

Along with everyone else, the Red Sox had their minds on the Sanchezes and the two murders, as they flew to the West Coast after beating Baltimore on Sunday. They can rest in knowing that Luis Sanseverra is safe and sound in his homeland. Not the Dominican, but Cuba. And his name isn't Luis Sanseverra either, it's Guillermo Valdez.

So Luis-now-Guillermo, who had been detained but not arrested, was able to use his credit card and fake passport to get a flight to Santo Domingo. From there it was a short hop back to Havana, where all was forgiven. The headlines translated to: KIDNAPPED PLAYER COMES HOME. Only a slight exaggeration. Within a couple of days, he was back with the *Industriales*, where he was firing his splitter better than he ever did in the not-quite-Carribbean summer in Maine. Perhaps he will be the the Dice-K of the next World Baseball Classic. . . .

COMMENTS:

KGNumber5 said: I was sure the kid was dead. Another dead body, that's all we need, right?

ConnecticutSoxFan said: Good for the kid. We always hear these seemingly heroic defection stories. This guy had to flee goin' the other way. If it was right for him—more power to him.

Gedman10 said: I hadn't thought of it that way. Defecting *to* Cuba.

CHAPTER

16

Byington had withdrawn $850,000 from a retirement account for which he was fined a substantial penalty. Later, he would have to pay taxes on the money. Money was not an issue for Byington though: Staying alive was.

Alberto Prido had called him on his cell phone within an hour of the discovery of Lagunas's body. Prido was succinct. He wanted the money owed him divvied up between his wife and his sons. He gave Byington the names of the banks and the account numbers. Then he was to mail a personal check for $20,000 to Machado in care of the Bahia Bar in Miami on Beachfront Avenue.

Prido told him, "If the money don't get to the banks in twenty-four hours, I come out there so I can put a hole through your ears, too."

Byington swore to Prido on his mother's heart that he would wire the money and send it the minute he got off the phone.

"You swearing on your mother's heart?" Prido asked him incredulously.

"Yes."

Prido could not control his laughter. There existed no capacity for empathy in his psychopathic mentality. "Maybe your mother she got no heart, rich boy."

That night, Prido and Machado used a little more of Jack Lagunas's hundred thousand dollars to enjoy a nice meal at the restaurant on the other side of the La Quinta's parking lot. They ate at the bar where they were more comfortable, and then they returned to the room they'd snagged. A week earlier, Prido had gotten hold of a tourist map and called all the hotels close by I-93, a highway that would would whisk them out of Boston easily, as long as they avoided rush hour which they would. The La Quinta in Somerville happened to have twelve free rooms as a spat between a soon-to-be bride and groom had reached proportions terrible enough, in the bride's view, to cancel the wedding. The bride's father was told by a La Quinta spokesperson that there wouldn't be a problem since he'd called ahead of the twenty-four hour deadline for canceling a block of rooms. His deposit would be refunded.

Prido followed a certain plan whenever he had a long trip to accomplish by car. He'd get a good night's sleep, set his alarm clock for 3 AM, drive five hours, stop for a big breakfast, turn the wheel over to Machado, stop five hours after that for lunch, at which time Machado's habit would have to be sated, and then drive straight through to Miami with a stop for dinner. He'd get home slightly before dawn, sleep all day, and then get back to his business—a line of work which took place in the dead of night.

Prido was thrilled to learn that this La Quinta was located behind a huge shopping mall. Prido found a dark, hidden area to park the SUV. From there, it was only yards from an access road to I-93.

George Sanchez and Carlos Vega were able to get a room at the La Quinta in Somerville, too. When they called La

Quinta, the hotel still had a couple of rooms reserved for the cancelled bridal block still available.

George and Carlos made a plan, similar in many ways to Rocky's. The biggest difference, of course, was that they had a room at the hotel. They'd taken a taxi there in the afternoon after spending a few minutes in Everett on the other side of Mystic River, and checked in under false names. Another difference in the two plans was that George and Carlos would put their plan into action at 2 AM, half-an-hour earlier than what Rocky had decided.

George and Carlos imagined beating up Prido and Machado within an inch of their lives, and then they'd tie them up, leave the hotel and go to Detective Patel like they'd told Emily. Neither George nor Carlos were violent men. But they had fed on one another's grief and fury until they'd convinced themselves that the men who killed Cinthia deserved something beyond an arrest, a trial, and a prison sentence. They were positive that the killers would receive a light sentence because they hadn't meant to kill Cinthia. Maybe her death might even be considered manslaughter. It was up to them to avenge her. They had no way of knowing of the federal charges against Prido and Machado.

At two o'clock, George Sanchez and Carlos Vega opened the door of Room 342, which was registered to Prido under another name. Carlos's cousins had learned what that name was from one of his sons, who he'd tied to a chair.

George used the key that he and Carlos had just procured from the lone and sleepy desk clerk, a student at Tufts. The clerk was now lying on the floor behind the desk, his hands tied behind his back. He'd been ordered not to move until Carlos and George returned. They promised him they would untie him then. They apologized to him.

The student was in terror, but was able to comfort himself

in the knowledge that the men who were registered in 342 had treated him like a piece of shit, when he told them he couldn't send someone up to fix their soundless TV. As he lay there, he was racking his brain as to who the fellow was who had apologized to him while restraining him. He knew that face. And then he thought, *The father* of *Baby Ted Williams?* (There would be some who would always think of Arturo that way.) The student's mind raced. He imagined himself in the center of a bunch of kids at school regaling them with the narrative of the night's excitement. This distracted him from his terror somewhat.

As George and Carlos entered Room 342, Rocky, his officers and the SWAT team poured into the La Quinta lobby. They came upon the Tufts student lying on the floor, awestruck. Marty looked down at him and said, "Holy fucking shit."

Once they had the desk clerk out in a car, he got to watch as the technicians trained their spotlights set up on the restaurant roof at the window of Room 342. He was further awe-struck.

The police now knew that George and Carlos were in the hotel. But of course, they hadn't checked in under their own names. The kid from Tufts hadn't come on duty until evening; there was no time to figure out where they might be. Or where they might have been.

Rocky would carry on.

⚾

Prido slept naked. Rather than the nudity causing him to feel vulnerable, he felt empowered even as he lay staring into the Smith and Wesson .45 pointed at him—the gun Carlos and George had bought on the street in Everett. He rose from the bed.

Carlos ordered, "Put your hands over your head."

Prido stood in front of them, as did Machado in his dirty underwear. George was closest to the bed, Carlos near the door.

Machado thought they were being robbed by someone who found out they had a lot of money on them—probably someone who was in the bar last night; Machado couldn't help but brag about it to the guys nearby when Prido was in the men's room.

Prido didn't recognize these two men. And obviously they weren't pros, which allowed for the click in his brain that signaled to him as to why they were there.

Hands still raised, he said, "It wasn't us did it, man. Another guy did it. A crazy guy. We're only here to get the money Jack Lagunas owe us. And this guy—the guy who did it—he kill Lagunas too. So we took off. Now the guy, he's looking for us. True! I swear it on my mother's heart."

"Who is the other guy?" is what George asked him, squinting, wishing he'd gotten a better look at the man he'd chased out of the reeds.

Prido could see the Q in the La Quinta sign through the crack in the half-opened blinds. "His name, Quirido. Listen, put that gun down. Somebody gonna get hurt."

Carlos clinched the .45 even tighter. He'd never fired a gun before in his life. And neither he, nor George, wanted to shoot anyone. They'd made a pact to that effect.

Meanwhile, Machado, who had no idea what Prido was talking about, found he was unable to shift his nervous gaze away from a spot near the door. There, propped up against the wall, was his shotgun. Prido had gotten annoyed when he insisted on bringing it into the room, but Machado liked the security of his big beautiful gun—a Browning A-5 semi-automatic—at the ready. You never knew what was on the other side of a door. Tonight, for example. Who the hell were these dudes? Machado knew Prido's gun was still in his suitcase. That was the trouble with Prido—he thought he was fucking God.

Outside, two cops were watching the Escalade. It's Florida plate had been replaced by another from Connecticut that Prido had paid for at a nearby chop shop. All was quiet. But inside, Rocky, Marty and two cops, plus the SWAT team came out of a stairway onto the third floor, and fanned out along the corridor.

In Room 342, Prido was pointing to a briefcase that belonged to the late Jack Lagunas. It was lying on the coffee table.

"There's almost a hundred thousand dollars inside there. Lagunas try to buy us off with that, but he owe us a lot more. Take it. Take it all, and I promise you I find Quirido, and I tell you where he is. I got proof he's the guy who did it."

Carlos could care less about a hundred thousand dollars. He asked him, "What proof?"

"He hit the girl. The paper said when he hit her he's wearing a heavy ring."

Prido had gotten rid of his ring when he read that. George and Carlos were listening intently, adrenaline rushing through them. George felt like he could throw up any minute.

"I bet Quirido still got that ring on. Hey, I'm sorry. That girl? She was crossing the street. We're in a hurry. We're going to the ballpark to leave a message there for Lagunas. You heard of that guy, right? We want him to know we can get into the ballpark easy. We want to scare him. This guy Lagunas screw us bad. We're so nervous, man. We drive around the girl. We don't mean to get so close to her. She so mad at us. She start yelling at us. Quirido he jump out and grab her. We only got a couple minutes to get into the ballpark. He got crazy. She's holding on to the stroller so he grab that baby too.

"She keep on yelling. Quirido hit her. He knock her out. We know they find the baby right away if we bring him into that ballpark with us. We leave him in there. There's a lot of people in there. Then we take off and we put the girl in these woods. Man, we don't know the place got all that water in it. I. . ."

Now Machado found his wits and with that, his voice. "We didn't mean none of it. We only wanted to show Lagunas he couldn't jerk us around. But Quirido. . . Like my friend says. He's nuts." He gestured toward the briefcase too. "Go ahead. Take it." Then he took a step toward them. He ached to get closer to the door, closer to his trusty shotgun.

Carlos raised the pistol just a little bit. He said, "You're both full of shit."

Right outside the door of Room 342, Rocky held his phone to his ear, waited five more seconds, and screamed, "*Now!*"

The lights on the roof across the parking lot blazed on, two cops slammed their bodies into the door of Room 342 and Jan O'Keefe burst through, tossing the stun grenade which went off with a huge flash and a very loud bang. The snake emptied out of the staircase, nine of the SWAT team poured into the room, while the rest filled the corridor.

Everyone in 342—George Sanchez, Carlos Vega, the two human traffickers and all the cops were momentarily blinded.

Despite his inability to see anything, Rocky shouted, "Hands in the air! Up!" And then he could see. He trained his own gun on the still naked Prido; Marty's was pointed directly at Machado's heart. The rest of the cops fanned out, and

now four Glocks plus eight varied SWAT weapons were lev-
eled at the men as well, including the two men no one expected would be there until seconds earlier.

Machado's hands flew straight up as if he were trying to
touch the ceiling to show the cops he was voting for absolute
compliance. Prido sent his arms up too, but then his right
hand darted out toward Carlos and he yanked him into a vise,
his left arm tight around his neck. With his right, he crushed
Carlos's hand around the gun he still gripped so tightly, and
pointed it at Rocky.

Carlos felt the vertabrae in his neck crack; he could barely
get any air into his throat. The cold muzzle of the .45 he'd
bought on the street in Everett was stuck into his ear.

To George, who had nearly been hit by the door when it
was smashed open, the tableau looked like a movie scene, the
room lit up like broad daylight, the action frozen, waiting for
the director to tell the actors their next move. George felt as
though some higher power had created the tableau, giving
him the prescience necessary to take everyone in; he became
instantly aware that the only pair of eyes not on Prido and
Carlos was Machado's. Machado seemed to be staring at the
wall behind George, near the half-opened door.

Rocky said, "Prido, don't do it."

Prido's look of desperation was not tainted with fear as was
Machado's; his face was twisted with rage. Carlos was gag-
ging. Prido started backing up, dragging Carlos with him.

He screamed, "Put your guns down on the floor. Put all
your shit on the floor. Every fuckin' one of you. Do it!"

And they did; they had to. The SWAT officers lay down
their panels, then placed their guns on the carpet.

Prido said, "I'm goin' out, and this guy here, he right with
me," and Prido dug the gun deeper into Carlos's ear. "If you

shoot me, the last thing I do before I croak, I pull this fuckin' trigger."

Rocky said to him, his voice level with the calm of Jesus blocking Shiva. "We know Cinthia Sanchez's death was not homicide. We know it was an accident."

"Yeah, well big fuckin' deal. Thas' really gonna help me. I tellin' you, just let me get out of here or I blow this guy's brains out."

Rocky kept talking, Jesus still holding back Shiva. "You're in the Commonwealth of Massachusetts. We'll give you the opportunity to bring down Jack Lagunas's illegal operation. We know you didn't murder anyone. We can make a deal."

"And who are you gonna charge with Lagunas murder? This asshole?" His eyes shifted for one split second toward Machado.

Marty had hoped by some miracle that it was someone else who'd shot Lagunas, yet another enemy of his, or if Prido had done it, he hadn't heard about the new information with regard to Lagunas's cause of death. Sometimes unrealistic optimism kept Marty strong.

Now Prido waved the gun crushed into both his and Carlos's hands. "All of you, you get your hands back of your heads. Now! And sit fuckin' down. Just sit down and keep your fuckin' hands back of your heads."

Everyone complied except for Machado. Rocky thought about the snipers on the restaurant roof. They could see everything. But as long as Prido was wrapped around Carlos, none of them would fire. Prido said, "Somebody make a funny move, I gonna pop this guy and then I shoot a couple of you while I go down."

George, sitting on the floor, hands on his head, inched a little closer to the door.

Machado took a few steps toward George. Prido lashed out with his foot and kicked Machado behind the knees. He fell in a heap to the floor. He looked up. "Why the hell'd ya do that? What. . ."

"Shut up. *Shut up!*"

Prido's hold on Carlos's neck eased enough for Carlos to breathe. He smelled the .45. He didn't know how it could smell so vile. The combination of cleaning fluid, powder and the steel of the bullets was indeed vile when a gun was up so close.

Prido looked at Rocky. "You!"

Rocky answered him. "What do you want?"

"You goin' to walk ahead of me. You goin' to walk with me to my car and then you goin' to let me drive away. This guy, he stay with me. Somebody shoot out my tire, I shoot this guy and I crash into so many cars as I can. I got a big Cadillac. I take a million people out with me. Now move the fuck over here!"

As Rocky stood, Prido stayed focused. "Keep your fuckin' hands in the air!"

George edged a little closer to the door.

Rocky kept his hands up high.

Prido screamed at him. "Now go to the door! *Slow, you hear me? Fuckin' slow!*"

Rocky did as he was told.

"Take one step in that hall."

Rocky took the step. The rest of the SWAT team in the corridor were staring at him, crouched, weapons pointed.

Prido dragged Carlos toward the door. He stopped next to the coffee table, and loosened his grip around Carlos's neck.

"Get the briefcase."

Carlos sucked in as much air as he could, leaned over and picked up the briefcase. The vise closed again.

Prido said to Rocky, "Shout to who the fuck you got out there to tell somebody. . . Tell somebody let me go to my car. Nobody stop me!"

Rocky looked down the corridor. He turned to Prido. "They heard you."

"I don't hear nobody makin' calls! Say to them to call who you got outside!"

And immediately, everyone heard the voice of the second point man six feet down the hallway yelling Prido's order.

"Now tell them to shut off the fuckin' lights."

And the order went out. Rocky was impressed by Prido's ability to calculate so carefully under the most dire of circumstances. But then, the man had been able to calculate how to get a boatload of people from Cuba to Florida in the middle of the night, while avoiding the Coast Guard. To say nothing of Fidel.

The hotel room was now in the dark except for the pale glow coming in from the corridor.

The one person Prido's back faced was George. George felt sweat dripping into his eyes. He blinked them away. Then Prido was in the doorway, about to step out. In the second Prido took to look down the corridor, George reached behind the door and with both hands grabbed the barrel of the shotgun. In the same motion, he leaped to his feet, and with more strength than he ever knew he possessed, he swung the shotgun as hard as he could into Alberto Prido's back, shattering his right shoulder blade.

THE NUMBER ONE PLACE
Tuesday, Noon

It's over. The barbarians who killed Cinthia Sanchez

have been caught. We hope some kind of good comes out of all of it.

I've been invited by Rocky Patel to hang out with him and his entire crew tonight for a drink, watch the game with them. Maybe they'll cheer me up. I was happy to be of some kind of help, but hopefully I won't feel too out of place as the one person there who didn't risk his life. Or her life.

I promised everyone I would try to get into baseball, so here's my feeble attempt. Red Sox vs. Athletics from the West Coast tonight at 10 to get us back on track and head for the stretch run. I wouldn't blame you this time if you went to bed early tonight. The whole city is stressed out.

COMMENTS:

RebGirl said: The cops did a great job. Pat 'em on the back for me. . .

AJM said: That goes double for me, Jay.

KGNumber 5 said: Especially the woman from the SWAT team! She's my new hero.

Jay said: Mine, too, KG.

MattySox said: Let's sign George up!

CopMarty said: Yeah, you'll be out of place. Don't worry about it.

CHAPTER
17

The next night, Rocky and Marty are drinking beer at Daisy Buchanan's, a couple of blocks from D-4. Marty has come to appreciate Rocky's favorite brand, Kingfisher, imported from India. Rocky said to him once, "It tastes so good because it's perfumed with jasmine."

Marty's response had been, "Please don't tell me about the shit's that in it, okay Rock?"

Rocky had smiled.

A huge crowd of cops were with them at the bar. They were still freaked at what might have been. The Browning had discharged when it made contact with Prido's shoulder blade. The projectile that blasted forth zipped beneath George's armpit, nicked Jan O'Keefe's right boot, then pierced the carpeted floor between two joists. It came out the ceiling in the room below, over the guest's head who was sitting up in bed wondering what the hell was going on, and through the man's laptop sitting on the desk, before lodging into the baseboard.

The Browning's round was followed by another from Carlos's pistol when it flew out of his hand and banged into the wall. The bullet skimmed past the helmets of the SWAT team in formation, and exploded the huge plaster vase full of fake flowers at the end of the hallway.

The cops in the hallway immediately charged Room 342, hopping over the screaming Prido, and trying not to collide with Carlos.

Rocky's words had impacted them all. Not a one of them fired a weapon. The last thing Rocky had said to them at headquarters after the chief had departed was, "In other words, you're getting the same order that was given to the Boston police in the ranks of volunteers in 1775: *Don't fire till you see the whites of their eyes.*"

Rocky loved American history, particularly the history of the force he served.

But blood covered Prido's face—he'd hit the floor face first and sustained a broken nose in addition to the smashed shoulder blade—so no one could see the whites of his eyes. Cha-Cha Machado's eyes were squeezed shut.

Now, at the bar, Rocky mused to his fellow officers: "So interesting that a person is able get off a shot—pull the trigger of his weapon—even when he has been shot *himself.* I have seen it. But Prido... "

Marty finished the thought. ". . .with his shoulder blade blasted away. . . Man, the nerves in his arm turned into instant spaghetti."

Then Jan O'Keefe said, "All I know is, that kid had a swing would've done Big Papi proud."

Mugs and bottles were raised high; they drank to George Sanchez's feat.

Jay the blogger, raised his glass. He'd been sitting quietly at the end of the bar. Now he said, "You should have let Prido go."

The cops' heads all turned.

"No way he'd have found his way out of that mall. You can't find 93 because the signs are all wrong. It's never been done. You need *radar!* People end up in New Hampshire.

Can't you guys get the traffic department to do something?"

The cops had to laugh at that. Jan said, "I told you we shouldn't have invited that dweeb." But she leaned over the bar, raised her bottle to him and sent Jay a wicked smile.

The cops all drank to the blogger, and the one sitting next to Jay smacked him on the back. His Red Sox hat went flying. It was quickly retrieved, and reverently brushed off.

Before Rocky left the others to go home, he told Marty he wanted to speak to him outside for a minute. Marty drained his beer and ordered another one. "I'll be right back," he told the bartender.

On the sidewalk, Rocky asked him, "Where's the briefcase?"

"The briefcase?"

"Yes, Marty. The briefcase."

Marty folded his arms across his chest, a big bull of a man.

Rocky looked up into his partner's face. "Tampering with evidence is against the law. I am not understanding this. You are not a thief, Marty."

"Uh. . . Rock?"

"What?"

"Our guys are brilliant, aren't they? A dozen guns in that room, another kajillion out in the hallway, and not one cop responds to a shotgun blast. . . Or what about a pistol bullet whizzing past their ears? Nerves of fucking steel."

"It is why no one was killed, Sargeant."

"Yeah. So if we screw up over a few little things. . . Hey, it happens. But not to worry. I bet the briefcase turns up."

Rocky shut his eyes for one second, a most brief *namaste*. When he opened them he said, "Good night, Marty."

"Night, Rock."

They shook hands and parted.

Under arrest, Machado told the story of what had happened to Cinthia, a story identical to the one Rocky and Marty had surmised, based on their experience and what they saw in front of them. Machado explained that the only card Prido had to play against Lagunas was the picture of Luis Sanseverra's girlfriend. But how to use it? How could they force a meeting with Lagunas and demand he pay them the money he owed them? He decided he'd go to Boston with the picture because that's where Luis was. He would tell the Red Sox Luis's papers were phony. He'd think of something.

Trouble was, Prido didn't know Luis was in Portland—he could care less where the players ended up. He only knew Luis's contract was with the Red Sox organization. Prido called the Red Sox business number and after two days, someone got back to him to tell him Luis played in Portland. He asked where Portland was and was told, "Maine."

Prido had grown frustrated. And then they noticed Cinthia pushing her baby in a stroller to the playground. Saw her again. Both times in the morning. He made his plan for the next day. He got a press pass from someone on the street. He bought a new backpack. But the next day she didn't come out. Then the next—Sunday morning—there she was. But with her husband!

Machado said that he and Prido sat in their car and watched them. The husband walked off in a different direction. They drove up next to Cinthia, Prido got out and grabbed the stroller.

But the girl wouldn't let go of it. So Prido hit her across the face and then hit her again. She lost consciousness and they got her into the car. They took off. Prido crushed a barbiturate and put it into the screaming baby's mouth.

And the rest? Everyone knew the rest.

Though charged with first degree homicide, Machado

protested to his court-appointed lawyer that he was just Prido's driver. He didn't know Prido's plan. He just did as he was told. The trial was scheduled for September, at which time he was found guilty, but with mitigating circumstances—his addiction that left him beholden to Prido's demands. He would probably end up serving a dozen years of his sentence. But then there were the federal charges. Machado would someday, no doubt, die of old age in the pen.

Alberto Prido, though under guard in his room at Mass General, still was able to jump from the third floor ICU window, plastic tubing trailing after him. Though he was aiming at the roof of a Ford Taurus which would have cushioned his fall, he missed, and after about five minutes succumbed on the sidewalk surrounded by medical staff and pedestrians. One of the doctors had to turn away to vomit.

So as it turned out, one of the perps did in fact die the day of the La Quinta assault, but not at the hands of the cops.

⚾

After sweeping the Colorado Rockies to win the World Series, the Red Sox players arrived at the clubhouse today, for the last time this season—the Duck Boats lined up on Yawkey Way, at the ready. The fans greeting them out on Ispwich Street couldn't figure out why they were wearing jackets and ties. At the 2004 Rolling Rally they had on jeans and sweatshirts. No one could imagine Larry Lucchino taking a page from the Steinbrenner hair and dress code.

Twenty-seven members of the Sanchez and Vega families had already arrived including the youngest, three months old, blissfully asleep in his godmother's arms. The Reverend Tom Connealy directed Jason Varitek to stand next to Emily, and the rest of the godfathers gathered on either side of them.

The ceremony began—not a baptism since the baby had

already been baptized by Sully, who was already wiping his eyes. Just as Father Connealy was about to begin, Emily passed the baby to Jason, whose eyes also filled with tears.

The priest intoned, "Graciously hear our prayers, we beseech thee O Lord, and by thy unfailing might protect this soul, Arturo Ted Williams Sanchez."

David Ortiz read from a card, the same words as the priest's, in Spanish.

Then Father Connealy said a prayer of acknowledgment of the baby's godmother, Emily Vega, and his godfathers, the Boston Red Sox.

The priest offered a blessing of the community of people gathered there, and finally a prayer for the soul of the late Cinthia Sanchez. Then he read an excerpt from George's eulogy for his wife, delivered at her funeral.

"Our Cinthia was a good wife who wanted to teach me to enjoy life. She never gave up on me though I tried her patience. She was a proud, perfect mother, and Arturo was blessed to spend the first twenty-seven days of his life in her loving arms."

There were no dry eyes at all.

Then, a prayer from Kevin Youkilis, who chose to honor Cinthia with *El Maleh Rachamim*, a Hebrew prayer for her soul. When he was finished, Daisuke Matsuzaka took out a slip of paper where he had copied the words his mother had written on a votive plaque. She'd hung it at a Shinto shrine when his own child was born. In a small rendition of *Miyamairi*, he read her wishes for her grandchild's good health and happiness, and was halfway through when he became choked up. Hideki Okajima took the paper from him and finished.

Curt Schilling opened his family's Bible. He concluded his reading of scripture with a line from the gospel of Mark:

Suffer the little children to come to me; do not hinder them; for of such is the kingdom of God.

Father Connealy looked over at his friend Rocky Patel. The Detective closed his eyes. Marty hoped he wouldn't disappear for too long. But Rocky came right back, and said the Hindu prayer of his childhood, translating as best he could in the instant available to him when the prayer left his brain and was produced by his voice: *O you compassionate ones, defend this one who is defenseless. Protect him who is unprotected. Be his friend and his kinsmen. Let not the force of your compassion be weak; but aid him forever more.*

The Sanchez family declined the invitation to join the team for the Rally. They would to go to the cemetery to lay the flowers they'd brought for the naming ceremony on Cinthia's grave, and the senior Arturo's grave too. They said their goodbyes, their thank-yous, and exchanged loving hugs. And then the players changed out of their suits and into jeans before heading for another ceremony on the field with the mayor and dignitaries. The waiting Duck Boats revved their engines.

Detective Patel declined the same invitation, explaining that his wife and friends were planning to watch the rolling rally from Boston Common. His partner Sargeant Marty Flanagan, however, accepted. Victor Hauck had seen to getting him a slot in the boat carrying the Red Sox front office.

But Big Papi ordered the sergeant to ride with him.

THE NUMBER ONE PLACE
Rolling Rally Day, 4:00 PM

Now that the parade is over and Papelbon has done his last victory dance, I can really take a good look back on what just happened. The way in which the Red Sox won another World Series doesn't seem that amazing—but only because the way we did it three years ago was even more incredible. Again we were one game away from losing the ALCS, and again we didn't lose another game from that point on. The '04 team is the only one to ever win a seven-game series after being down 3-0, but the '07 team is one of just a handful who won after being down 3-1. And like in '04, we swept through the World Series with ease against a team many people were very afraid to face.

All this coming after the amazing night at Fenway when we won a game, after which the fans stuck around and watched the Yanks game on the scoreboard. Their loss clinched the division for us, and the players came back out on to the field and celebrated with the fans. I'm so fortunate to have been there that night. I was ready to head out when my girlfriend—her name's Jan, I met her this summer—decided we should maybe stick around. As usual, she made the right decision. The Champagne cork I got, popped by Dice-K, will be handed down to my grandchildren and theirs—my will shall state that it won't ever be allowed to be sold on eBay.

And of course, the Yankees are "bugged out" of the

playoffs, making it seven years in a row without a World Series. (Seven years, ha! We could do seven years standin' on our heads.)

I'm hearing a lot of, "2004 was for all the past generations. This one's for us." I say both championships were for all Sox fans—young, old, not yet born, dead, whatever. Nothing can ever be as meaningful as '04, but '07 was just as fun.

And it's no longer a secret who this "friend" of mine is—the one with the good seats. Or should I say "the best seat." You may have seen Jan and I sitting next to him at Game One of the World Series. . . .

That's right, it's Victor Hauck, who my family has known since well before he took a front office job with the Red Sox. Victor has opened a trust which will pay for Baby Ted's, no, sorry, Arturo's education.

Also today, the Jimmy Fund received an anonymous donation of a hundred thousand dollars in baby Arturo's name.

COMMENTS:

MattySox said: Jay, you sonuvabitch! I remember thinking on the night of Game One, "It's too bad Jay's at the game, if he was watching on TV like the rest of us, he'd surely have something to say about this new, young guy chatting up 'blazer guy' in the stands behind home plate." And it was you! No wonder you were always noticing that guy. . .

Melanie said: I thought that, too! I haven't been able to
stop watching the people behind the plate since this
blog and its readers pointed them out to me. And I
feel like I knew in the back of my mind it was you
back there! I mean, you did post a jpg from that
night from a great perspective, but I guess I figured
you just snuck down for a second or something.

KGNumber5 said: Jan! You mean SWAT Jan! You
dog, you! What a year, eh?

ConnecticutSoxFan said: Jay, nice job getting that
sweet seat. I took the day off and came up for the
parade today! A rolling rally every few years: I could
get used to this! Now to find the nearest Yankee fan
so I can rub it in. (If it's anything like 2004, I bet
they'll all be hiding!)

Jay said: I'm sure they will be, man. But they'll be
back next year, same as always. And we wouldn't
want it any other way. . . . I'm psyched for the next
hundred years of this rivalry.

BostonDetective said: The Boston Police Department
would like to thank Jay for his inquiries into illegal
human trafficking. If this trafficking had been prevented by Major League Baseball, or exposed
forcefully in the media, Cinthia Sanchez would not
have died. A crime is a deadly cancer. Its evil cells
consume everything in their path. Their tentacles
spread, contaminating all. We hope Cinthia has not
died in vain, and this criminal practice ceases. This
blog and its sources, in revealing the whereabouts

of the late Jack Lagunas, allowed us the time we needed to bring our investigation to a close. The Boston Police Department is always grateful for the help of our citizens. May Cinthia Sanchez rest in peace, and her son Arturo, thrive within the love this entire city has come to feel for him.

BabyTedFan said: Off-season is officially upon us. Rather than football, my main hobby is charting genealogies. I decided to do baby Arturo's. Through church records, I have found that his grandfather, the first Arturo Sanchez, was born in Hidalgo del Parral in the state of Chihuahua, Mexico. Arturo's father's first cousin, Natalia Hernandez, married Pablo Venzor, whose family had emigrated a century earlier from the Basque region of Spain. Pablo and Natalia had nine children, several of them born in the United States after the family emigrated first to Texas, and then west to Santa Barbara, California. One daughter, called Maria Elena, and later to be known as May, was born in El Paso just before the turn of the century, in 1893. May married Samuel Williams in 1915, and the couple moved to San Diego. Their son, Theodore, was born soon after on August 30, 1918. He was called Teddy. Hence: Baby Arturo is the third cousin of Ted Williams, twice removed. So someday, Jay, we might be cheering on "Baby Teddy Ballgame" from the stands at Fenway, watching him make a run at .400. I hear he's already swinging his rattle left-handed.

EPILOGUE

Rocky placed a photograph, face down, on the desk. Marty raised his eyebrow. "I have good news followed by bad news."

"Fire it on me, Rock."

"My friend at the FBI has found who it was that saw to Guillermo Valdez making his way home. This person visited him a month ago."

He turned the photograph over, a picture of three people: Guillermo Valdez, aka Luis Sanseverra; a pretty girl who was clearly the woman in the picture Michael Kim held up to the *ESPNews* camera; and an extremely attractive woman with a sweep of caramel-colored hair and a perfect smile—very white teeth and very red lips.

Marty took in the picture, looked up at Rocky and said, "I told you she was gorgeous, right?"

"Words to that effect."

"The bad news?"

"Again, the FBI. They had been very interested in the missing link, one that concerned them very much."

"Which link was what?"

"The person who recruited the Cuban players; convinced them to risk their lives; leave their families and come and play baseball in the United States where they would be stars."

Marty leaned back and stretched. "Yeah? So'd they find out?"

"They did."

Marty had been reading Rocky's eyes since they'd been teamed up three years earlier. His gaze remained steady for many moments until finally Marty said, "You are shittin' me."

It was not necessary for Rocky to answer.

"Where is she?"

"Last seen in Spain. Malaga. She was able to thoroughly document her new identity with funds from hidden WorldWide Baseball accounts. She absconded with quite a large amount of money."

Marty picked up the photograph. "Can I have this?"

"I don't see why not. It's a copy." He slid it over to him. "And Marty?"

"Jesus, Rocky, will ya shut up?"

"I'm almost finished." Rocky smiled. Marty had gotten past his feelings of burn-out—he'd found comfort from a source other than Rocky. Rocky said to him, "The missing briefcase was found. In the La Quinta dumpster."

"Hey, no kiddin'."

"Empty."

"Wicked surprise there."

"May I ask you something? Just to satisfy my own curiosity?"

"Rock, you know damn well you can feel free to ask me anything you want, whenever you want."

"I just wanted to be sure. So let me ask this: How much of your own money did you have to put in to make the sum a round hundred-thousand dollars?"

Now Marty smiled. "Hey, I'm a single guy. Don't remember. I got money to burn. It's the Jimmy Fund. Who's countin'?"

Rocky began to speak, but Marty held his hand up. "Uh. . . Rock?"

"Yes, Marty."

"Does that FBI agent of yours ever come around? Poppy Rice?"

"She hasn't been to Boston in a while. But if she does get up here, she'll drop in. Why?"

"Does she really look like Nicole Kidman?"

Briefest of *namastes*. Then Rocky answered him. "Although it might be difficult to believe, I would say she is even more attractive than the movie star."

"Oh." Marty went into a little *namaste* of his own, and then he asked his partner one more question: "She single?"